REVIEWS

THE LAST DANCE - Reviews

I was quite surprised and pleased that the skill of Ms. Enox kept me fully engaged throughout the book. Overall the style reminded me of early Marcia Muller. I would definitely recommend this book to anyone enjoying contemporary mysteries. Janes is certainly an unusual character and worth following in subsequent outings. I look forward to more from Lonna Enox. – Jack Quick, Readers Favorite

This book was wonderful! It was fun, light-hearted and captivating! It kept me second guessing my predictions all the way to the end." – Reader

The Last Dance, by Lonna Enox, has been awarded First Place for Debut Novel of 2013 – Chanticleer Book Reviews

Kept me in suspense until the end. I couldn't put it down. Can't wait to read more by Lonna Enox – Reader

Lonna Enox captured the modern Southwest culture, wrote a great mystery read, and had well-developed characters. The clues held the suspense and I can't wait for the sequel. Hope it's soon! - Reader

Winner of Chanticleer's Book Reviews for 2015 Grand Prize for Clue Awards.

BLOOD RELATIONS

Lonna Enox

Lonna Enox Publications
lonnaenox.org
Roswell, NM

Blood Relations
by Lonna Enox

First Printing – December 2014
ISBN: 978-0-9977424-3-5
Library of Congress Control Number: 2014921964

*To my husband Ron who always believes I can do anything,
and to my children who inspire me to do it.*

ACKNOWLEDGEMENTS

My editor, Sandy, has guided me through my sequel with a firm yet encouraging hand. It hasn't been an easy job for her, but I appreciate every note. Her patience is greatly appreciated!

How could I know that all those years ago one of the "slumber party crew" would grow up to become a police officer? Special thanks to Officer Shannon Snuggs and her husband, Officer Mike Snuggs, for always being available to answer questions through the writing of my novel. Maybe all those spooky stories I told Shannon "by candlelight" paid off for both of us!

My cousin Joe Foster had no idea that his email to me about his genealogical search of our family would inspire this novel, "Blood Relations." I appreciate the inspiration, Joe.

My dear friend, Lucy Nials, has again given me a recipe. The tamale recipe came not only with detailed directions, but also gave me the social aspect of preparing tamales at Christmas time. Lucy taught Home Economics next door to me for several years, and we have shared children's school activities, graduations, weddings, and now grandchildren.

My loyal friends, both longtime and new, have been the backbone for this dream's success. I thank all of you, and the hundreds whom I can't fit on here. Your reviews, your encouraging comments, your faith in this book and me is such a gift.

My children—Monica, Marissa, Nathan—and my grandchildren—Brooke and Drake—inspire me. They've proudly traveled to book signings, encouraged their friends to "check out Lonna Enox", and cheered me on. My husband, Ron, keeps the household moving when I am at the computer and keeps the computer operating when I can't.

Finally, my three kitties—Oliver, Emma, and Elsa—offer inspiration for Flash and Van.

My profound thanks to Lane Anderson of Cloudstone Photography, Lubbock, TX, for the back cover photo.

"Knavery and Flattery are blood relations." Abraham Lincoln

PROLOGUE

The intruder pulled the collar of his jacket up over his neck. Fall was the best time for this small job, but he'd forgotten the chill of autumn evenings. Denim, while it blended into the darkness, didn't offer much protection against the damp air.

He stuffed his hands back into his jacket pockets, keeping his eyes on the window. Even with the blinds closed, he could detect slight movement inside. He slid back behind the hedge and counted minutes on the luminous watch dial. Three . . . four . . . five . . .

He parted branches in the hedge until he could once more see. No lights in the front room now. That small gleam must be the hallway. Could be his adventurous prey had plans for the evening.

As if on cue, the garage door began its ascent, clanking to a grumpy halt. After the small car backed out, the door slid into place again. The driver paused in the street, as if reconsidering the trip. Finally, the car shot forward down the street.

He stepped out around the hedge in time to see the left turn signal blinking at the end of the short block.

Then he dashed around back. It would be too easy if he knew how long he had. Even a trip to the convenience store, however, should take fifteen minutes. At this time last night, his trial stop there had taken twenty minutes. Of course, he had to consider the number of customers. To be safe, he had allotted twelve minutes for tonight's activities.

It only took two to open the back window and climb into the photography studio. Then he wasted another two gaping at the sheer beauty of the framed prints on the walls—mostly water birds, except for a whimsical grouping of small critters: squirrels, raccoons, field mice, and rabbits. Talented. Very talented. Had he any conscience, he might have retreated then.

His low-light beam glanced against a door. A closet? He crept over and turned the knob. Locked. He had it open in a few seconds and peeked inside. Surely he could have chosen a better spot for the safe than tucked into the corner behind an aged file cabinet. Most people kept only what they thought of as valuables in the safe— money, jewelry, old coins. He would get those if time allowed, but he had more valuable things to nab.

Shelves at the top of the closet held photography supplies and magazines in cardboard boxes. A quick peek revealed nothing of interest. He checked the file cabinet next. Folders were arranged neatly but not in alphabetic order. The first one, obviously the most used, was labeled Invoices. This guy must keep copies of every receipt.

The will had its own folder and even contained a duplicate copy in an envelope with a strange name clipped to it. Titles of the house and vehicle, retirement benefits, credit card information, insurance policies, passport—he scooped those and stuffed them into his inner jacket pocket. A clock chimed and he glanced at his watch. Five minutes left.

Luckily, the safe was merely a reinforced box with a fairly simple lock. He pulled his tools from an outer pocket and made quick work of opening it. Pay dirt! From inside a nondescript plastic envelope he pulled a birth certificate and adoption papers. He didn't look at the details. Just grabbed them per instructions. A quick look through the rest of the safe offered an envelope filled with about a thousand dollars in cash. Probably trip money. He removed three one-hundred dollar bills. He doubted the guy would notice anything else . . . at least not right now. He could use it all, but caution made him leave the rest.

Just as he moved to close the lid, he saw a yellowed envelope. Inside was a tiny photo. He held it under the flash light and studied it carefully. Excitement coursed through him. Perfect! He stuffed it in with the rest.

Tempted though he was, he didn't tour the house or snoop through drawers or other closets. Instead, he carefully pushed the safe into its original spot, arranged the folders in the file cabinet, checked the floor of the closet for leaves or grass he might have carried in on his boots, and closed the door.

The window opened easier from the inside. He wished he could latch it, but that was beyond his expertise. Maybe it wouldn't be noticed. People tended to get a little absentminded with age. He brushed his gloved hand over the area beneath the window, obliterating footprints. Done!

He sprinted back toward the hedge and then alongside the fence to the dark alley. The dog across the alley should be indoors, but he'd brought a treat for him just in case. A dumpster rattled as he sprinted past, and he tensed and skidded to a halt. Peeking out were a pair of big yellow eyes. Just a cat. He couldn't resist lunging toward it, laughing silently when it jumped past and whizzed down the opposite direction. No more time to play!

He closed the door of his rental car with a minute left. As he drove through the intersection, he glanced toward the third house on his right. A car was pulling into the garage.

He grinned, adrenaline still pumping through his veins. Tonight called for a drink. Sadly, that would have to wait. He had a plane to catch. Then he grinned. They do sell drinks on the plane.

CHAPTER ONE

I could wait in the Jeep no longer, in spite of its cozy warmth. Several dozen people had already gathered in the predawn wonder this Saturday morning—opening day at Bosque del Apache Festival. This was my first visit and I wanted to experience the morning take-off, a "can't miss" according to the brochure. And I certainly didn't plan to watch it from the Jeep. So I zipped my jacket, turned off the motor, and grabbed my camera bag.

Most of the dozen or so who had already gathered on the water's edge were older than I. Many held small notebooks in their gloved hands, but a few had electronic tablets. They chatted quietly and nodded as I wove through them until I found an opening on the pond's bank.

Birders. I'd met them before when photographing on wildlife refuges. They were usually retired, traveling alone or in groups, most of them keeping a list of the types and numbers of birds they'd seen. Almost always, they were friendly and helpful to newcomers.

I saw another photographer farther down, setting up a tripod. I preferred to be more mobile.

Photography wasn't completely new for me, but I'd only decided to pursue it professionally when I moved to Saddle Gap. Previously, I'd spent a large part of my life in front of the camera instead of behind it. In my other life, I'd been a television crime reporter then news anchor in Houston, Texas. That was before my husband's murder, my own near death, and the inheritance that had given me a new life.

"Look at that sky!" my nearest neighbor exclaimed. "The colors! And that line of fluffy clouds!"

I quickly pulled out my camera. The first few orange streaks shot across the still darkened sky, providing a peek at the dark mountains across the water. Thousands of snow geese floated on the shallow pond, busily grooming and splashing in the frigid water. Resisting the urge to snap photos as quickly as possible, I scanned the scene ahead. A distance shot would give me an idea of whether my lens was the right choice. Not for the first time, I wished John were here already to lend advice.

"Your first time?" Again, my chatty neighbor.

I lowered the camera and smiled. "Yes." I nodded.

"It will be quick," she said, pointing at the pond at the geese. "When they decide to leave, it's instantaneous. Over in a minute."

Pink, fuchsia, and peach blended with the orange streaks, tinting the cloud bank as I hunkered down to shoot a chatty group of bathers to my left.

I could hear the soft murmurs amid camera shutters clicking. The group along the bank had grown to several dozen, but they kept their voices soft so as not to spook the geese. Some snapped shots with their phones.

I turned my focus toward a gorgeous pair closest to me. Unlike their neighbors, these two splashed, stretched their wings, and scrubbed vigorously with their beaks.

All around, heads pulled out from under wings. Within seconds, the whole pond transformed into a blanket of white fluffy bodies in various stages of bathing.

"Not long now," my neighbor cautioned.

I shook off the irritation her chattiness stirred inside me and clicked off a dozen more shots. Finally, I stood.

My pocket buzzed. I touched my pocket but left my phone inside. Nothing was too important to interrupt this moment. Whoever it was could leave a message.

Fleetingly, I wondered if it was John. I'd expected him to be here when I arrived yesterday. He'd had a longer drive—all the way from Branson, Missouri—and I'd only driven a few hours over from Saddle

Gap. Still, he'd planned the trip and talked me into joining him. It hadn't been hard to do. John and I had been friends since my college days when he'd befriended a shy freshman and convinced her she could do anything she dreamed. He'd kept in touch after we moved, he to pursue his art and me to pursue my journalism. And when my world fell in, John had flown to Houston and taken me to Branson to heal.

A gasp pulled me back. Then all murmurs ceased as everyone stared, motionless, at the show before us. I couldn't decide who gave the signal, but in unison thousands of snow geese stilled, gazed up at the now golden, pink, and lilac sky, and then—whoosh! Frantically snapping, I forgot focus and simply aimed. Within seconds, loud honking filled the sky above the emptied pond. The feathered group circled a few times and then headed toward the west and the cornfields the rangers had planted.

I lowered my camera. "Morning Celebration," I murmured. That would be the perfect name for this collection of photos.

All around me, people turned toward parked cars, chatting softly. My neighbor had moved closer. "I'll bet those are going to be gorgeous photos."

"I plan to put them in my small shop," I told her, capping the lens and stowing my camera in the bag. I slipped out of my gloves and reached in a side pocket for a card. "It's in Saddle Gap, near the Mexican border. If you're ever that way, I'd love for you to stop by. I'm Sorrel, the owner, but it's set up more like a co-op of sorts."

We parted at the graveled road. I walked toward the Jeep. She joined a group loading into a refuge van. Engines started up and everyone headed to the next location on the schedule

The next stop was near a shallow pond across the highway from the refuge area where we had been. Apparently, the sandhill cranes preferred this spot for their nightly rest; every spare inch of the pond held a large gray crane, hunkering down and balancing on one spindly leg.

Although the sun had risen over the mountains that formed a ring around the refuge, it was still early. My breath formed puffs in the chilly air, tempting me—almost—to linger in the warm vehicle. But I'd arrived ahead of the caravan of birdwatchers, so I hustled to grab a good spot. High above, the squawking snow geese urged their sleepy neighbors to get up. A few cranes had begun to stir, pulling their heads from under wings, shifting long stick legs and slapping sleep from gray bodies. Others held onto the last moments of sleep before heading off to breakfast with their noisy neighbors.

I took a quick moment and scanned the arrivals. Maybe John had missed the alarm, I thought, and would join me here. But I knew I was only fooling myself. John never needed an alarm. He would have been first to arrive at the other pond. In fact, he'd have left a message at the bed and breakfast down the road where I'd booked a room for the week.

A gasp around me caught my attention. The cranes—urged on by the cacophony of the geese—were taking off. I knelt to capture the preflight exercise—wings spread out and flapping, one foot up, beak and long thin neck arched forward, a few moments frozen in this pose. As if they were counting down, each bird suddenly started an awkward trot forward, his neighbors moving out of the way, and then—whoosh! With the smoothness of a giant jet, each crane lifted up into the pink-orange sky to the cheering of his raucous neighbors. My chest tightened. If only I could capture a fourth of this majesty!

Close to an hour later, I repacked my equipment. Most of my companions had already left for the refuge headquarters where an outdoor country breakfast awaited them. The lure of hot coffee enticed me as well. Only a few cranes still needed to take off. These stragglers had made a couple of half-hearted attempts but had aborted at the last moment. Giggling, I'd taken some comical photos to add to the gorgeous ones.

"Show offs!" a deep voice commented behind me.

Reed! I jumped and almost dropped my bag, but he caught it swiftly.

"What are you doing here?"

"Happy to see you too." I tried to pull the bag out of his hand, but he held on and started walking toward my Jeep. " Let's go sample that country breakfast I heard people talking about," he said.

"When did you get here? Why are you here?" I repeated, matching my stride to his since he didn't seem inclined to stop.

Reed reached the Jeep. He took a deep breath before turning back toward me. "I've driven a long way on a couple of cups of coffee. Bad coffee. And it's sloshing around in my belly. Can't we just get something to throw in with it and talk? Like civilized people? I just called to let you know—again, by the way—but you didn't pick up."

With the early morning sun in his face, I could see the lines fatigue had made on his face. He set my bag in the back seat and motioned across the road. He'd pulled off onto a muddy shoulder and parked at an angle—like he'd been in a hurry. But he wasn't looking at me. His eyes drifted toward my shoulder and behind, watching the last birds lift off.

"It's John, isn't it?" I asked.

No answer. I grabbed his jacket tight in my fists and yelled. "Tell me! It's John, isn't it!"

He didn't answer. Instead, he pried my hands loose from his jacket and pulled me into his arms.

"It's John," I whispered, my body suddenly wracked with shivers.

We stood that way for a few moments. I'd missed him—the clean soap smell, the way he threaded his fingers through my hair, the strong heartbeat, his arms strong yet gentle around me. It had been the craziest thing—to start out as enemies and end up falling in love. At least, that's how it had been for me. But not for Reed.

When Teri told me he'd left the police force, I'd just laughed. "It isn't April Fools' Day," I'd reminded her. "Reed wouldn't quit the department. He loves it. What else would he do?"

"He's working with the sheriff's department," she said. "Jose is close-mouthed about it. I couldn't get anything more than that out of him."

Jose and Reed had been best friends since high school. In fact, Reed was the godfather for their twin boys. Teri worked for the same newspaper that I provided photographs for and helped run my gift shop. Reed had been totally opposed to our working together in the beginning—when he still thought I might be a murderess.

The love stuff surfaced during the mystery and danger that followed. Until he cancelled our first official date to leave town that first summer on family matters, that is. I had only seen him twice since then until now—November—when I was clinging to him once again.

I shoved—hard. He stepped back but kept his hands on my arms. "Let's eat first," he said. "We can leave the Jeep in the lot here. And, yes, it's John."

"What?"

He clammed up. I hated this obstinate, arrogant . . . sexy man. "I won't eat a bite," I told him. "You always do this—treat me like some kind of child. If something's happened to John, I have a right to know. I'm not waiting until after breakfast!" I pulled my arms out of his grasp but moved up until our noses were almost touching. "What's going on?"

Reed didn't step back. "You can watch me eat then." He sighed. "Sorrel, it's complicated. I've been on the road and I'm exhausted. Please trust me."

Had he ever said please? As for the trust part, I'd trusted him with my life before. Trust didn't come easily for me. In fact, the only two men I could remember trusting were Reed and John.

"Don't patronize me then," I finally whispered.

"I promise." Reed walked over to his truck, opened the door, and waited for me. "Patronize is a word that never comes to mind when I look at you."

CHAPTER TWO

By eight o'clock, the refuge's Cowboy Kitchen had already served dozens of hungry birdwatchers and wildlife photographers. A few latecomers cradled cups of hot coffee at the scattered picnic tables. The kitchen, set up outdoors between the road and refuge headquarters, was staffed by volunteers. Signs proclaimed that proceeds from the food benefitted the wildlife refuge.

When Chris Reed and I lined up at the coffee pot, a stocky guy with a cowboy hat almost bigger than he was hurried over. "Ready for breakfast? There's plenty of sausage gravy, biscuits, and eggs." Without waiting for a reply, he grabbed a paper plate in one hand and the gravy ladle in the other.

"I'm—"

"—hungry!" he finished for me. I heard Reed chuckle.

"Gotta feed these fillies, son," the cowboy told Reed. "They'll waste away while trying to make up their minds. They don't realize a man doesn't want to cuddle up to a beanpole." He dished up scrambled eggs alongside the biscuit covered in gravy.

"Speak for yourself, Sam!" A tall, thin woman took the plate and smiled at me. "Do you want this or do I have to eat it?"

The cowboy grimaced. "She will too. Can't seem to fatten her up no matter how much she eats."

Laughter erupted from a nearby table. "You're doing a good job on yourself!" someone called.

My stomach growled. "Smells great." I smiled. It had been a long time since dinner last night, but I didn't feel much like eating. Still, I needed to try. Reed already had a loaded plate.

A couple at the nearest picnic table—Stan and Mary, they immediately introduced themselves—waved us over to join them. "I'm Chris Reed," he said, "but almost everyone calls me Reed. Guess that's what I get for having two first names." He put an arm around me and gave a casual hug. "And this filly is Sorrel." That drew appreciative chuckles from the cowboys. We had hardly sat down before Sam came by with a couple of Styrofoam cups and a big speckled coffee pot. "It's real coffee," he said. "Brewed over the fire instead of run through one of those fancy machines."

"Guaranteed to put hair on your chest," the thin woman remarked, setting creamer and sugar nearby. "I'm Betty, by the way." She gestured toward Sam. "But the coffee doesn't work on the head. That's why he keeps his hat on." Everyone, including Sam, laughed.

They both settled at our table, hopping up to serve the stragglers coming through the line and then returning. Amid their ongoing banter with each other and everyone else, I relaxed a bit and amazed myself by clearing my whole plate. Reed even refilled his, reminding me of his long road trip last night.

He must have been thinking about it too.

As he finished, he turned to Stan. "Sorrel was expecting to meet up with an old friend here," he continued. "We haven't seen him."

"Lots of folks here on festival weekend," Stan said. He and Mary had driven here for the weekend from Phoenix, where they wintered. A retired engineer and nurse from Michigan, he and Mary explained that their single son lived in their Michigan home while they were gone. "The lady running the gift shop said over a hundred had already registered. Lot more will come today."

"They have a good variety of activities," I said. "Did you go to the early take-offs this morning? Amazing!"

"We were here cooking since before dawn," Sam said. "Amazing how much you birders can eat!" He grinned and rubbed his belly.

"We're more sunset worshippers," Stan said, the corners of his mouth hinting at a grin. "Mary couldn't possibly get her hair and make-up done for a sunrise event—no matter how amazing it might be."

Mary whacked him on the arm with her palm.

Reed tried again. "Sorrel's friend, John, bragged about this kitchen. He's been here several times before. Photographer."

"You from around here, Sorrel?" Mary asked.

"Not originally. But I live over near the Mexico and Arizona border now, running my own gift shop and chasing my dream of wildlife photography. John and I knew each other when I was in college in Missouri—"

"The Professor?" I jumped and looked toward the voice close to my elbow.

"Sorry, didn't mean to startle you. But I've been keeping an eye out for him as well. He promised to donate a print for our auction this afternoon, but he didn't show two days ago when I expected him. Then I heard you and thought the coincidence was too great for two Johns who were college professors." Another hand shot out toward me and I shook it. "Sorry. I'm Esperanza. I run the gift shop and am co-director of the festival."

She was so tiny I almost could look down on the top of her head. And her energy reminded me of Teri. She looked to be in her fifties or thereabout.

"Sorrel," I told her. "That's John. He mentioned that he would be donating a print. I told him I'd be in on Friday and we planned to meet up. He's my mentor of sorts and a really good friend."

I could have told them that he was more a savior than a mentor. When my husband, Kevin, had been murdered in Houston a year ago, the police thought I had been the target. As a crime journalist, I'd angered the local branch of a Mexican cartel. For my own protection, they insisted I go into hiding. I'd refused protective custody and settled on staying with John in Branson instead. We'd kept in touch all these years since I'd been in his college classes, even after my move to Houston and his retirement to Branson, and I knew he'd give me the space I needed just then.

He'd been in the station when the police finally finished questioning me. My own father had died years earlier, so John had filled that space. During the next few weeks he'd listened, fed me good meals, soothed me during nightmares, and driven me to therapy appointments. He had never let me down before. And I knew he never would. Something had happened.

Reed had been reading my expressions. He put his arm around me and gave a warning squeeze. "He must have gotten carried away with some photo shoot, honey," he said. I tried to pull away, but he gave me another warning squeeze. Then he glanced toward the couples across the table. "I'm sure he'll turn up. But if you run into him before we do, would you tell him Sorrel and Reed are staying at the little bed and breakfast up the road?"

I forced myself to smile—sort of—and make general chit chat for another few minutes. Reed caught my hand as we headed toward his truck. I started to pull away, but he had me in a tight grip so I forced my hand to relax.

When we reached his truck, I reached for the door. Still locked. Then I heard that telltale chuckle. "I figured the best therapy was a good mad spell."

I whirled around, too mad to notice how close our noses were. "Some nerve!" I hissed, remembering to smile for the audience. "Do you think you can just dance back into my life—"

"I received a couple of letters you need to read, Sorrel."

"Are they about John?"

"One's from John; the other, from his attorney. And I'm not sure how they fit with John not being here. But, Sorrel, if something has happened to John, we can't wear our emotions on our sleeves, as my grandma used to say. I know you've had plenty of experience with role playing." He glanced around. "We need to act as if nothing is wrong—just be casual—until we can think this out a bit."

"Then you do think something has happened—"

Did he think kissing me was the only way to shut me up? Did he expect me to melt into his arms? I guess role playing came easily for Reed. It didn't for me—at least, that's the last thought I had for a bit. Reed was a great kisser.

CHAPTER THREE

"I feel like an actress in a bad soap opera!"

I didn't look at Reed, but I knew he was grinning. It wasn't the first time he'd taken advantage of a situation where I couldn't do anything more than play along with him. We'd both discussed the wisdom of playing our cards close to our chests—something we'd done a few months earlier when I'd first come to Saddle Gap. But he always managed to sneak in a kiss, a hug, a look—something I'd learned was pure acting. But he was so hard to resist.

"You're not dramatic enough."

"What?"

"For a soap opera. At least not outwardly." He started the motor and didn't speak again until we were out on the highway heading back toward the pond where I'd left my Jeep.

It was only a few miles up the road, so I held my tongue and stared out the window. What had happened to John? What did he know? Why couldn't he just—

"I don't know much, Sorrel." His voice was soft and gentle. He pulled his truck into the parking lot beside my Jeep, turned off the engine, and sighed. "I've been working undercover—away for a while, if you hadn't noticed."

I had but I was still too mad at him to admit it. Instead, I stared out my window and nodded.

"So I wasn't home when the letter arrived, and mail sure wasn't being forwarded." I could hear the rustle of paper as he dug the letter out of his pocket. "Open it," he said and shoved it into my hand.

It was John's handwriting. He had a sloping style that I'd know anywhere. Why was John writing to Reed? I glanced at the postmark. It had been mailed last month from his home in Branson, Missouri.

"Read it." I could clearly hear the exhaustion in Reed's voice now.

I pulled out the single-page handwritten letter.

> *Reed, I'm embarking on what may turn out to be a wild goose chase. It's been on my mind for a very long time, and I've decided it's a "now or never" thing. I've waited until Sorrel was settled and safe. And she is. So now is my time. But in the event something unforeseen comes along, I need you to be there for her. I had thought things were heading for a more permanent situation with you two—and I don't want to get into your personal lives—but even though it hasn't developed, I know that you will help her should she need it. I know she thinks she's strong and independent—and she is—but all of us need family at times in our lives, and she's become part of mine. I plan to meet up with her in a few weeks for a photography weekend. But first, I've decided it's time to follow my heart and search for some family roots. It seemed unlikely that I would find anyone, but recently I have received some interesting results. My curiosity won't allow me to just ignore them. So I plan to follow up. I haven't told Sorrel about this just yet— want to see if it's legitimate first. Besides, she's a mother hen type. I've been contacted by someone but want to check the person out first. It won't interfere with our weekend. But if I'm off the mark and she needs a friend, I trust you'll be there, John.*

I read it through twice. At the end, John had written the name and phone number of his attorney. Sometime during my reading,

Reed had left the truck. I spotted him standing near the edge of the shallow pond where a handful of ducks sailed along, periodically diving for bugs and calling to each other. He didn't say anything when I joined him, just reached for my hand.

"I'd been awake so long I just crashed," he said. "Didn't even start on the stack of mail until I'd slept twelve or fourteen hours. Figured I'd better at least open the utility bills unless I wanted to be in the dark. This was in the stack."

A group of snow geese flew high above us to another field. I watched them go, clinging to his hand. I knew there was more, but I couldn't will myself to speak.

"There was a letter from his attorney as well, asking if I'd call." He took the letter from my other hand without turning me loose, tucked it into his jacket, and then pulled me close.

"Tell me."

"I don't know. The attorney just said that he'd been instructed to get in touch with me in the event that John made any changes in his will."

"And did he?"

"I guess so but I don't know what they are. The attorney just requested that I notify you."

"Why didn't he notify me himself?"

"You'll have to ask him . . . or John."

"Did the attorney mention why he needed you to notify me?"

"No."

"Something's very wrong, Reed." I could hear the quiver in my voice. Apparently Reed heard it too.

"When did you expect John to join you here?" he asked.

"I was joining him! He planned to be here last Monday, but I didn't want to shut down the store that early. With Thanksgiving the week after next, I'd planned to close it for the next two weeks and then reopen for the big sales the Friday after Thanksgiving. John was coming for the holiday and the sale."

"Where were you meeting?"

"At Quail Run, the bed and breakfast in that little town just off the main road. But when I checked in yesterday, the clerk said he'd not shown up. They couldn't keep his room past the day his deposit covered—Tuesday—because with the festival, rooms are much in demand."

Reed released my hand and wrapped his arm around me, gazing at the pond. "Did he leave you a message?"

"No. I thought maybe he'd been delayed and had forgotten to cancel . . . that he'd just be here today. This is the big day and he'd talked about showing me the refuge. Maybe he'd decided to pull his camper after all and just stay there."

"Sorrel, has he ever not told you if he wasn't going to show up?"

"No."

"When did you speak with him last?"

"He'd left me a message at the store instead of calling my cell. I didn't notice it until shortly before I left. It was odd, now that I think of it. He said he'd see me and Flash soon. He knew I'd never bring Flash along."."

A group of birders had arrived. They waved in greeting but looked at us curiously, not sure if they were intruding. "We can't just stand here," I said, and turned back toward the Jeep. "Something has happened, and we have to figure out what to do." Reed nodded toward the birders and fell in step beside me, his arm draped loosely around my waist.

"You're right, Sorrel. Obviously, we can't get in touch with the attorney on a Saturday." Reed motioned toward the Jeep. "I'll follow you to the bed and breakfast. Let's talk with those people first, just to get the times and facts down. We need to call Branson too. Do you have a point of contact there besides John?"

"He has a couple of neighbors who look after things when he's gone."

"Great!" Reed waved at the group who had assembled with cameras at the water's edge. I climbed into the Jeep's driver's seat. "Let's not dwell on the worst until we must." He reached in and patted my shoulder.

I looked at the smudges under his eyes. "Why don't I do all that while you get some rest? I don't know much about what you're doing workwise, but isn't this—"

"I had some time coming."

Still no explanation for why he'd left so suddenly months earlier. I wasn't sure whether I was madder at him for just taking off when things were beginning for us or at myself for being so glad he was here with me now. He glanced at me. "Let's just put all those questions steaming in your brain into storage, Sorrel. We need to do what we do well—team up and help our friend."

"We won't be much help if we're exhausted."

"You didn't sleep?"

"I don't usually sleep well the first night in a strange place. And I'd expected to meet up with John already, you know."

"We could—"

"Reed!" I felt my face warming. There it was again. Chris loved to tease me, but that seemed to be the extent of our relationship. He'd saved my life, we'd shared some steamy kisses, and then he'd vanished.

I led the way down the two-lane highway from the refuge, my mind swimming with the unanswered questions.

CHAPTER FOUR

Quail Run was no help to us. John had booked a room there a couple of months ago. I'd talked to the owner earlier when I had been looking for John. She knew him because he'd stayed there on previous visits. She seemed uncomfortable that I was questioning her once again, this time with Reed standing next to me, and was quite clear that it was John who had lost his room because he hadn't cancelled. Why he hadn't shown up wasn't important to her. After all, it wasn't unusual for people to change their minds and she could easily rent the room during this busy time.

I thanked her and left a card with a hastily scribbled note on the back to give to John should he come. She nodded and placed the card with the other messages for guests.

We decided to leave my Jeep there at Quail Run in the parking lot. Should John come in late, he'd surely recognize it. I grabbed my camera bag and the pass I'd received earlier to get back into the refuge loop.

Back in the truck, Reed noted that we still needed to call John's neighbors in Branson. "Unless you've already done that," he said.

"No. I wasn't really worried last night. Sometimes John just wanders upon something he can't resist and alters his schedule. I expected him to come along this morning."

"And he might. I know he's what . . . six days late? He could have planned to go somewhere else first then got caught up in a photography session and lost track of time." He was silent a moment or two. "Are you uncomfortable calling his neighbors? You know them, don't you?"

"Unless they've moved. People tend to live temporarily in Branson. But the couple across the street has lived there a long time, and I did become acquainted with them. They're elderly." I could already imagine their reactions. He had a bad heart and she tended toward the dramatic. "I'll mention that I'm thinking of coming for a visit but haven't been able to reach John. That way, they can let me know if they're watching his place and I don't have to alarm them unnecessarily. Everything is just conjecture right now."

Reed agreed. "How about we just go back to the refuge and drive the loop. John may be there shooting right now. It's a big place and this is prime time."

"I know." I felt guilty about the momentary twinge of regret that I was missing out on the festival, but I knew I'd not do my best work either.

"We need to be sure that we're not panicking needlessly here." Reed's voice was consoling and I wanted to believe what he was saying—I wished I could—but we still needed some sort of plan. Reed was an experienced police officer, then detective, and now sheriff's deputy. He knew what to do. He was also stubborn.

The refuge headquarters parking lot was now full. Families wandered through the outside exhibits, photographing their children with the wild rescue critters in the background. Shuttles were loading up for tours, and the cooks we'd met at breakfast scurried around the open air kitchen creating delicious smells.

Reed slowed down to pay at the gate. "I have a pass," I reminded him and handed it over. "This your first trip?" the volunteer asked Reed. When Reed nodded, he advised, "Keep this pass handy. It should be good for the whole festival."

We had only rolled a short distance forward when Reed stopped. "Look!" he said. I followed his gaze in time to see a big buck stroll across the road. In spite of the unusually large groups of people, he stopped in the middle of the road and scanned his surroundings. Two vehicles had already lined up behind us, their occupants hopping out with their cameras. "Where's your camera?"

"I—"

"Isn't this why you came here? We can look for John, who is probably traipsing around some wooded area somewhere, but you can't recapture these moments."

I needed no more urging. I whipped my camera out of its case, slipped out the door, and began focusing.

A few minutes later, as we continued to ease around the big loop and stray down side roads, I felt the tension that had been building release completely. What a treasure trove!

After a half hour or so, we parked beside a large pond and walked to the elevated stand. Out in the middle of the pond, on a post of sorts, roosted a couple of eagles. I switched lenses to get a closer view. Time stood still as I shot frame after frame—until they decided to fly. I continued snapping as they lifted high above.

"Amazing." I'd forgotten Reed completely. I'd certainly not noticed his arm around me. He hugged me close and crowed, "You can't imagine this beauty. You have to see it!"

I smiled up at him, suddenly happy to have him here to share this moment.

"Look at those honeymooners," I heard an older guy say. I looked around to see the couple, but the guy was looking at us.

"We need to keep looking," I said, pulling out of Reed's hug. He didn't say anything, but I saw that grin tugging at his mouth!

Back in the truck, Reed handed me a bottle of icy cold water from a cooler behind the seat and drank thirstily from one of his own. I gulped mine also, surprised at how the sun had warmed me up in spite of the cooler temperatures.

Reed stuffed his empty bottle in a bag and started the engine. "John would want you to enjoy this time, Sorrel. Whatever has delayed him must have been important. Maybe he's out of cell tower range. You know how it is in these remote areas of New Mexico. But he'd expect you to do just what you did—snap amazing photos to share."

I knew Reed was right. But I still felt guilty—and anxious. "Let's drive around to the fields where the cranes and snow geese eat," I said. "John talks about how amazing it is. Maybe he's there."

My words sounded hollow to my own ears. But Reed backed out and we continued on the loop, stopping to wait for an occasional deer crossing the road or to admire a raccoon up a tree. When we reached the fields, Reed cruised slowly, both of us checking not only license plates but also people. "Let's get out and walk a bit," he said. That wasn't a bad idea. Sitting was making me even more nervous.

We zipped up our jackets, locked the truck doors, and started down the long frontage, taking care not to step in front of photographers.

"Reed! Sorrel!" We both swung around. It was Stan, one of our early breakfast companions. "Come join us!" He motioned toward some empty folding chairs among a group across the road.

"We're still walking off breakfast!" I called. They were nice folks, but we were too worried just now to join their group. Reed put his arm around my shoulders, the intimate gesture rewarded by a chuckle or two from the group. He leaned in and whispered, "Sorry but this act seems to be the best way to avoid the socializing."

I'm a lousy actress, I reminded myself as I moved a bit and slipped my hand in his, but this did seem easier just now. People expected lovers to be less social. "On to Plan Two," I said as we reached the end of the field and crossed the road to start back.

In spite of the cool weather, Reed had unzipped his jacket to check his cell. "No messages."

"When do you have to be back at work—whatever that is?"

Reed grinned. "Nosey Rosy." Before I could reply, he continued, "I took a few days. In fact, the case I was working is finished . . . at least the field work is, which is what I was doing. So I'm taking some days owed to me for the holiday before heading back to Saddle Gap and the sheriff's office."

"Do you miss—" A gray snow goose whooshed up, spooked by my voice. Instinctively, I lifted my camera. "Come on, baby. Turn back this way. Let me have a look at you." I followed him, clicking shots quickly as he circled high and low and then headed toward a ditch that had been plowed between this field and the next to allow for water.

"Excuse me," a deep voice said. I moved over to give him room, a little irritated that he hadn't just walked around me. Some people didn't know protocol for photography. When I could hear his breathing still, I stepped a couple of yards further over and waited until he passed. Then I returned to the birds. I'd missed a good shot, but that wasn't totally unexpected. I focused. "Reed?" I called, trying to keep my voice from portraying the horror I was feeling.

"Right here," he said, walking up behind me and placing his hands gently on my shoulders. "I've been admiring—"

"Reed!" My voice echoed my fear. "There's something along that ditch!" I nodded toward the water as the snow goose landed just a few feet from the still form. "It looks like a man—"

But he was already heading that direction. Luckily, my long legs could keep up with his.

"Hurt?" He stopped at the edge of the water, unable to get any closer.

I focused my lens. "Not moving. Face down." I handed Reed the camera to see for himself.

"He's dead, I think. But he looks like he's been posed. Few people fall down dead and have their legs lined up evenly with their toes pointed behind. And he's not dressed for here. Looks like the soles of dress shoes."

Reed handed the camera back to me. "Let's find a ranger. He'll contact the proper authorities."

We hurried to the truck. "Sorrel," Reed said, as he started the engine. "It isn't John, you know. He looks like a much younger man. John's likely just late getting here."

CHAPTER FIVE

The good news was that it wasn't John. Of course, it wasn't good news for the dead man. In fact, I felt guilty again—Was this the new norm for me? Feeling guilty?—because I was so relieved to see this stranger's dark hair instead of John's salt and pepper gray. He also looked heavier than John and shorter. Even from a distance and through the camera lens, he didn't look like John.

We drove back to the entry booth as casually as we could. Reed pulled the truck to a small area beside the booth so others could go on through, and then we walked around to speak to the lady inside. We explained as calmly as possible what we'd found. If this were some sort of hoax, we didn't want to upset the entire festival. The lady at the booth wasn't sure we weren't doing just that and asked us dozens of questions before finally calling headquarters. "Wait right here," she said after hanging up. She'd kept her voice low but her eyes on us.

The park ranger wasn't happy to see us when he sped onto the dirt beside the booth. "What's this you two think you saw?" he asked without bothering with an introduction.

Reed stuck out his hand. "Chris Reed."

Grudgingly, the ranger replied. "Jack Willowby."

"We think we saw a dead body," Chris said. "Sorrel," he said as he turned toward me, "Janes and I were walking past the snow geese and sandhill cranes. She was shooting with her high power lens as they flew. When she glanced through them, she noticed him."

"Do you have the camera?" He was still addressing Reed.

"Yes, I do," I said, offering my own hand. He shook it grudgingly as well. "I've got the camera in the truck." I turned to go get it, but he stopped me with his hand.

"I can get it. You just stay here."

Reed didn't like his attitude or the direction this was taking. He pulled back his jacket and started to reach inside. Willowby's stance changed immediately. "I'm with the sheriff's department in Saddle Gap," Reed said. "I was reaching for ID as I realize this is an unusual situation here. You can call and confirm. Sorrel owns a gift shop there and sells her wildlife photography in it. We just came for the festival."

Not exactly true but I silently agreed. "My camera case is on the passenger seat," I offered, this encounter seemingly stalled as the men bristled. "I'd prefer to find the photo for you, though, as I've gotten some wonderful shots I wouldn't want accidentally deleted."

Willowby appeared to be in his fifties and enjoyed his food more than he probably should have. He also looked more like a grandpa than a lawman. I wondered if he encountered much more than kids sneaking onto the refuge for drinking or sex—and maybe vandalism. When he didn't answer right away, I could feel Reed's irritation and impatience rise.

"It could just be some sort of prank," I said. "I'm not the professional you guys are. Sometimes things look different through the lens."

He bought my act and visibly relaxed a bit. "I'll get the camera bag," he said. Reed clicked the lock and we watched the ranger cautiously lift it out.

He handed it to me with all the caution of a bomb squad leader. I pulled out the camera, clicked it on, and found the first of the shots I'd taken of the birds flying up in the field a few minutes ago.

"Here. Look through here and push this button to move the images."

Willowby gave the briefest of sighs, his skepticism returning once he was no longer worrying about guns or bombs. But he tensed when he reached the first frame with the body. He studied it closely, noting on his pad the date and time printed on the screen once he'd handed the camera back to me.

"I'll follow you back," he said. "I don't want to cause a big furor in case this isn't what it seems to be." So he thought it was a body as well. He turned to Reed. "I'd like to see that ID now, if you don't mind."

Reed showed him his ID and badge. "I know you don't want to call for back up or scare people unnecessarily," he said, "but some other photographer may discover this as well. Sorrel is a former investigative reporter, so she reacted quicker than most."

Willowby didn't answer, but I noticed as I climbed into the truck that he was on his cell phone while he walked to his SUV. We didn't talk as we led Willowby around the narrow roads, but Reed reached over and squeezed my hand.

By the time we reached the field, white with snow geese and gray, gawky cranes, the crowds had grown enough that it was impossible to park close by. We pulled into the nearest photo shoot area, Willowby right behind us. He was out of his SUV before Reed could put the truck in park and waited impatiently as we climbed out and locked up.

"No camera," he told me. I'd locked mine in the truck and told him so. "After my back-up arrives," he continued as if I'd not spoken, "you'll have to wait here with the deputy while we investigate."

No sooner had he spoken than a pick-up truck with a sheriff's department insignia pulled in on the other side of us. Willowby stepped past us and drew the sheriff and his deputy off to the side, speaking softly and urgently. I shivered. It wasn't that cold, but a chill settled between my shoulders, as my aunt Rose used to say.

Finally, the sheriff stepped over and shook hands with Reed. Once more, we were asked a series of questions: Why we were here? When we noticed the body? What aroused our suspicions? How long had we been here? With his sunglasses hiding his eyes, he seemed almost bored at first. He was younger than Willowby—closer to Reed's age—and shorter than both of them. "Could I see the camera?" he asked, finally acknowledging my presence. At my stare, he added, "Sheriff Joe Garcia."

I nodded. "It's in our truck," I said. "I'll get it." I turned to ask Reed for the keys.

"Ma'am, I'll do that." The sheriff's deputy, a young Hispanic who walked with a military air, stepped between us. Reed handed him the keys and instructed him on the whereabouts of the camera case.

"I will turn it on and show you the photos," I told him, turning toward the sheriff with a smile I didn't feel. "Those photos are important to my business, and I don't want them accidentally deleted."

Our group had drawn curious looks at first, but now cars and people were starting to wander closer.

It took the deputy only a few seconds to return with my camera. I made quick work of turning it on and finding the photos. The time and date showed clearly on the screen and this time Sheriff Garcia jotted them down.

"Have you been here before?" he asked.

"No. This is my first trip. I saw the ads about the Fall Festival here and it looked like a great photo opportunity." I didn't want to mention John just yet.

Garcia turned to Reed. "Did you come here together?"

"I couldn't get off as early," Reed lied smoothly. He casually slipped an arm around my waist. "Got in this morning in time for breakfast." Then he repeated the information he'd given Willowby earlier about his job.

"Okay." Garcia finally turned to his deputy. "You stay here and do some crowd control," he said.

I must have shivered because the sheriff stared at me. "Would you like to wait for us in the car?"

"I'm fine."

His eyes traveled over me. "Yes," he said. Reed's hand tightened on my waist.

Garcia finally turned and walked back to Willowby, who was standing with some crime technicians I'd not noticed before. The young deputy strutted over to the gathering crowd. "Cameras off," he repeated over and over.

"Are you shutting down the refuge?" someone called.

"Not at this time," the deputy answered. "You may photograph in other areas. However, you will be asked for some information by the officers who are at the entrance when you leave."

"What's going on?" another voice called.

"We don't know. Someone may have had an accident."

At that point, the refuge tour bus driver called out, "All aboard! Eagle Pond is next!" His voice startled me. I hadn't even noticed the bus.

A large number of people broke away from the onlookers and climbed aboard. I envied them. I'd been looking forward to photographing Eagle Pond. My fingers itched. Then I felt my phone vibrate in my pocket and began to reach for it.

"Let it go to message," Reed murmured without even moving his lips. He leaned into my hair as if to kiss me and whispered, "The less we say or do to arouse suspicion may be better right now."

I knew he was right. I'd spent years around crime scenes and, as illogical as it seemed to us, we were certainly suspects. "It's probably just Teri anyway."

After the deputy cleared out the onlookers, he stretched crime scene tape across the narrow road. In spite of the coolness, I felt my face and neck warming in the bright sun. A coroner's van arrived after half an hour, along with deputies from nearby Socorro. Reed gave me a bottle of cold water from the cooler in the back of his truck and offered one to the deputy.

Finally, Garcia returned. When he reached us, he straightened his hat and stood with his hands at his waist for several moments. We both politely stared at his sunglasses. "You may go," he finally said. Then he thrust a paper toward us. "But, first, do you know this name?"

Reed took the slip. "Marvin Mitchell. Nope. Can't say I do."

Garcia turned to me. "It isn't familiar," I said. "Is that this man's name?"

"We can't confirm his name at this time. We may need to ask you questions again," Garcia told us before strutting off toward the deputy.

Reed and I casually headed toward the truck. Both of us sighed when we finally clicked the seatbelts. Then he asked, "What do you think we should do next? I think I'd like to go on to Branson and check out John's place. You might want to stay here and finish out the festival. After all, you've paid the fees and you're planning to use the photographs for your store."

I was torn but I doubted I could concentrate while I was worried about John. I shook my head. "With this latest development, they may close the festival early anyway. Phone calls are fine, but looking at things there may be more valuable."

"My sentiments exactly," he said.

"Besides," I continued, "I'd be more likely to know if something is out of place. And I'd go nuts waiting here wondering about what you were finding."

I packed an overnight bag at Quail Run and informed the front desk clerk that I wanted any phone messages for my room forwarded to my cell. She agreed to do that.

CHAPTER SIX

I loved Branson's curious combination of country and class. Once a quiet mountain town, it had transformed into a bustling tourist attraction. And, as is often the case, the layout and streets of the town didn't quite match the billboards and flashing lights that advertised well-known television and music stars.

John's modest two-bedroom house nestled in one of the older neighborhoods near a lake in older Branson. A single car garage, built by John himself, crowded his neighbors. He joked that he'd looked for a house with a front yard that he could swipe twice with the mower and have the grass cut—and he'd found it.

Reed and I parked in John's driveway, covered with soggy leaves. His flower buckets overflowed with wilted flowers and more brown leaves. Newspapers littered the front steps, and a note had been stuck to the front door.

"Probably a utility notice." Reed reached over and squeezed my hand. " Let me go first," he said.

"Those may be wilting pansies in that flower pot, but I'm not one!" I snapped, yanking open the door and hopping out.

I pulled out my key ring and sorted through keys until I reached the one with a red dot. Reed reached for it. "What's this red dot?"

"Nail polish."

He laughed. "Only you—"

"I don't use it often. In fact, I haven't been back to Branson since I moved to Saddle Gap. Just wanted to make sure I had it on my key ring still." It was perfectly reasonable to me! I noticed his lip still twitching.

"Willowby wasn't too happy with our leaving."

"Where did that pop up from?" Reed asked.

"Figured you needed a new subject before you stepped into my wrath."

Reed laughed and winked. "Willowby must be better at managing a refuge than he is with law enforcement," Reed commented as we walked up to John's door.

"I hope he doesn't get into a lot of hot water over it," I said.

"Better he instead of we," Reed quipped. "Maybe it's a good thing we slipped out when we did."

We had left just as the state police portable crime unit had arrived and the festival had been shut down. Poor Willowby wouldn't be a popular person with either the visitors or the vendors. I couldn't help but sympathize with both sides.

Both Reed and I had also received our share of suspicious looks. We weren't suspects or anything, of course. I'd just unluckily noticed the man. Nothing connected us to him.

The dead man wasn't necessarily a homicide either. The sheriff had classified him as a suspicious death until the investigation proved otherwise. So it had been a good time to drive to Branson.

Now, standing at John's front door, I didn't feel any better about his whereabouts. People like John just didn't take off on a whim without seeing that things were arranged.

My calls to John's neighbors hadn't calmed my nerves. He'd not told them he was leaving, but he'd obviously hired someone to collect his mail and feed the cat. That was unusual and Cathy Barnes had sounded affronted. "We don't charge him. Why would he hire someone who doesn't even love Van?"

"How do you know he didn't take Van with him?" I asked.

"Because he sits in the front window. Or did. Haven't seen him in a couple of days. Whoever is taking care of him must keep strange hours, too, because we don't see anyone coming and going. And the city is getting picky about how things look. John might get a fine for all those weeds and high grass."

Cathy and her mother had been friendly to me during the weeks I stayed with John but only after she'd "looked me over" as she told me. "They don't call us the Show Me state for nothin'," she'd said.

I doubt they knew why I'd been there, but they'd recognized grief and terror well enough. I'd only been in Branson a couple of weeks before I was invited over to Cathy's house to play Chicken Foot. "You're kidding!" I'd told John when he'd relayed the invitation.

"It's a game with dominoes," he'd laughed. "You might enjoy it."

I had, along with stories about Cathy's middle school classroom, her mother's trips to the chiropractor, and her continually botched matchmaking plans for Cathy. Soon the horror I'd seen had drifted into less terrifying memories.

Now those memories had returned with John's unexplained vanishing act.

"Sorrel?" Reed called. As I stepped up to the door, Reed pulled off the notice, which was about the lawn, read it, and pocketed it. "John may have been gone longer than we thought."

He stepped forward to open the door after I unlocked it, but I pushed him back. "Van may not welcome a stranger," I told him.

"Weird name."

"Van Gogh."

He snickered. I ignored him and stepped inside.

There's a certain air in a house that has been closed up for a while. I'd figured John had left less than a week ago, but his house felt uncharacteristically chilly and musty. Although a neat housekeeper, John lived alone. His coffee cup on the table beside the recliner wasn't unusual, but its lying on its side with dried coffee residue spilled on the table was. A mystery novel had fallen on the floor beside the chair and his reading glasses lay on top of it.

"Van?" I called softly. "Here, kitty, kitty."

"He's here somewhere," Reed called from the kitchen.

It was a small room through an arched doorway straight ahead, with a small alcove for a table and four chairs. Reed pulled on gloves before opening refrigerator and cabinet doors and handed a pair to me. "Just a precaution," he said when I gave him a questioning look. "Better to always err on the side of caution." Then he grinned. "I know, the cop in me is alive and well."

I wasn't fooled. He was trying to lighten the mood, but he wasn't optimistic about what he'd already seen.

One lower cabinet door stood open and a bag of dry cat food lay half in and half out, the side torn open and food spilling out onto the tile floor. I smiled. "Van."

"Meow?" A scruffy yellow striped head peeked around the cabinet door. Yellow-orange eyes glared suspiciously. I ignored them and squatted down to pet the partially chewed up ear.

"Van Gogh," Reed chuckled. "I'd have called him Cassius Clay. Looks like he's a fighter."

"Was," I murmured, rubbing under Van's chin. His purr, like the rest of him, was rough. "He dragged himself up to John's door a few years ago, almost dead. John nursed him back to health. And now he's a lover. What has happened here, boy? John wouldn't abandon you."

Reed found a dish and opened a can of cat food. Van immediately abandoned me and attacked it. "He's thirsty," Reed said, eyeing the empty water dish. He took the dish to the faucet and filled it quickly.

"Something is definitely wrong," I murmured. "John wouldn't have left Van without proper care."

I turned and walked back into the living room and down the narrow hall on the right. John's bedroom was just past the small bathroom. I stopped inside the door and let my eyes slowly sweep the room. His bed looked like it hadn't been slept in, the colorful Navajo blanket smooth and taut. Another pair of reading glasses lay atop a book on Mayan ruins beside his reading lamp and recliner. John bought them four or five at a time—the generic instead of the prescription glasses. I could hear him saying, "I never seem to keep up with just one pair!" I glanced quickly around the room, but nothing looked disturbed.

"Let me look in the closet." Reed spoke from the door. He stepped in and opened the door. I walked over and peeked around him. "Anything look different? Does it look like clothes are missing?" he asked.

"Well, obviously I'm not too familiar with the closet. But John has lived on his own for a long time and he tends to be neat. That," I indicated a hanger on the floor, "is odd. And the clothes sticking out, like some have been pulled out in a hurry, that doesn't seem like John. And he would have taken that jacket." I pointed towards a camouflage jacket.

"Good." Reed looked up at the shelf at the top of the closet. "Looks like something's been pulled out from here. Do you have any idea what he kept here?"

"Not really. He kept all of his business stuff in the office, the spare room next to this one. That's where I slept—on a day bed—when I was here."

Reed was already out the door. "Let's look at it."

I followed him, trailed by the now full Van. John's office looked as neat as usual and I told Reed as much.

"Where does he keep his files?"

I pointed to the closet door. John had removed the clothes rod and moved in two filing cabinets. Behind those, next to the far inner wall, was a small safe.

"Locked," Reed said, pulling at the file cabinet drawers. He reached back and pulled on the safe door. "Everything seems to be undisturbed. Doesn't look like a robbery or anything."

"Unless someone made him open them."

We worked the next few moments in silence, checking the room for any signs of disturbance.

Finally, Reed said, "If an intruder visited here, he was meticulous. I see no sign of any trouble here."

We walked back into the living room. Van met us and wove around my legs. I bent down and picked him up, scratching under his chin. "Wish you could talk, boy," I crooned. "Where's John?"

A sharp rap at the front door made me jump. Reed held his finger to his lips. Another rap. A thud. Then footsteps and a truck starting up. Reed stepped over and peeked out the window. "Fed Ex." He opened the screen and lifted the large envelope up from where it had been dropped between the screen and the door. "Blood Relations," he read. "Located in Ohio. Ever heard of it?"

"No . . . wait! Didn't the letter mention that he was researching family or something? This may be one of those places that look up your ancestors."

"I should leave it here," he said. "If something comes up that a crime has been committed, the police might want to see it."

"Let's take it," I said. "What if someone else comes in and takes it?"

"Who? Sorrel, all we can see is that John may have gone off on a shooting trip."

"And Van?"

"Maybe whoever he hired isn't doing a good job. There's just not enough to indicate anything is amiss here."

They were reasonable observations, but I couldn't let go so easily. "Call it woman's intuition but something's not right here. If there's no crime, what would we hurt by taking it with us? And I'm not leaving Van here on his own."

Reed sighed. "Where's the carrier? But once I look at this Fed Ex stuff, I'll decide whether or not we should show the police."

"Garage. He didn't use it often. And all I was saying was to just see what's inside."

While I boxed up Van's food, litter, and a jug of water, Reed retrieved his travel carrier. I had to lure him inside with a treat that I'd found, but Van wasn't happy. As an afterthought, I dropped the treat bag in the box as well.

Cathy met us as we stepped out on the porch, curiosity lighting up her face. "It doesn't look like anything's amiss," Reed told her. "But we're taking the cat since whoever is taking care of him isn't doing such a good job."

"Or the yard," Cathy generously addressed the small handkerchief patch. "Should I have the man who does mine clean his? Once snow falls on all these leaves—"

"Yes," I said and reached inside my purse for my wallet. "Let me leave some—"

Cathy stopped my hand. "We've been neighbors for a long time. John's always helping us. Besides, it doesn't cost much."

"How long has it been since you saw John cleaning the yard?" Reed suddenly asked.

She thought a moment. "Well, leaves in the fall are a problem, so we do a weekly clean up usually. But, come to think of it, I don't remember him out here in at least three or four weeks. Of course, I've been helping out with my mom a bit and haven't been noticing as much."

We declined her offer of food and settled Van in the truck seat with us. She stood in the yard and waved as we left, clearly not convinced that everything was all right. "Something's just not right," she'd said when I hugged her goodbye.

I whispered the same thing as we pulled out.

"We'll figure it out," Reed murmured. Sometimes, I decided, he wasn't as irritating as other times. Having him here right now was a relief.

CHAPTER SEVEN

Van Gogh wasn't happy with being rescued, and his yowling drowned out any conversation. Or maybe he just didn't like the carrier. Either way, with exhaustion weighing heavily on both of us, finding a motel was our first priority.

We couldn't stay in John's little house because we weren't sure whether or not it was a crime scene. Besides, it felt strange to be there without John.

Just outside the older residential area was The Landing, an area with classy shops, trendy restaurants, and several motels. We turned off the main street into the lot of a mid-priced motel with a "pet friendly" sign.

Reed got out while I cajoled the disgruntled cat. When he came back, he held one key. "It's November, they said. Rooms are scarce as tourism is high just now. But it has two beds."

"I'm so tired I could almost share a room with Godzilla."

"That's a good thing," he said, "because I think we are."

Van complained all the way into the hotel room. When I opened his carrier door, he shot out and hid beneath one of the beds. Reed dumped his duffle bag and my small suitcase inside the closet while I set up food and water bowls in the bathroom. "Shower first?" I called.

No answer. I looked around the door. Reed had removed his clothes and crawled into bed. Nestled against his back was Van. Both of them snored unless—was Van actually purring?

I grabbed pajamas from my bag and returned to the bathroom. A shower would be good, but removing my clothes took a huge effort. How many hours had we been awake, taking turns driving cross country? We'd napped briefly in the truck amid RVs at a Wal-Mart parking lot somewhere in Oklahoma and showered at a truck stop in Joplin. Reed had grabbed food and reminded me to eat.

The hot water warmed and relaxed me as I stood in it longer than usual. I squeezed the shampoo sample the motel provided and massaged my long, red hair. It was longer than I'd worn it when on television but easier for my new life. Kevin had wanted me to cut it short. I had a classic face, he'd said, that could wear almost any style. But I hadn't. Maybe because of my dad and his love of my mane, as he called it.

I stepped out finally and dried off. The warm pajamas I'd packed for my birding trip felt good. I yawned as I braided my hair and secured the ends.

Still, exhaustion couldn't shut down my brain as I crept into bed. I turned on my side and hugged the spare pillow.

I heard Reed get out of his bed. Then his arms pulled me into a hug and his warm body cocooning mine opened the floodgates. I released the pillow and turned into Reed's arms. Finally, I cried. Reed's big hands rubbed my back as he gripped me closer, quietly waiting for me to stop. We lay there for a while, Reed's t-shirt soaked and me reduced to what my dad called snuffles.

"Tell me about John," he finally whispered. "How you met, what he's like, whatever you want."

And so, hesitantly, in whispers at first and then growing into a softer voice with a giggle or two interspersed, I did. I told him how I'd wandered into the wrong building—and class— as a terrified college freshman only to rush out fifteen minutes later when a man walked out from behind a screen and stepped out of his robe and I realized I was in a life modeling art class. John had helped steady me when I bumped into him. "Can I help you?" he'd asked.

"I think I must be in the wrong building!"

"Do you have your schedule?"

And within minutes, he'd walked me over to the Liberal Arts— not Fine Arts—building and up to my correct classroom. When I exited half an hour later, he'd been lounging in the hall outside. "How about we go for a soda in the Sub, and then I'll show you around to your other classes." I'd hesitated and he'd stuck out a hand. "I'm John and I work here when I can't get out of it." He'd smiled at a professor passing by us. "You can vouch for me, can't you, Hank?"

Hank had looked like a professor should, not like pony-tailed John whose jeans and t-shirt could have been student attire. He'd paused a moment, looked at me, and asked, "Freshman?"

I'd nodded.

"John's a freshman advisor and sometimes art professor," he'd said. He'd clapped John on the shoulder. "He can help you get settled in."

And he had. During those early weeks, John had occasionally appeared in the hall outside one of my classes to ask how I was doing. When Thanksgiving approached, he'd invited me to dinner when he learned I was staying on campus. His house, filled with others who hadn't gone home for the holiday, had smelled like my mama's house. It had also rung with laughter. Everyone had pitched in to cook or clean, and afterward we'd wedged into his tiny living room and sung songs while he played his guitar.

It had been the beginning of a tradition for my college years. As I became more involved in classes, work, and friends, I'd seen less of John. But he'd always been there when I needed someone to talk to—about the class I'd not done so well in, the boyfriend who'd wanted too much or too little, the career I craved but was timid about following—and we'd become a strange combination of friend/ advisor/mentor.

When I graduated and accepted a job with a television station in Houston, John and I had celebrated with a special dinner the night before I left. "Sorrel," he'd said, "you are such a combination of brains and heart. Let the brains guide you to the spot you want to go, but make sure your heart is happy with where you're heading." He'd patted my hand and said, "You can always find people who love to be with you, but the ones who love your heart are rare. Find that one."

I'd blithely promised to do just that, hardly thinking more of it than that John was just being fatherly. Our relationship after my move had become distant with the long hours I was working—cards, an occasional phone call—after that. I'd invited him to Kevin's and my wedding but had been secretly relieved when he sent his regrets. Kevin, I'd suspected, wouldn't have been comfortable with John's casual dress.

I'd created the life I'd dreamed of and, until I found myself staring down at Kevin's murdered body years later, I'd thought it was all I'd ever want.

By then, John had retired from the university and moved to Branson. He'd sent me photos in his Christmas cards of his small shop, Heartstrings, where he sold local crafts and his own photography. I'd wondered, briefly, if he was happy.

And then he'd walked through the doors of that police station in Houston—ponytail almost white now, jeans and sneakers still—and I'd run into his open arms. Spending a few weeks in Branson with him as a haven against the threats made against me, I'd finally understood what John had asked me to promise so long ago.

Soon John's love for wildlife photography had captured my imagination. During the days tramping through wildlife refuges, cold mornings spent huddling in bird blinds, and evenings framing prints, John and I had become closer than before.

"Kevin never asked about John," I whispered into Reed's chest. "Why didn't I know that was strange?"

I felt a light kiss on my hair. "We'll talk about that—and a few other things—another time." Reed moved his hand up, cupped my face, and kissed me lightly. "Now, I think we both need to sleep so we can continue our search for a special friend. I think he's waiting for us somewhere."

I started to pull back. "I'm not going anywhere," Reed said. "Just turn your back to me and we'll spoon sleep, as my mama called it. We've got this spot all warm and cozy."

I noticed, just before dozing off with Reed's arms still around me, that Van had curled against my knee, his raspy purring a sort of lullaby.

CHAPTER EIGHT

Reed and I overslept, waking to the sound of a vacuum in the room next to us. Maybe that was good because it was awkward to find myself snuggled up to someone I'd thought would be someone special until he'd vanished without a word.

Reed hopped up and took a quick shower while I dressed, packed up our meager belongings, and placed Van back in the carrier.

"There's a drive-through place on the way out," he said, dropping the room key on the dresser and picking up our bags. "We'll grab coffee and breakfast sandwiches."

"Sure." I stuck a finger through the wire of Van's cage and was rewarded with a lick from his raspy tongue. I knew things weren't perfect in his world, but I prayed we could restore it for him.

In another couple of minutes, we'd loaded the truck and were headed toward the main thoroughfare. "We'll stop by the police department," Reed said. "I'll have them keep an eye on his place."

"Do we file a missing person's report?"

"We could try," he said, turning into the drive-through, "but that would meet with resistance. We have no evidence that a crime has been committed. He was scheduled to meet with you yesterday. They'll argue that he hasn't been gone long enough—only a day— to warrant that kind of report. He probably just got caught up in shooting somewhere and lost track of time. At this time, they may be right." He turned to place our order into the speaker. "Do you want cream for your coffee?"

"Never."

"And I have another reason," he continued. "Say we report him missing and—since he's fairly well known around here—someone leaks the information to the news? The likelihood of John's house being burglarized goes up. Or if he really is in trouble and someone is watching the house, they would know that we weren't just scheduled house sitters. Then we could have problems."

He handed me the coffees, balanced the paper bag on his lap, and pulled into a parking space. He put the truck in park but left the engine running. I handed him his coffee while he dug out the sandwiches. We stuffed everything down as if we hadn't eaten in days.

"Sleeping together makes an appetite," he observed.

I almost choked on my last bite. "Just for that," I answered when I could talk again, "you can do the dishes!"

He chuckled as he put the truck in gear and headed toward the police station.

It was hard to stay mad at Reed. He was a lot like John, I thought. When I'd traveled through those dark weeks following Kevin's death, John had teased me into an occasional giggle. "It's no crime to laugh, even in the saddest times. Laughter is its own medicine," he'd told me. But caution crept in around the attraction I felt toward Reed. We still hadn't addressed his disappearance and the secrets we'd been skirting.

We weren't in the police station long for a couple of reasons. First, it was too cold to leave Van in the truck for a long time. Second, and the primary reason, was that the officer to whom we'd spoken, although polite, clearly didn't think we had a missing person. "I've met him," he said. "And you."

As soon as he said that, I realized he'd been one of the officers assigned to my case. From the skeptical look on his face, he obviously thought the drama queen was back with another goose chase.

Reed quickly filled him in and simply asked if someone could drive by John's house occasionally during the next few days. "Just as a precaution," he asked. The officer agreed—and I hoped he'd keep his word.

"He's probably off photographing something and lost track of time," he said as we stood to leave. "Few people are truly missing.

But if you do want to file a report, just let me know. We'd search the house and ping his cellphone."

A light rain had started while we'd been inside the station. Van growled a greeting and I reached to pet him through his carrier. "Flash will be happy to see you," I told him, pushing a treat through to him. He gave me a disdainful look; we both knew that Van and Flash, although having reached a truce, weren't huge buddies. But he ate the treat anyway.

"Ready to hit the road?" Reed asked, pulling out into traffic.

Branson in November bore no resemblance to the previous spring when I'd stayed a couple of months with John. Traffic bottlenecked the narrow streets, and downtown already looked like a Christmas wonderland. Billboards advertised several holiday shows, and stores glittered with Christmas lights and tinsel. We drove by John's tiny shop, which looked forlorn among its festive neighbors.

At the last second, Reed pulled into the parking lot and into a spot close to the shop. "I almost forgot," he said and hopped out. I followed him onto the sidewalk.

John's shop, nestled into a tiny shopping center, had a sign advertising store hours as 9:00 to 4:00. But another sign had been taped to the door inside. "Temporarily closed for repairs," Reed read aloud.

We peeked inside the front windows but saw no evidence of repairs. Neither had any Christmas decorations been added. The whole scene bore an air of neglect. "When's the last time you spoke with John?" Reed asked.

I had to think a moment. "We talked about the Bosque trip a few weeks ago," I said. "He was excited about replenishing his photos before Christmas season began."

"No mention of repairs?"

"No."

Both of us jumped a little when someone said, "That shop is closed. But we're not."

We turned toward the cheery voice. "Hate to see that," Reed answered. "We'd heard his photos are a treasure."

"They are indeed." The voice belonged to a plump lady dressed as an elf who stood in the doorway of a children's toy store.

"Know when it will be open again?" I asked. "We're from out of state."

"No idea. In fact, it's not unusual for him to take off on a shooting trip—especially during the early fall—but he usually stops by to let the rest of us know."

"Doesn't he have someone keep the shop open?" I'd wandered into Elves Wonderland, drawing a deep whiff of chocolate delights.

"Yes, especially at this time of year. But it says repairs. Maybe he's having a plumbing problem or something." She paused. "All Christmas decorations go up November first in Branson. John was a real wizard with them. We wondered if he'd decided to close down when he didn't decorate."

Other people had entered behind us, and she was clearly distracted. We wandered a moment or two, hoping to question her a bit more. I found a wooden puzzle of Santa's workshop for Teri's twins, and I saw Reed had picked up books. I raised my eyebrows. "Teri fusses at me when I get the boys toys," he said. "So I throw a book in to pacify her."

Teri and her husband, Jose, were Reed's closest friends, and he was godfather to the preschoolers. Although she worked for the newspaper where I was contributing photographer, she also helped me with my gift shop and sold her own line of lotions and scented products. When I was away, like now, she managed the shop.

"You'll love this puzzle," the cheery shop owner told me as she stuffed our purchases into a bag. "They're made by an old gentleman who grew up here."

I gave her my card and told her I also had a gift shop in New Mexico. "It's more a craft shop," I told her. "I'm also a photographer."

"Oh, then it's really bad that you missed the shop next door," she said. "I'll keep this and let him know when he returns. He also has a website, you know."

I did but I'd forgotten, and I could tell Reed hadn't known. We thanked her and walked back to the truck. We didn't speak until we'd turned back onto the main road, headed toward the highway.

As he stopped at a traffic light, Reed said, "I'm beginning to not have a good feeling about this, Sorrel."

"I haven't had a good feeling since he didn't show up at Bosque," I said. "But I think the problem must have started before that. John is a person of habit and is particular about his home and his shop. And he adores Christmas. I hadn't even thought of the Christmas decorations until she mentioned it, but he would have had someone at the shop. I mean, this is a huge holiday here, and I imagine he depends upon it for a huge part of his yearly profits. Why would he leave it right now?"

"I thought he might have had a family emergency at first. Or that he'd gone to meet some family from his research. Didn't he say he was following some leads on family?"

"That would be news for me. As far as I know, John never married and didn't have any children. I've never heard of any relatives."

Van gave a mournful meow, as if to correct us.

CHAPTER NINE

We left Branson with more questions than answers, some of them not even about John, although most of them related to him in some way—except maybe the dead man in the field.

Reed called Bosque to check in with the authorities there and let them know we were returning. I'd paid for the whole week when I'd arrived at Quail Run, and my Jeep was there as well. As Reed pulled out onto the country road, I tried to just enjoy the countryside—as well as the curves.

We switched off drivers near Joplin. Reed answered voicemails concerning work, his voice quiet and private.

After a sandwich at about eight o'clock that evening, we decided to travel a couple of hours longer. Reed took over the driving and turned on a country music station. Van occasionally meowed along with the guitars.

Teri's call startled me. As always, she jumped into a long, uninterrupted chatter without pausing for replies: The boys were terrors as usual. Jose hadn't heard from Reed. She'd been helping Tia make tamales and had left a couple of dozen in the refrigerator for me. Just when I thought she'd never get to why she had really called, she said, "A registered envelope arrived for you Saturday. They left a notice at the door and then another today. You have to go sign for it."

"It's probably just something left over from the sale of the Houston house," I said.

"No," Teri said. I could hear the curiosity she'd been tamping. "The sender is some weird place. Blood something."

"Doesn't sound familiar. It's probably one of those places that are trying to sell something. Or more likely, ask for donations." I felt Reed's sudden stillness.

"A charity wouldn't usually send it certified," Teri said. "Anyway, the notice says they'll hold it for your signature. You can pick it up at the post office when you get back. How's the shooting going?"

"Great." I didn't want to go into anything about John or my trip to Branson over the phone.

We chatted for a moment longer before a loud noise and wails erupted behind her. "World War 98 has begun," she laughed. "And their dad's nose—and his ears—are buried in the ballgame."

"What's going on?" Reed asked, as soon as I hung up.

"Typical Teri." I relayed the bits of chatter she'd shared. Usually Reed chuckled at Teri's updates, but he waited impatiently. "She mentioned that I have a registered envelope from Blood Relations. I wonder if it's the same company as the one on John's." I'd tried for a casual tone, but Reed knew better. We both knew we'd removed a Fed Ex envelope at John's with that return address.

"It really could be an advertisement, Sorrel."

"In a registered envelope? And I've never heard of this place until we looked at the return address on that envelope delivered while we were in John's home."

"You're right," Reed finally said. "It's a little too odd to be a coincidence. Why would they just drop off John's and make you sign? But we have a few miles yet, so we can't panic."

"Who said I'm panicking? I never panic! Even when I had a knife to my throat! Even when you vanished without a word just when things were—"

"—taking off for us?" He sighed. "Isn't it crazy how we prioritize things? I mean, keeping my job seemed important at the time. And eating . . . and a place to park the truck . . ."

I glanced over. "And me?"

Reed flipped on his turn signal and pulled into a roadside park. He put the truck in park and stared out the windshield for a while. Then he turned to me and reached for my hand. "Sorrel, you needed time . . . time to grieve for all you'd lost . . . time to come to terms with things like a new career and a totally new home. Accepting the job at the sheriff's department was a big change for me as well, and you well know that changing jobs comes with a cartload of paperwork and training. Maybe we should be thankful for my job interfering. Both of us have had some experiences behind us that should—"

"—shove caution into the wind and grab the moment while we can?" I interrupted.

"Meow!" came a raucous yodel from the cat carrier.

We looked over into glaring yellow eyes. We both burst out laughing, but he wasn't amused and continued his "meowish" yodel. I reached in the box and pulled out a treat. He sniffed it disdainfully, so I dropped it in his carrier.

"I guess Van's reminding us that we need to get our focus back on business," Reed murmured. "Hold the thought?"

And I did as we crossed the miles to New Mexico . . . and Bosque.

CHAPTER TEN

I sighed. It was a gorgeous day for shooting, and I'd not yet visited the pond the eagles frequented. The problem with shooting is that you either have to give your mind up to it completely or avoid it completely—and my mind was certainly not up to it. Neither was my heart. I hoped I'd gotten some good shots of the cranes and snow geese, but it all felt insignificant now.

We'd pulled into Bosque late last night. I'd stayed at Quail Run, while Reed and Van had driven into nearby Socorro for a pet friendly motel. Yet in spite of the exhaustion from the long road trip, I'd not settled down easily last night. The inconsistent details we'd found in Branson ran through my mind. We must have missed something. I had little doubt that John had left Branson—likely not of his own volition—but he was resourceful and bright. Worrying gave him no real support. I had to draw on my years of investigative reporting, as well as Reed's law enforcement expertise, to help John.

Sometime during the night I must have dozed off for a few hours, waking just after six with heavy eyelids and a growling stomach.

After a hot shower, I followed my nose to the breakfast area. I could have had regular coffee, but the featured coffee was Pumpkin Spice.

"I'll have that one," I told the young waitress. She smiled and left a menu which offered both traditional choices and breakfast burritos.

"Mmm. That smells wonderful!" I told her when she returned.

"Just like pie."

Willowby! How had he known I was here? I looked up and asked, "Would you like to have a cup with me?"

"Don't care if I do," he said and plopped into the opposite seat. I hoped it would hold up.

The waitress came back with another cup. Either she knew Willowby well enough or she had big ears. "I'll have French toast," I told her.

I looked across at Willowby, but he shook his head. "I'm heading back home in a bit and my wife will be upset if I don't have an appetite."

I spent a moment or two trying to visualize a brow-beaten Willowby, but he interrupted my naughty thoughts. "I'd asked the management here to let me know when you returned."

"Got in late last night."

"Any word on your friend?" I could hear the skepticism dripping.

"Just didn't clear his schedule for the festival," I lied. "November is one of the busiest times for Branson. Of eight million or so visitors each year, a huge number come for the Christmas season."

My toast arrived and I poured syrup over it and then cut it into squares. Willowby followed my movements with hungry eyes. "Sure you don't want some?" I couldn't resist asking.

He looked away and took another sip of coffee. "The man you discovered is still a John Doe."

I resisted the urge to ask questions and stuffed a bite of toast into my mouth.

He waited another beat. "I guess you're free to go when you want. But we'll call if we have more questions."

I wondered why he, and not the sheriff, was here telling me this. Maybe it had something to do with jurisdiction. "I want to take more photos anyway," I said as casually as I could.

"So you're staying on?"

"I'd planned to be here a week. I'm not sure yet if I'll follow that plan though. My business is entering its busy time, so I doubt I can stay away too long."

"Hello, Ranger Willowby."

Reed looked around for a chair to pull over but Willowby stood up. "Here, you can have my seat. I've finished my coffee anyway." When Willowby didn't immediately move away, Reed put out a hand.

Willowby shook it reluctantly. "Ms. Janes was telling me about your quick trip to Missouri," he said.

"I told him we didn't have any luck in getting John to come on down. Season just too busy in Branson."

"Place is crammed full of tourists," Reed agreed. He remained standing.

"Your friend coming another time?"

"He didn't say."

It was beginning to feel like a bad comedy. The waitress returned with the coffee pot. "I'd like another one," I told her. "And Reed would like one too . . . black."

She reached over to a nearby table and nabbed the cup from a place setting there, poured his cup, and refilled mine. "Let me know if you want something to eat," she told us.

"Any progress on the body?" Reed asked.

"John Doe." Willowby still stood. When he finally spoke, his voice trembled a bit with outrage, "Probably a shooter for the festival. Totally ruined it. Lots of disappointed folks."

"Well, hope you get it cleared up soon," Reed answered, his tone polite but dismissive. "You have our numbers if you have any other questions."

Willowby finally nodded and turned toward the door.

The waitress returned when Reed sat and took his order: eggs over easy, bacon, and biscuits with gravy. "Good night's sleep?" he asked and took a drink of coffee.

I nodded and waited for him to swallow. "How's Van?"

"Great! He's a decent roommate." Another sip of coffee. "I dropped in on the sheriff after we checked out of the motel."

"Is that why Willowby was here?"

"I doubt it. More than likely he got a call though. This is Willowby's turf. The sheriff really doesn't have any reason to talk to us unless something else comes up. He did say the guy had been there a few hours, likely through the night. They're treating it as a suspicious death, but there's no outward sign of foul play."

"Then why the suspicious death?"

"No ID on him. No vehicle. How did he get there?"

He waited until the waitress put his food down and refilled our cups. "Thanks." She smiled a bit longer than necessary before moving away.

Neither of us spoke the next few minutes while Reed ate. My inner reporter was curious about the poor guy, but at the same time I was relieved that it wasn't John and that Willowby and that the sheriff no longer seemed interested in us. The next order of business was . . . what we should we do next?

"I've been thinking about that." Reed had this uncanny thing about reading my mind—sometimes.

I sipped my coffee. "I think we need to go back to Saddle Gap so I can check on this registered mail from Blood Relations. And you can get back to work . . . whatever that is."

"Why not just open the one we have in the truck? It would save us another long trip."

"It's addressed to John." I'd snooped in other people's mail before, but I wasn't ready to admit it to law enforcement.

"I know but it might give us a clue—"

"—and maybe not. But it will either give us a place to start or move us in another direction. Besides, we need to settle the cat and start a real search. That's easier done there where we're not camping out in hotels or being harassed by—"

"One other thing," a now familiar voice interrupted.

"—Willowby," Reed finished.

We both turned. "I forgot to leave money for the coffee. Don't want any appearance of impropriety."

"There's no need to pay for the coffee," I said.

"Can't accept gifts," he replied. I didn't know how much he'd overheard, but he was clearly snooping. He either had suspicions or was just nosy.

Reed waited until Willowby walked through the door. "For lack of anyone else, he hates to move on. How long will it take you to pack up? We've got an unhappy cat." He grabbed the bill and headed toward the register.

"I had a call from Teri," I told him. "She wondered if I wanted her to pick up Flash as she's working in the store today. So he won't be too unhappy for long."

I put Van in the Jeep with me. "I can take him," Reed said.

"He'll keep me company," I told him.

"If you insist. But turn on the country music station. Van likes that."

CHAPTER ELEVEN

Home looked more like Santa's Christmas Wonderland than Branson had. Even though I'd told Teri to wait until I returned, she'd gotten impatient. Christmas lights lined the windows and roof, Santa rested against the small chimney someone had constructed, and every window winked and glittered.

"I'm glad I don't have to pay your electric bill," Reed said, when he pulled in right behind me.

"Is that all you can say?"

Reed reached in my Jeep and took out Van's carrier. He leaned in and addressed the big cat. "Boy, the first thing you have to learn about women is that anything you say is never right. When you have that down, then you need to know when to—"

"—shut up," I finished for him.

Reed's laughter followed me to the door, only to be replaced by an ecstatic feline howl. Flash almost tripped me as she wove around my ankles, meowing constantly. "Hi, baby," I crooned, bending down to pick her up. "Were you happy to have Aunt Teri rescue you?" She purred loudly, rubbing her cheek against my shoulder as I cradled her.

That lasted only a minute or two until she caught sight of Reed and the carrier. Every hair stood on end and she jumped down, hissing and growling. "Don't you remember Van?" I asked.

Reed set the carrier down and opened the door. "Is it safe?"

"Sure. They finally became friends when I stayed there. By the time we get unloaded, they'll be accustomed to each other again."

The door between my kitchen and the shop opened and Teri burst through and into the short hall. "Sorrel!" she called. "Am I ever glad to see you! Business is booming!" Then she stopped in the doorway. "Reed?"

"I'll just finish unloading things," he said, "and you and Sorrel can catch up."

"Coward," I hissed toward his back.

Teri watched his hasty retreat and then turned to me with her brows raised.

"I really appreciate your picking up Flash at the kennel," I told her, giving her a hug and ignoring the eyebrows. "We've been driving with one disgruntled cat since Branson," I told her.

"Branson? I thought you were going to Bosque!"

"I did. I was meeting John there at this wildlife festival, but he never showed. Then Reed came to the refuge to tell me that John had sent him a letter concerning me. . . and then we went to Branson where John lives, but John wasn't there and after we talked to the police, we knew we needed to come home—"

The bell to the shop door jangled. "Let me take care of this customer and then we'll close a little early," she said as she rushed off. "Dinner at our house."

Reed stuck his head in after she'd left. "Safe yet?"

"Coward," I said again, but a yawn weakened the delivery.

"Nope, just wise. Once Teri gets going . . ." He rolled his eyes.

I nodded then noticed he was holding my bag. "Just dump my suitcase in the bedroom there," I told him.

"I put the photography stuff out in the workroom."

Reed looked as tired as I felt. "Do you want something to drink?" I asked. "I don't know what there's here to eat. I left the refrigerator sort of empty."

"Coffee?" he asked.

"Sure."

I headed to the kitchen, while Reed settled into an easy chair in the living room Having him here felt comforting. With everything that had happened in such a few short days, my world felt tilted.

When I carried in our cups of coffee a few minutes later, Reed had a cat on each knee.

"How do you do that?"

"Cats are discriminating creatures," he said. "They recognize intelligence—"

I snorted and handed him his cup. "There's food down for you discriminating creatures," I told Flash and Van. Both headed to the kitchen as I sank down onto the couch.

We sipped the hot brew and just sat for a moment or two. A cloak of exhaustion settled on my shoulders, chased by the return of worry. I caught Reed's eye and saw the same emotions reflected there. "We need to get that registered letter."

"Yes, we do. But it's too late tonight. The post office closes at five. By the time we get there—"

"—it will be closed."

Neither of us had noticed Teri. She came in and sat beside me on the couch. "You two look exhausted."

Reed nodded. "Sorry about the dinner invite, but—"

"I ordered pizza," she said. "Jose is picking it up and will be here shortly. I locked up the shop, but I need to shut things down." She hopped up. "We'll wake you."

It seemed only seconds later that she touched my shoulder. I'd curled up on the couch and someone had draped a throw over me. Flash curled against my feet. I opened my mouth, but Teri put a finger to her lips and motioned toward the worn easy chair. Reed was sprawled out with his feet on the ottoman, snoring through his slightly open mouth, Van curled up on his lap.

Teri grinned. "He'll never admit he's snoring," she whispered.

Jose had brought two large pizzas, cheese covered breadsticks, sodas, and beer. Except for small talk, everyone plowed into the food. Teri caught me up on the store sales and the twins' preschool activities. Finally, she could contain herself no longer. "So what's going on? Did you get some good shots at the festival?"

"I got a few but I haven't had a chance to look at them yet. I really was only there for the first morning before Reed arrived."

All eyes turned to Reed. "I've been working undercover," he said, "which I still can't discuss. But I got a personal text to my cell. When I got back to the place I was staying and saw it, I was able to take some time. It was just about finished—my part anyway—because I'd gotten about all of the info they thought I could. Then, I'd also received a letter from John. He wanted me to know that he was starting out on a project, tracing his ancestors, and to give me a heads up in case Sorrel had problems or needed my help." He drained his can before looking at me. "I drove to Bosque without coming home because I knew Sorrel would need a friend."

"You never told me about that text, Reed," I complained. "Why not?"

"What—" Teri began.

"Because I knew you'd react like this." Reed interrupted.

"It's John." I turned to Teri. "He was supposed to meet me, remember? But he never showed. I thought maybe he'd gotten tied up, but then he would have called me. And then Reed came—"

"—but first Sorrel found this dead guy at the refuge—"

"—so of course the ranger in charge and the sheriff thought we must be involved in the murder—"

"—and after the sheriff questioned us we went to Branson. John's not there but his home looks suspicious." Reed finished the round robin.

"Foul play?" Jose asked.

"No, not so you can notice," I said. "But some things just aren't like he would leave them for a trip. He would never leave Van unattended."

At the mention of his name, Van padded over. "Poor cat," Teri exclaimed. "Look at his poor ear!" Van identified another softie and moved toward her, taking the bite she held down.

"He's John's cat, Teri. Van Gogh. He wandered up without the ear and John and he adopted each other."

"Poor kitty," Teri crooned.

"You two can drool over the cats later," Jose finally interrupted. "I want to hear the rest of the story!"

"There's not much left," Reed said and then filled them in about the odd address on the Fed Ex envelope delivered while we were at John's, the police report, the neighbors, and Teri's call about the mail waiting for me.

When he finished, Jose asked, "Have you looked at John's letter?"

"Not yet. Thought we'd look at Sorrel's first."

Jose rose, picked up his plate, and headed to the sink. "Then I suggest we get this cleared up and let you get some rest . . . unless you need a bed for the night?"

"My place is likely full of dust and spiders," Reed said. "I'll go there in the morning. Figured I'd just camp out on Sorrel's sofa tonight, if she doesn't mind. Don't know if I can drive another mile."

If Teri and Jose thought that had been laid on a little thick, they didn't comment. Instead, they quickly cleared up and told us good night, with promises from Teri that she would be back to open the shop in the morning.

"You hop in the shower," Reed told me when I offered it to him. "I'll get my bed set up."

When I got out, he'd made cups of herbal sleepy time tea for us and fixed a bed from one of Aunt Rose's quilts on the couch. Van had already snuggled at the foot of it.

"Hop in bed and sip this," he said.

I was too tired to argue and sat on the edge of the bed. As Flash snuggled in beside me, I obediently took a couple of drinks from the cup.

"Reed, I need to know about the text."

"It said, 'Rescue has located a Sorrel horse that needs help.'"

I gasped. "Do you think John was telling you he's in trouble?"

"Sorrel, if he was able to send that message, he's okay. Maye in a tight spot but okay. We both need to rest. Then we'll tackle this tomorrow."

I nodded. He gulped his tea, took my half-empty cup, stood up, and yawned.

"Van and I are pooped," he said. "Like the interesting nightwear!"

I looked down. I'd put on mismatched pajamas. "Fashion statement!" I said.

He threw back his head and laughed. "You'd better get under the covers before I leave the room," he said.

He was probably right. I climbed in and then reached for his hand. "Reed, thank you," and felt my eyelids dropping.

I must have imagined a light kiss on my forehead as I dozed off.

CHAPTER TWELVE

My mama always said that sleeping on a problem is sometimes the best solution. Things seem different—and usually brighter—in the morning.

I woke to the smell of coffee and bacon and a missing cat. I found them a few moments later. Reed looked up from the stove, a smile twitching as he caught sight of me. But he exercised unusually good judgment and kept his mouth shut. Flash wove around his ankles.

"Don't say a word!" I snapped.

"I can't even say—"

"No!" I pushed the hair out of my eyes and glared at my contented traitor cat. Then I headed back into my bedroom.

"Your mama got up on the wrong side of the bed," he told Flash in a loud stage whisper.

When I emerged again, dressed in a pair of jeans and sweatshirt and my hair bunched in a ponytail, Reed was seated at the table finishing up his breakfast. He started to rise but I quickly shushed him.

"I can wait on myself. I've never seen a wilting violet, but I'm certain I bear no resemblance to one." I poured a cup of coffee and sat down opposite him at the table. Flash flopped down on my feet and glared at Van munching on dry food across the room.

"Looks like both our girls woke up grumpy, Van." This time the stage whisper was difficult not to smile about.

I reached for a slice of crispy bacon and took a bite. "I'm not grumpy. And I'm not one of your girls!"

No one said anything for a bit while I finished the bacon and spread jelly on a slice of toast. Reed poured himself another cup and silently sipped it.

"Did you sleep?" Reed finally asked.

"Some."

"I haven't forgotten John, Sorrel. And it's okay for you to laugh with friends. John would want that."

"How do people know what someone would want?"

Reed sighed and sipped his coffee. "I know you've said that John has been more a dad to you than a friend." I chewed on the tasteless toast.

"Sorrel, you don't talk much about your dad—or any of your family."

"Neither do you."

Reed looked down in his cup. "Got me."

"My dad was older than Mama" I finally said. "He'd been in the military—still was when I was born—so he wasn't there all the time. I had an older stepbrother, but he lived with his mother and the few times he came to visit, he seemed jealous of me. And bossy!"

"Like me?"

My mouth twitched. "You're worse."

Reed wisely didn't address that. "Do you still keep in touch?" he asked instead.

"No. I have no idea where he is . . . or when I saw him last. He didn't even come to Dad's funeral. I was in elementary school when Dad died.""

"Tough."

"Well, Mama was a teacher so we had her salary. We sold the ranch and moved into town into a little house. It must have been a challenge for her. The ranch sale money paid the mortgage on the house, but Dad's military retirement checks stopped. She was a wonderful teacher and loved her job. That's probably why we stayed in Montana instead of moving here closer to Aunt Rose."

I swallowed the last of my coffee and continued. "Mama died, and I went to college on a scholarship in Missouri. I met John and he helped me through those first weeks—just sort of stepped in. He was a wonderful teacher, but he also looked after those of us who were sort of lost sheep."

"Seems like a long way to go to college," Reed said.

"I'd applied for journalism scholarships all over, but with Mama gone, I'd accepted the one farthest away. It is also one of the top journalism schools in the country. I realize now I was running away."

We both started when a car door slammed. "Teri, I imagine," Reed said. "You'll want to go over store things with her. And I need to report in. Want to meet up for lunch or something?"

"I'm going to pick up the letter. Why don't you just come here when you've taken care of things?"

"I'll pick up something and bring it to you," Reed said and left.

The door had scarcely closed when the bell between the shop and my house rang and Teri bustled past me with her usual chatter and energy. Sales had really taken off since the first of November. My framed wildlife photos were selling well, but Teri's own line of lotions and soaps far exceeded them. I'd stocked my shop with consigned crafts from a variety of people in the area, including seniors from retirement homes. Vendors either paid a fee or volunteered in the store. Teri handled the work schedule and I took care of the books, which had worked well for us so far.

"I've scheduled several more workers from the senior center for the day after Thanksgiving," she told me when I commented on last week's sales. "And we need to start playing Christmas music, don't you think? It gets people in the mood to shop."

"If they've driven all the way out here, they're in the mood."

She either didn't hear me or ignored me—probably a little of both. "I've put those Christmas bells on the door to warn us that people are here. "

"It's a small shop, Teri, and we're out here in the country on our own. When a car drives up, we know it."

"Tia could set up her travel trailer by the pavilion," Teri continued. "Posole and tamales . . ."

Sometimes I wondered if Teri ever heard anyone else. Then she turned to me and said, "Sorrel, it's going to be okay. I lit a candle for John at mass. He's probably just lost track of things like you do when you're taking your photos. Oh, and Mr. Byrd needs you to stop by soon so he can schedule you for some photos for his Christmas special edition."

"Thank you for your prayers and thoughtfulness for John, Teri. As for Mr. Byrd, I don't know if I'll have time. I guess it depends on when he'll need them. Did he mention anything specific?"

"No, he just asked you to stop by. I did tell him you were on a photo shoot in Bosque, though, so if you called instead of dropping by, I'm sure if would be fine." Mr. Byrd was the editor of the local paper. I supplemented my income with freelance work for him since my shop was so new and business was sparse some months. He'd fired me once—and I still felt a coolness in his attitude—but the public loved my photos.

I added a note to my phone to call Mr. Byrd. Then I waited until Teri took a breath and asked, "Teri, I need to go to the post office to get that registered mail. Are we set for workers today?"

She sighed dramatically. "Have you heard anything I've been telling you? I'm here this morning and we have the quilting group this afternoon."

I laughed. "Okay. And remember that we have two felines at the moment. I know that Flash knows not to venture into the shop, but Van is new to the game. If you have to come in here, be careful he doesn't run into the shop and escape. I don't know if he'll scratch if you try to catch him."

"Aw, Sorrel, he's a softie."

"Even softies have claws, you know."

Teri impulsively grabbed me and hugged. "I've got things under control here. You go on and do what you need to do. Oh, you might want to contact the phone company."

"What's the problem now?"

"Hang ups. Lots of hang ups . . . but I guess they won't do anything about that, will they?"

"I doubt it but I'll add it to my list."

The front door jangled and Teri hurried out. She was already greeting the new customer as I locked the door between my house and the shop. As I headed through my living quarters to the outside door, I saw both cats snuggled up in the easy chair, their backs to each other like bookends. They had apparently decided to be friends after all.

"Flash," I said, "as usual, you're in charge." She answered drowsily, "Purr-meow."

I could stall no longer.

CHAPTER THIRTEEN

"We can approach this several ways," Reed said.

I must have jumped a foot. "Reed!" I squealed. "You scared me! Have you been lurking—"

He laughed. "You were walking in a fog. Probably didn't hear me with your ears ringing from Teri's chatter. We can either ride together or you can go on your own and we can meet up later and discuss whatever—"

"I thought you were going by your place!"

"I was. Then I got a call so I just pulled over in the roadside park and talked. I'm clear with work. They'll probably need me to testify and they'd like me to keep a low profile. So I turned around to see if I could still catch up with you."

"I don't need a babysitter, Reed."

"I know but I figured that two brains might be better than one. I don't like the feel of this." He winked. "Okay, I'm also nosey. Helps with my job, though."

I silently agreed with the nosey part. Reed followed me to the Jeep and reached to open the door. "I'll drive," I said and opened it. Reed sighed and walked around to the passenger side.

Two more cars had pulled into the parking lot. Business was good but I couldn't rejoice in anything just now.

I flipped the stereo knob to a popular country music station and turned out on the highway. Reed stared out the window as I drove the few miles into Saddle Gap. At the post office, I whipped into a parking spot on the side and hopped out as Reed answered his cell.

It must have been the busiest day of the year for the Saddle Gap post office. Fifteen minutes later, I returned. Reed shut his phone as I opened the car door and slid in, gripping the large envelope and fighting the urge to rip the thing open right there.

"Do you have any other errands?" I finally asked.

"Why don't we find a quiet place to look this over and talk?" I looked at Reed. Something in that phone call must have disturbed him, but I already knew he wouldn't tell me until he was ready. And he was right about one thing—a crowded parking spot in front of the post office wasn't a good place to talk about it.

I started the Jeep and pulled out. "Let's go back home," I said. "Teri doesn't disturb me during work hours unless it's something she can't handle."

Almost every parking place out front was filled when we pulled into my place. Silently, we walked through the enclosed porch I'd converted into a workroom and into the living room.

"I could use a cup of coffee," Reed said.

"I think the pot is empty, but I have instant."

"I'll pass," he grimaced.

I scooped Flash up and curled up in the big chair. She snuggled in my lap. Van trailed behind Reed as he re-entered with a steaming cup in each hand. He handed me one and then sat on the couch. "This is the last of the breakfast pot. It might be too strong."

I took a sip and grimaced. "Ewww!" I set it on the small table beside me. Then I picked up the envelope I'd placed on my lap and looked briefly at the return address. "Columbus, Ohio." I tore it open and pulled out a letter, a couple of other stapled pages, and a self-addressed envelope.

"Dear Ms. Janes," I read out loud. "Thank you for choosing Blood Relations for your DNA testing. We are not only the most reliable company in the business but also the most discreet, as you know. Therefore, although it is most unusual for a client to request DNA testing results be sent to your father before—" The letter fell from my fingers and onto the floor. "This isn't funny!"

Reed picked it up and handed it to me. I looked once more at the return address and the letterhead. "There's a phone number. I'd call and give them a piece of my mind, but I'd only get a little receptionist or someone—"

"You could ask for whoever signed the letter."

"I know that, Mr. Christopher Reed. You know that I spent several years as a top-notch investigative reporter. I've made a few ... 'not friends' . . . and they've decided to pull a joke on me. I have never liked cruel jokes!"

"Sorrel—"

"Of all times for someone to do this!"

"Sorrel—"

"What?"

"Isn't this the same place that sent John the Fed Ex envelope?"

"And your point is? Reed, maybe this is one of those bogus marketing schemes where they act like you've purchased something just to pull you in. Maybe they sent one to John as well."

"Kind of an odd coincidence." Reed got up and sat down beside me. " Here." He handed me a tissue.

That was when I realized I was crying. I don't cry well and I hate it. When I was small, I would run out to the barn and rake the horse stalls until the storm passed. But now two arms pulled me tight and there were no stalls to rake. The tears ran silently as I held myself stiffly in his embrace.

Finally, Reed eased his arms a bit. "I don't want to sound like a sissy," he said, "but I don't usually wear my shirts while they're being soaked."

I pulled back to look at him, but he wouldn't let me get up. Sure enough, I'd soaked the shoulder of his shirt. "I'm so sorry. I—"

"I didn't mean I didn't like it. This knight in shining armor thing just takes a little care not to rust."

I managed a weak smile. "I'll go wash my face." This time he loosened his arms.

"Looks like I need to make some fresh coffee," he said. "No woman just washes her face."

He was right. When I re-entered the living room with a clean face, I'd also reapplied lip gloss and combed my hair. "Ready for battle?" he joked.

I sat down, forced myself to sip the fresh coffee, and picked up the fallen letter. I glanced up at Reed.

"No, I didn't snoop, although I was tempted."

I took a deep breath. "Reed—"

"Don't say it, Sorrel. I'm doing my best with this knight thing. I didn't lose it with the waterworks, but when you look at me like that . . . I just might forget that you're the contrary filly that you are and ride off into the sunset with you over my saddle."

I smiled at his bad John Wayne imitation.

"That's better. Now read this thing. I'm dying to know what the rest of it says."

"Okay, but you need to know I didn't have a DNA test done. They must have the wrong person. I don't know how this stuff operates, but—"

"Sorrel . . . the letter?"

I reread the first part, my voice quivering a bit on the word *father* and then continued, "before sending it on to your attorney and you. You will find your results as well as the names in our database that indicate that they are your blood relations. The results will indicate the percentage of chances that they are related as well as whether they are brothers, aunts, cousins, etc. Only people who have been tested with us are listed, so you could have other relatives as well. Also enclosed is a form for you to sign if you want your name to be sent to these who have already signed consent forms. Please let us know if we can further assist you."

"Are you sure you didn't do this?"

"Reed! Don't you think I'd remember if I sent my DNA off! And my attorney—and I have no idea who this Henry Brown is—certainly doesn't live in California. Like I told you, someone has either played a joke on me or the company has mistaken my identity! My father? He's been dead for fifteen years!

As I vented, Reed had reached for the stapled sheets and begun reading through them.

"Why would anyone think this was funny? This is a nasty, unfunny joke!"

"Sorrel."

Something in Reed's voice hushed me and I looked over at him. He was gripping the letter so tightly his fingers were whitened. "You need to look at this list."

I reached over and pulled the sheets out of his hand. The first name on the list, with a ninety-five percent chance of accuracy, was labeled Father. The name was John's.

CHAPTER FOURTEEN

"This is crazy!" I looked at the paper again. I had heard of elaborate hoaxes, but this one was the most ridiculous I'd ever seen. "These people are good," I told Reed.

Reed continued reading through the paperwork. "Really, someone just has to do some creative computer work," Reed said. "It wouldn't be hard to do. They could order results for someone else and then just scan, cut, and paste."

"And my information? My blood type, my social security number—"

"Easy if you know how to search. What we need to be figuring out—"

But the ringing of his cell phone interrupted him. He looked at the number and raised his eyebrows. "Willowby," he said and punched the speaker button.

"Sheriff Reed? This is Ranger Willowby."

"Not sheriff. I'm only a deputy. How can I help you, sir?"

"Oh. Well, deputy, I think it's how I can help you." He gave the statement a weighty pause. When Reed didn't respond, he continued. "A package arrived for your friend, Ms. Janes. I could forward it, but I'm going to be in the area anyway this week. Mrs. Willowby and I are visiting friends in Tucson. We've never been to Saddle Gap, so we thought we'd take an alternate route—maybe even go over to Tombstone."

"Ms. Janes is right here. Why don't I let you explain things and she can decide about her package."

Reed handed me the phone, leaning in to whisper, "Curiouser and curiouser."

I listened to Willowby's explanation. "What a nice offer, Ranger Willowby! But you really don't need to go to all that trouble, sir. This is such a busy time for you. Can you forward it? Or hold it until I come back that way"

But Willowby began detailing his protestations again until I finally agreed. "Well, Ranger Willowby, if you don't mind . . . you have the address. . . . tomorrow? Okay, I'll see you then."

I handed Reed his phone. "The ranger doth protest too much."

Reed laughed. "From Dr. Seuss to Shakespeare."

"You read Shakespeare?"

"Don't look so surprised. I'm not a total heathen. Besides, Mrs. Knowles held the power."

"Graduation requirement?"

"Worse. Football eligibility . . . had to keep the grades up to play."

We were both quiet for a moment. "Reed," I said then. "It's time to open John's mail."

Inside was a certified letter. The envelope had been resealed with wide tape. Reed pulled out his pocket knife, eased it under the tape, and then handed the envelope to me. I looked at the mailing date. March of this year! I'd still been staying with John at that time, waiting until the authorities thought it was safe to leave.

The letter enclosed was the same form letter I'd received, explaining how to interpret the results they had reached. I shuffled to the next page. About twenty names were listed, each with contact information as well as the individual's possible relationship to John. One name caught my eye. Patricia Stevens, a lady in Tennessee. She was on my list as well! I could feel from Reed's stillness that he'd also made the connection. What could all this mean?

I picked up the list from my letter and compared it to John's. Except for his name at the bottom, we had the same list. "It would be hard to fake all of these numbers. We need to check them out."

Reed had been quiet as I processed the information, his brain searching for answers as mine was. "John could have sent your DNA in, Sorrel," he finally suggested. "A strand of hair with the follicle still attached—"

"Why? If he wanted my DNA, why didn't he just ask? Besides, John had no idea who I was when I started college. It was pure chance that I ended up there! "

"Why did you choose that particular college? Had you been looking at it?"

"It had a great television journalism department. I was class valedictorian and received scholarships but not enough to pay the whole thing. I'd almost decided to just start at the junior college at home when—"

"—you received a big private scholarship?"

I felt my throat close. "Yes. An endowment."

"From?"

"The family wanted to be anonymous," I whispered. I got up and walked toward the door. "I think I want a few moments to think," I said.

"Don't forget your coat. It's chilly out there in the gazebo."

I hadn't noticed that the sun had started down. I grabbed a jacket and pulled up the zipper. "Reed, could you let Teri know that I . . . have a headache. This is our last day for the shop until we reopen the day after Thanksgiving. Tell her I'll call her and we can talk about the plans . . . later."

The gazebo was nestled just behind my little house. Teri's family had built it in the spring in the same space that an old building had occupied, a building burned down by a killer. The gazebo had become my haven. I sat down on one of the handmade benches and admired the pots of pansies. They would grow here all winter, filling my space with purples and yellows and crimsons . . . and peace.

But peace wasn't coming today. Questions flew around in my mind faster than I could contemplate answers. If this were true, then my dad . . . hadn't been my dad at all. And my mom had lied. Both were inconceivable. Everything I knew—the essence of who I was— would be a lie!

I'd cried plenty lately—the strong girl who seldom shed a tear. Now, I just ached all inside and there wasn't enough room for tears.

It had grown dark and I shivered in the cold. The twinkle lights had automatically switched on, but they didn't lighten my spirits like they usually did. Then I felt his presence behind me.

"I made a pot of potato soup," Reed said. "My mama's recipe. It always lifted my spirits. Ready to sample it?"

I wiped my suddenly wet eyes on my sleeves. "I love potato soup," I said.

CHAPTER FIFTEEN

The red numbers on the clock glowed ominously. 2:11 . . . 2:12 . . . 2:13. I reached over and clicked on the lamp. Flash protested, blinked at me, and then settled back into the warm bed.

I'd actually gone to sleep quickly after Reed left last night. Reed and I had spent the evening researching Blood Relations on the Internet. They seemed like a legitimate company. So I'd finally composed a letter and emailed it to their help desk. Someone had submitted my DNA—or had pretended to submit my DNA. How would Blood Relations know that it was mine or an imposter's? When had it been submitted? I hoped they would or could answer my questions.

While I'd done that, Reed had made a few calls, including one to the Branson Police Department. They'd had nothing to report, although they had made a few inquiries. They had no real cause to suspect John had been taken against his will. The people they had spoken with had all said the same thing: he often took off without telling anyone for his photography trips. They had seen nothing suspicious.

I walked into the kitchen and rummaged around until I found the box of herbal tea guaranteed to help one sleep, silently thanking Teri. She had stocked my tea supply, convinced I drank too much coffee. I put a mug of water and a teabag into the microwave, all the time trying to figure out what was niggling at my brain.

The microwave beeped. I added honey to my tea, carried the steaming mug into the living room, and curled up in the overstuffed chair. He wasn't wrong—it was perfect for snuggling into when I needed to cuddle. I blew into the steaming mug and took a sip. As usual, Teri was right. I loved it.

A movement—a shadow–on my left made my heart stop. I eased the mug to the side table. Out of habit or economy of movement, I'd put my cell in my robe pocket. My forefinger found the keypad and I pushed 9—

"Meow?"

I gasped. A huge battered feline eased from behind the couch. "Van! I almost had a heart attack!"

He padded over to me, leaped onto my lap, and gazed wordlessly with huge yellow eyes. I stroked his head, and he curled into a ball against my chest. "It's going to be okay, Van," I lied. "There's no need for you to worry." Maybe he believed me, because a rumbling purr vibrated against me as he snuggled closer. It reminded me of those weeks when I'd stayed with John after Kevin's death. Van had comforted me then.

I sipped my tea, stroked John's cat, and watched the mental movie play in my mind. Things had worked out. And they would again. I just had to be my resourceful self. My years as a television journalist gave me an edge, and I had to use those skills. If John was in trouble, tangled up with unsavory characters or just hurt from some accident, then my panic would only hurt him more. How would I approach this dilemma were he a total stranger?

I emptied the cup and carried it to the kitchen, Van cuddled up in one arm. I yawned. "Time to get some sleep, Van Gogh," I whispered. "We have lots to do tomorrow to reunite you with your partner."

Flash hardly moved when I settled Van next to her and slid into bed. Ranger Willowby and Mrs. Ranger would be here tomorrow. I envisioned an oversized tyrant ordering Willowby around while he scurried to please her. The thought brought giggles, and both cats raised their heads to gaze balefully. I settled back under the quilt my mama had made. To believe those crazy DNA results would negate everything I had known my whole life. It couldn't all be a lie! But why? What would possibly motivate someone to create false DNA results? Neither Mama nor Dad had amassed a fortune in their lives. John certainly wasn't rich. So we could rule out money as a motive.

The motive must be related to the one common denominator— me. I'd naturally stepped on a few toes over the years, if not completely antagonized others.   I'd worked for the local station during college, more as a general fetch-and-carry slave, until my senior year when a co-ed had disappeared. Her car had been left at the airport, and no one could provide a clue. Yet there had been no evidence of foul play. Local authorities had finally let the file go cold.

I'd passed her dorm on my way to class one morning just as a van parked in the loading zone. Her parents stepped out, the pain weighing on their faces. "Can I help?" I'd asked. They'd looked at me blankly then quickly shook their heads. "Are you packing? I can help. I'd like to."

They'd just sort of shrugged their shoulders, so I'd followed them upstairs and started filling boxes. They'd seemed relieved to not have to touch her things, hauling furniture instead. When they lifted her desk, a letter had fallen out—a letter with a Canadian postmark. I'd picked it up. "Pitch it," her dad had said. Instead, I'd followed the lead. And the station had allowed me to broadcast the story of her rescue.   And the rest—as they say—was history. My story had been picked up by a national network, and Houston had made their offer.

I yawned again. Teri's tea had performed its magic. Just as I was drifting off , a stray memory that had been niggling in my brain all evening surfaced. The break in. We had never tied the break in here during the spring to anything relevant. Someone had gone through my office.   Nothing much of importance had been disturbed—or taken—except the small trash basket by my desk.

CHAPTER SIXTEEN

Someone hovered over me. I tensed and willed myself not to move. I could feel warm breath against my neck. Eyes bored into mine, checking for any twitch of a muscle or flutter of an eyelid. Had my breathing changed?

Someone leaned forward and lightly touched my cheek. He jumped when my phone started ringing. I opened my eyes and stared deeply into big green ones. "Flash!" I yelled. "You terrified me!"

She stared at the bedside table and my phone. The phone! I grabbed it. "Hello?"

Silence.

"Hello? May I help you?"

Silence. Then the soft click.

This was my landline. Thankfully, I'd had Caller ID installed but when I checked it read UNKNOWN. I reached for my cell and checked for missed calls. There were two messages.

I scratched Flash behind her ears as I listened to the first message. It was Teri. "Sorrel, I know we need to talk about the sale on Black Friday. Let me know when you want to get together and I'll put you on my schedule. I'm helping with the boys' Thanksgiving program at their preschool and there's the family tamale marathon. Hope you're sleeping in." Teri, as usual, ended with a giggle. As part of a huge family, she was always juggling several activities at once; yet she was still a good—no wonderful—friend and helper with the shop. We were unlikely cohorts, coming from such different backgrounds, but we had jelled.

The second one was from Reed. "I'm doing some office work. If I'm not there when Willowby gets there, give me a call."

I glanced at the clock. Eight o'clock. "No wonder you two are singing the 'I'm starving!' chorus," I told my furry buddies. "I'll be there in a minute!"

By ten o'clock, the cats and I had breakfasted, I'd showered, and they'd groomed each other and snuggled for a nap. I'd even managed to vacuum and dash around with a dust cloth. Aunt Rose had practiced the sniff test. I sniffed and . . . it passed.

"And just in time," I told the felines as tires crunched in the driveway. I walked over and peeked through the door peephole but couldn't see a vehicle.

Then I heard someone knocking on the front door of the shop. The knocking grew louder. "Just a minute!" I called and hurried around booths Teri had moved closer together for the Black Friday sale.

Ranger and Mrs. Willowby stood uncertainly outside.

I unlocked the door. "Hello!" I smiled my television-reporter-about-to-interview smile. "I'm so sorry. My private residence is at the back and I forgot to warn you. Just come on in and we'll wind our way to my quarters."

Mrs. Willowby stepped into the shop, her eyes scanning the various displays. The ranger followed. Neither of them spoke.

Teri's uncle had built wooden waist-high booths my consignees had filled with a variety of crafts. Many of the crafters lived at the local nursing home and helped out in the store. I explained all of this as we stood there a moment and then turned to relock the door. "We're closed until Thanksgiving and will have a big sale on Black Friday," I told them.

Before I could turn the lock, however, the door was pulled open by a big hand. "Ranger Willowby," Reed said, reaching past me to shake hands. "And is this your wife? Chris Reed." He touched the brim of his hat, a gesture out of an old western movie that I'd never seen him use. It worked.

Mrs. Willowby smiled. "Sheryl."

So she could speak! "I'm sorry, Sheryl. I've been rude. My name is Sorrel." I included the whole group in my smile. "Would you like to come on back for a cup of coffee? I'd invite you into my office," I gestured toward the tiny cubicle at the back of the store, "but I'm afraid it would be a bit crowded."

"We wouldn't want to put you out," Willowby said.

I started weaving my way toward the back. "Of course it isn't a problem," I assured him. "I just made a fresh pot."

The Willowbys settled on the couch I'd bought from one of Teri's cousins, and Flash strolled over to greet them. "I didn't ask if you're allergic to cats. I can put them up," I said. "I have Flash there and I've collected my friend's cat, Van, while he's away."

"No need." Sheryl reached out to stroke her shiny back. "We have some of our own."

I'd need to give Flash an extra cat treat, I decided, as I watched Sheryl Willowby relax. "How many coffees?"

A few moments later I came out with a tray and set it on the coffee table. A lively conversation had started while I'd been in the kitchen. I'd even heard Sheryl Willowby laugh. I suspected Reed had exerted his charming side. He'd offered to help me, but I knew he'd be a greater help here.

"Help yourselves," I said and stepped back into the kitchen for the brownies I'd stirred up earlier.

My dad always said you get to know a lot about a person over a cup of good coffee. As usual, he was right. During the next few minutes, I watched Willowby sneak half a dozen brownies from the plate and wash them down with coffee doctored with cream and sugar. Sheryl declined the brownies and accepted a cup of black coffee. She sipped it carefully and studied my coyote collage I'd arranged on the wall opposite her. "You're a good photographer," she remarked.

"Thanks. I love it. I took some courses in college, but the last several years I've not done much. I'm rusty but you have great subjects with nature."

"Yes, they are," she said.

I nodded. "Still, I've got a lot to learn."

Willowby had been eavesdropping. "You ought to see Sheryl's stuff," he said. "She likes to draw animals on fabric."

"Sort of," she corrected him. "I make tapestries," she told me.

"Wow! That's a lot of work," I said. "I don't have any of those in the shop, but a lady in Arizona makes needlepoint pillows and framed pieces. My shop is consignment, so if you'd be interested in selling some of your work sometime, you're welcome."

"I saw those needlepoint items." She seemed to warm up a bit. "I'd like to take a closer look sometime."

"Any time."

"They couldn't be better than your stuff," Willowby bragged. I could like this Willowby, I decided, seeing the affection in his smile.

Sheryl patted his hand and reached for her cup. She wasn't as shy as she'd seemed at the front door, I decided. Instead, I suspected she was the boss of their outfit in spite of her waiflike body. Willowby, on the other hand, resembled a bear, with his round face and watermelon-sized tummy. Both of them looked to be in their fifties. I was tempted to extend the conversation. People interested me and it was difficult not to spend time finding out more about them. But it was time to move this visit on.

I met Reed's eyes briefly and read the same thought. I spoke first, "You said you had something for me? It came to the refuge?"

Willowby set his cup on the coffee table and reached over for the jacket he'd laid on the arm of the couch. "UPS actually. It came to the bed and breakfast. They were going to mail it on to you, but we were coming this way anyway . . . we're going over to check on Sheryl's parents in Arizona and visit with friends there."

"It's not a good time," Sheryl interrupted. "Dad is down with shingles and Mama doesn't drive any more. So I'm going to stay for a bit. Honey Bear can come back at Thanksgiving and take me home."

It took my years of training to keep my smile from breaking out. I didn't dare meet Reed's eyes, but I noticed he took a gulp of coffee. I murmured polite sympathy.

"Here it is," Willowby said and handed a padded envelope over to me.

I took it and looked at the label. John's name and Missouri address were typed in the return address box. It was addressed to Sorrel Janes. The envelope was light and about the size of a piece of typing paper. I held it a moment longer, then casually laid it on the coffee table.

"You didn't need to take all this trouble," I said as I reached for my coffee cup. "Anyone want a refill?"

"I'll get it," Reed said. Both of the guests declined and thanked me politely.

Willowby was clearly curious about the envelope but didn't press the point. When I asked him about the dead body I had discovered at the refuge, he was vague. "That's still under investigation."

"Have they identified him yet?" I asked.

Willowby shook his head. "That takes a bit," he said. "We're following all of the usual avenues. Actually, the sheriff's office and the state crime lab are working on it. We may not know for a bit." Then he added, "Odd that no one had seen him until you spotted him."

After a few minutes more, both of the Willowbys rose and said they needed to get back on the road. I led them out the front door of my house and around to the front of the shop where they'd parked. Sheryl chatted about some of the things she'd noticed in the shop. "I'd love to take some time and shop," she said.

"You're certainly welcome to look around now," I lied. Well, maybe I didn't lie, but I fibbed. Willowby clearly still suspected that the stranger lying dead in his refuge was connected to Reed and me. And I could hardly restrain myself from racing back to open and read the letter.

Sheryl took me at my word and agreed, so I unlocked the door while she chattered happily and moved from booth to booth, inspecting items and even buying a needlepoint for her mother. "We don't exchange gifts at Christmas," she confided, "because she has too much stuff already. I usually bake something instead. But this will brighten her up."

I felt guilty about my earlier brusqueness. Sheryl wasn't a bad person at all. It gave me fresh hopes that Willowby may not be so bad either.

Reed smiled and waved as they backed out. "Thank God that's over," he said through his toothy smile. Then he turned toward me. "I have some news for you."

CHAPTER SEVENTEEN

"News?" I sputtered. I'd held it in until we were inside the door. Then I turned on Reed. "Is your phone broken?"

Reed grinned. "I thought I'd wait until we'd gotten rid of the Willowbys. I never figured you'd have a tea party."

"Coffee. Coffee and brownies. After all, Willowby hasn't been too friendly and I figured I'd catch a few flies with—"

"Honey Bear?"

My giggles erupted and Reed's laughter joined in. It felt good to laugh, but I felt a little guilty as well. The Willowbys were nice people, and they had gone out of their way to deliver the mail.

Reed must have felt the same. As he picked up his cup, he remarked, "They did save you a trip. He obviously dotes on her. Not always the case with people who have been married so long. He told me they've been married over twenty years."

He came back in with Flash under an arm and sat on the sofa.

"News?" I prompted.

"I got a call from Branson."

"And?"

"There was a break-in at John's shop."

"Anything taken?"

"That's the odd part. Nothing seemed to be missing, although you'd have to know the inventory. But to the police, there was no apparent robbery. Whoever was there rummaged through the paperwork on John's little work desk."

"That doesn't seem worthwhile."

Reed sighed. "I know. I told the officer that John is very neat, so having the paperwork in disarray is odd. They figure it was some kid thinking to find spare change." He took a drink from his cup.

"Except?"

"Except it may not have been a break-in at all. Sorrel, the shop appeared to have been opened with a key. The only reason the police responded is that the silent alarm wasn't turned off. By the time they got there, the door was closed and nothing seemed amiss otherwise."

"And their take is?"

"They think we may be panicking. Maybe John isn't really missing, just wants some privacy."

"Because of the key."

"Yes."

"Which we know is crazy. First, John had planned this trip for a while. In fact, he had to talk me into it. I mean, I wanted to go, but with the store open less than six months and the biggest holidays of the year approaching . . . well, he didn't convince me to go easily. Then he doesn't show up? No phone call, no messages—"

"—the package the Willowbys brought!" we chorused.

I looked around Reed. It was still on the coffee table where I'd laid it. I walked over, picked it up, and examined the envelope, one of those square postal envelopes for speedy delivery. I could feel Reed close to my shoulder, but he walked past and sat on the couch. I appreciated that he was giving me space.

I ripped the flap and looked inside. "It's empty!" I said. I opened it wide and turned it upside down. A tiny square floated down to my feet. A black and white photo. I bent down and picked it up.

A chubby baby smiled up at the photographer, her toes hidden in a footed sleeper. The baby must have been about six months old. He or she wasn't able to sit up yet. A slim arm supported her. My mama's arm. Was it my baby picture? I'd never seen it before, but I was her only child.

"Sorrel? Are you all right?"

I couldn't pull my eyes away. I heard Reed rise and walk my way. Gently, he reached out and took the tiny photo. "Cute hairdo," he said. I looked at the photo he was now holding up. "Mostly bald as an onion," he continued.

"Why do people say that? Bald as an onion, as if an onion should have hair!" I snatched it out of his hand.

"Well, you're not an onion now," he said.

"Who says this is me?"

He squinted. "Well, it looks sorta like you."

I scarcely heard him. "Reed, we've let ourselves be distracted with all of this—Blood Relations, photos, break-ins—"

"—while we should be focusing on the motivation behind it all," he finished.

"Right! We're missing something here. And we've lost precious time!" I took a deep breath.

"Slow down. Let's sit down and recap a minute." Reed walked back over to his chair; I sank onto the couch, the tiny photo still in my hand. "First, John didn't show up for the photo shoot he'd invited you to share with him. How long did the two of you plan to be there?"

"We planned to meet on Friday afternoon. The festival started that morning, but we weren't really interested in the opening events."

"Did you call when he wasn't there?

I thought a moment. "No, I didn't. John often doesn't leave his cell on when he's shooting or traveling. I assumed he'd gotten a late start . . . and I was tired. I'd been up really late on Thursday making sure things would be all right here and then the long drive there, so I crashed about eight o'clock. We'd planned to catch the first flight out on Saturday morning."

"But he wasn't there."

"No, I looked over the lot at the bed and breakfast, but his truck wasn't there. So I drove on over to the geese pond and cruised up and down the road. I didn't see him, but it was still pretty dark. So I parked and took photos. I thought he might have just decided to do the early morning shots on another morning."

"How long did you plan to stay?"

"We were booked until the next Friday morning." I'd been reciting my answers while looking down at the photo. Now, I laid it gently on the coffee table and looked over at Reed. "Whoever is behind this has planned very well. He—or she—had to know about John's plans for Bosque and how I would react and rush to Branson. Now the mind games have started—the certified letter, this photo, the hang-ups, the—"

"—hang-ups?"

"Haven't I mentioned the hang-ups?" For the first time, I noticed the pad and pen in Reed's hands. "You do agree with me now, don't you, Reed. We do have a crime on our hands."

"Maybe. But we can't let that distract us, Sorrel."

"Right . . . do you think that body . . ."

"Sorrel, let's not get distracted. One thing at a time, okay?"

"All right," I said but I couldn't just sit there. "You keep talking and writing. I'll make another pot of coffee."

CHAPTER EIGHTEEN

"Vicente, how are you?"

"Sorrel? Are you back? I've been waiting breathlessly—"

"Look at your caller ID, Romeo!" I smiled. Vicente never changed, able to lighten the atmosphere even in serious situations. And in this crazy world of mine lately, I could smile about that. "I must be sick, but I miss you," I told him and was rewarded by his deep, sexy chuckle.

"Ah, *mi amor*, I thought you'd never say that!"

"I didn't either! Working with you all those years, I'd dream of ways to send you on a one-way trip to—"

"Never, *chica*! I saved your pretty neck a few times. Those of us behind the scenes make you poster gals look good!" Then, on a serious note, "How can I help you?"

"I need a favor," I said.

"What's in it for me?" The accent vanished as the television producer mentality took charge.

"It promises, maybe, to be a story for you."

"Uh . . . aren't you married with a dozen kids by now?"

"It's a missing college professor," I said.

I could almost hear his brain clicking in the silence. He was tempted but he didn't bite.

"Again, missing persons are sad but unremarkable—especially so far away. I'd like to help you sweetie but—"

"—you're right," I interrupted. "It's really better suited to that mystery series out of New York. It's just hard to bypass old loyalties..."

"Why would it interest them?"

I knew I had him now. Briefly, I recounted the past few days. He listened quietly, interrupting to ask me again about Blood Relations. When I reached the part about the baby photo, I stopped and waited. "You want anything I can find about this John, this company, and you," he said. "And maybe your parents."

"Yes," I said. "And I don't need to tell you we need to move quickly and quietly."

"Mum's the word." Another pause. Then he spoke seriously, "Hon, that contract on you by the drug cartel? The guy that was killed was their assassin. Depending on what was at stake, the contract may still be out there. You need to be very careful. Keep your name out of things. I know I will. In fact, I'll do the work on this one myself on my own time."

"I can't tell you, Vicente—"

"Then don't. Love ya, girl. Stay safe."

I hung up and turned to Reed. "It's in motion."

"Good. I'm hungry."

I laughed. "I can do scrambled eggs, but I'm afraid the larder is sort of empty."

"Better offer than that. Teri called when I was on my way here to invite us to dinner."

"Tempting. I just don't know if I want to spend the evening fending off her questions." Teri was notoriously nosey.

"Easy. Just get her on the store."

"You're right! We have the sale coming up, and she'll have a thousand ideas."

Reed fed the cats while I brushed my hair and put it into a ponytail, dabbed perfume on my wrists, and finished with lip gloss. An evening with Teri and Jose meant playing with the twins, a pair of rowdy little guys whom I'd adored on sight. I usually ended up on the floor, playing a boisterous game of Twister or helping them construct a skyscraper with their giant blocks.

"Good choice," Reed commented while he watched me set the alarm. I was still wearing my jeans but had changed into a bright green sweater. "Bet this Vicente wouldn't recognize his glamorous news anchor."

"Oh, he's seen me casual. The glamor is only for the cameras, you know." But he was right. I had changed in my months away. My naturally lean body hadn't changed, but the hours devoted to make-up, nails, hair—

"Do you miss it?" Reed asked, opening the passenger door of his truck.

"Like a swarm of mosquitoes."

He chuckled. We rode into town without saying much more until he pulled in front of Teri's house. "I'm having a change of heart here, I think. The real test tonight will be fielding Teri's nosy questions. That girl is a bloodhound when she catches a whiff of a good story."

"Like you said, I'll get her diverted onto the store."

"I was thinking about myself. She's been the self-appointed president of the Getting Reed Married Club for a while now. Part of me is thrilled she has you in her sites." He laughed and ducked as I made a fist.

"I think we need to change our plan," he said as we got out and started toward the house. Right before we reached the porch, Reed caught my hand, pulled me to him, and kissed me.

"What are you doing?" I tried to pull my hand away when he came up for air, but he held tight.

"Creating my own little diversion—just in case yours doesn't work," he said and kissed me on the cheek. "Did you see a curtain twitch?" he whispered.

Unlocking my door later that evening, I had to admit that Reed was a genius. Instead of fielding questions about John, we'd spent our evening amid Teri's veiled looks and veiled comments.

Of course, she'd still fed him countless questions about his job while I escaped to play with the twins. Reed suffered through as much as he could handle before coming to join our Lego building.

Dinner was easier, although she mentioned how much we'd looked like parents.

"We need to shop," Teri whispered when she hugged me goodnight. "Why did you get rid of all your sexy clothes when you left Houston?"

We held ourselves together until we drove away. Reed pulled over a couple of blocks down and we both exploded with laughter. "I know we needed to divert Teri," Reed gasped, "but she's already looking at those bride books. We may have opened up a can of worms we can't control."

"First, she's worrying about my sexy wardrobe . . . or lack thereof."

That set us off again. When we sobered up, Reed started driving again. "Well, dinner was great and I love those little guys. I've missed them all. Even if we have to lay low for a little while with Teri."

"Have you forgotten she's there almost every day getting ready for the Black Friday sale?"

"Better than dodging Willowby's questions."

"Yes. Teri's questions are still a bit easier. I don't know about you, but I feel relaxed."

Reed's lips quirked a bit, and his eyes—if possible—were bluer than ever when he left me at the door. "I'd come in," he said, "but I guess you're going to have to go shop—"

'Chris Reed! I've been broadminded—"

"Really?" He looked shocked.

"—but I can only put up with—"

"Flirty television producers?" he asked.

I closed the door on his loud laughter.

It had been a nice break from the tense days we'd had, I conceded later that evening as I brushed my teeth. The cats, both fed, curled up on the foot of my bed taking elaborate baths. I looked at the loose pants and oversized t-shirt I wore. I rinsed my mouth and turned to the kitties. "What do you think? How do you think Teri would rate this nightwear?"

Both stopped, looked at me, and then returned to their baths. "You're no help," I muttered, clicking off the bathroom light and padding over to bed.

I doubted Teri wore anything different either, with the busy little boys in her house. That sent me to a mental picture of Reed chasing a couple of little ones of his own. Why hadn't he already settled down with a wife and a half dozen? I giggled at the thought of Reed with a half dozen little girls. Red-haired girls? What was I thinking!!

I pulled back the covers and started to slide in when I saw the blinking light on the answering machine. Since most personal calls came on my cell, I'd placed the office/residence phone over on my miniature desk.   I walked over to check.   Three messages. Immediately, I thought that it might be Willowby or even Sheriff Garcia. It wouldn't be John. He always called the cell.

I punched the button. Three hang-ups. Unknown callers. It seemed a little early for Christmas advertisers! I'd had my business and personal lines combined to simplify things. Sometimes I don't make such good choices, I thought before sleep invaded.

CHAPTER NINETEEN

"I'll bet it's what happened to my cousin," Teri told me the next morning. "Some guy gave her number when he went into the emergency room and when he didn't pay, it went to collections. They called until she had to finally change her number."

"Did they leave messages?" I thought of the silences on my answering machine.

"No. If you answer, they ask for whoever they are wanting, but they won't leave a message. And when you tell them the person doesn't live there, they never take it off their records."

"How horrible!" And just what I needed right now. "A business number is pricey to change, and by now it's listed in the Yellow Pages. Besides, I'd combined it with my personal number—a promotional deal. Guess I'll have to change them both and separate them, but we really don't need to change them right now. "

Teri shrugged. "Maybe it's Reed's ex-girlfriend—"

"Hush!" I said. "Does he have a lot of ex-girlfriends? Wait! I don't want to know!"

Teri's giggles eased the tension. We were in my office, putting the final touches to our Black Friday ad for the newspaper. "So this is finished?" she asked finally. "I need to get back to the paper. Today's only a half day for me, and I have a bunch of things to finish before the monsters get out of school."

"Are they in preschool every morning?"

"Two mornings and one full day. On the full day, they have a field trip."

"Sounds fun. Four-year-olds! Are they liking it?"

"Yes, even though they complain when they have to get dressed. It was hard for their *abuelita* at first, but she'll never admit that the boys are getting harder for her." Teri had packed the ad into her case and started toward the door. "Call if you need me."

"Teri? I don't want you to overwork. You have your hands full already with the twins, the paper, and making your products."

She laughed and waved. "The store gives me an escape." I waved back but felt a little ashamed. During our short friendship, I seemed to have been the focus. Teri had been such a sweet support to me. I vowed to see what I could do to ease things a bit.

I stood up and stretched. Reed was catching up on paperwork or something at the sheriff's office this morning. We had a strategy to explore this afternoon, but I had a couple of hours on my own. One look outside at the sunshine and I headed to the bedroom to change into my running gear.

I'd always liked running, but my years on the track team in high school had turned liking into loving. My tensions eased and my mind always cleared when I pushed my body on the track.

Kevin, early in our marriage, had been horrified that I ran in a city as huge as Houston, even as I'd argued that I'd run in other large cities. "It isn't safe!" he'd argued. Yet he'd been murdered while in the safety of his home.

I stowed water and my cellphone in a fanny pack, gave the cats a treat and instructions that they were in charge, and stepped out into the gorgeous fall morning. November had brought cooler weather, perfect after the hot summer days. I'd always loved the fall with its colorful changing leaves. That's one thing I missed. I'd grown up with lots of trees. Here, grassland stretched on, now a dull yellow.

As I stretched, I thought about going back to the Chiricahua National Forest, down the road fifty miles or so. But I just didn't have enough time right now.

There wasn't much traffic out on the highway this morning, so I could have easily run alongside it. But the pasture road beckoned instead. Aunt Rose and Uncle Jim had once owned a section of land behind the shop when they were younger. He'd made a road—just a pair of rough ruts—so he could drive the truck over to drop off feed for the cows. I followed the barbed wire fence that stretched from my driveway west along the highway until I reached the primitive road. I'd never seen any trucks on it that I could remember.

The new owners didn't have cows in the pasture just now. Plastic store bags and other trash had blown in and settled. Littering was a big problem in the rural areas. Mr. Byrd had sent me with Jason to photograph the areas where people had traveled across the border, leaving their trash—food wrappers, clothes, even soiled disposable diapers—along the way. Even though I empathized with their desperate trek toward a new life, I could also empathize with the ranchers whose cattle were often slaughtered for a meal and whose pastures were trashed.

I'd reached the big metal watering tank—only partially filled with greenish water—and started back when I felt my phone vibrating. I pulled it out. It was a text from Reed: "Where R U?"

I slowed and typed slowly so I could keep an eye on the road. "Run."

"Pasture?" He responded

"Y."

Stuffing the phone back in my fanny pack, I realized how tired I was. I'd been running for almost an hour and was at least another fifteen or twenty minutes from home. "Wuss!" I gasped and took a couple of sips from my water bottle.

I'd gotten soft during these past few months. True, I'd tramped through wildlife areas with my photography; but the business had kept me in the office too much. I needed to shape up, I mentally scolded myself.

But, as it always did, the run had helped clear my mind. I'd looked at the recent events as I ran, and felt conflicting emotions.

Optimistically, John may have hired a college kid who had just neglected to care for Van. Or John may have been unable to resist a photo shoot and headed out. That wasn't unusual. True, he'd made plans to meet me in Bosque, but Branson was especially gorgeous in the fall. He may have lost track of time. That wasn't unusual either. Still, he would have let me know.

This Blood Relations part was harder to rationalize. This whole testing thing was too elaborate just to be a joke. Someone had gone to considerable trouble to have my DNA tested or to falsify the tests. I knew my father and that paper saying John was my dad was crazy. He and my mother didn't even know each other! And I bore a family resemblance to my dad. It was all so crazy. And niggling at me the most was the motivation. What possible reason would someone have to do this?

And where was John? I pulled out my phone and dialed his cell. Immediately after the first ring, it went to voicemail. A nasally female voice intoned, "The person whose number you have dialed has a full mailbox." Odd. Still, maybe he was out of range of a cell tower. And that was the most frustrating thing about it all. Almost everything had a rational, easy explanation!

My stop had given my muscles time to stiffen up a little. So I stretched a bit before heading down the road, keeping my head down a bit to watch for rattlesnakes. In the fall, they tended to come out of their holes more than in the hot summer. A startled rabbit crossed not far from me.

My thoughts and my concentration had distracted me, so when the tires crunched just ahead of me, I caught my breath. Looking up, I saw Reed directly in front of me—on a dirt bike!

"Hello, stranger!" he said.

"Where'd you get that?"

"My garage." He reached behind and handed me a helmet. "Here. You'll need this."

Immediately, my contrary bug bit. "Why?"

Reed sighed and answered in a long-suffering tone. "Because I have this thing for safety? Or maybe I thought you'd like a ride?" He turned to stow it behind. "But as usual—"

"All right." I could hear the grudging tone in my voice, and I hoped he didn't hear the eagerness behind it as I reached for the helmet. This morning's exercise had tired me more than it should have. "What's the agenda?"

"Right now? Thought I'd give you a lift back to your place . . . unless you want to run beside me?"

I fastened the helmet and climbed onto the bike. "I'm tempted," I lied.

"It's bumpy. You might want to put your arms around me." I could hear the wicked pleasure in his voice. This was a side of Reed—among others—that I'd missed the past couple of months.

He was right. It was a bumpy ride.

I'd cooled off a bit, but Reed's broad back was warm and he smelled of a leathery soap. I resisted the urge to bury my face into his back, even though the wind against my cheeks was chilly.

We were home in a short time. Reed started rolling the bike toward the tailgate of his pickup as soon as we'd both gotten off. "I changed the oil and checked it over. Figured it needed to be driven a bit," he said, following me to the door.

Reed stepped past me while I turned off the alarm, and both cats rushed forward to greet him. He picked up Flash and made a mock stagger. "What are you feeding these creatures?"

I reached down to pet Van. "Just lots of love." Van's gravelly purr vibrated his whole body. I straightened up. "Would you like something to drink? Water? Soda?"

"Coffee?"

"It's going to stunt your growth." I warned as I started toward the bedroom, "Just give me a minute."

"I can make it. Do you want some too? I can make a pot."

"Sounds good."

As I stepped out of the shower a few minutes later, the aroma had already crept into my bed room. I pulled on jeans and a shirt and put my long hair up into a ponytail. I then applied a light lotion on my face and gloss on my lips. For some reason, I squirted a floral spray on my neck.

Reed was seated in the overstuffed chair, both cats squeezed in beside him, while he munched a cookie.

"I see you found the snicker doodles," I groused as I walked into the kitchen and poured a cup of coffee.

Reed waited until I sat down. "I didn't empty the jar," he said, "but I couldn't resist. My grandma made these."

"So did Aunt Rose," I said. "I'm actually glad you found them so I don't have to eat them all myself. I made them planning to take them to Bosque because John loves them, but I forgot them." I noticed the blinking red light on the phone. I reached over, lifted the set, and punched in the message button. No message. I set it down.

"Bad news?"

I took a sip. "A hang-up."

"Guess someone thought the store was open."

"Maybe."

"What's on your agenda?"

"As in?"

"Well, I finished up the paperwork. Until this other stuff is cleared up, I'm not on a regular schedule at work. Of course, with the business here . . . "

"Teri and I finished the ads for the Black Friday sales so I'm okay. What's on your mind?"

"I thought we might take a little road trip."

"Branson is a long way—"

"—I thought we might want to go back up to Socorro. You never finished your shoot—"

"Have you gotten a call from Willowby?"

"No." He drained his cup and walked into the kitchen. I heard him rinsing the cup. "Do you have a thermos?"

I followed him in. "What's on your mind?"

"How did you go to Socorro?"

"Took 10 out of Lordsburg and picked up 25 north of Hatch. A few jogs on small roads but not bad."

"That's how I went too. Couple of hundred miles."

I wasn't following him totally, but I knew him well enough by now to wait him out.

"Hilly drive around Silver City. I didn't notice too much since I was driving it at night—and was tired." Reed seemed to be debating within. Then he looked at me. "There are two national forests, Gila and Cibola, so the area isn't heavily populated. Beautiful area for photographers."

"You think John may have decided to go there and then circle back to Socorro," I said. "But why wouldn't he do that after the festival?"

"I don't know. I don't know John as well as you do. Would he change his plans, go off on an adventure spontaneously?"

"I'm not sure on this one. He has done it before, but—"

"Maybe he just wanted to explore a bit and return later when he'd have more time." Reed leaned against the counter and seemed to measure his words. "And while he was exploring, he may have encountered something that kept him away."

I didn't want to think of that. "John's smart," I said, my voice rising. "He's really smart in wilderness survival—goes backpacking, camps out in the rugged areas—"

"Sorrel, it wouldn't hurt to take the drive."

"The rangers or the authorities would have—"

Reed had moved closer. "—found him? Maybe but it's rugged out there. And like everything else, cuts have meant fewer personnel." He gently touched my cheek, making me look up at him. "He may have just lost track of time. But a look wouldn't hurt us, would it?" He dropped his hand. "Now, where's the thermos? I'll pour up the rest of this coffee—no need to let it waste. You might pack a light bag. Include—"

I'd already disappeared into the bedroom. When I came out, Reed was shutting off his phone. "Jose and Teri will care for the kitties," he said. He'd found a basket and filled it with the thermos, apples, sandwiches, and a Ziploc with the rest of the snicker doodles. "I've already got water and soda in the truck," he added.

"Flash," I said as I headed toward the door with my bag in one arm and a jacket in the other, "You and Van are in charge." Reed stifled a chuckle. "Want to grab my camera case there?" I asked.

CHAPTER TWENTY

The cab of Reed's truck smelled delicious. "You've been to Teri's *tia*."

Reed smiled. "Guilty. I always order tamales, so when I called in my order, she told me to come by and pick them up. She's keeping the other couple of dozen in the freezer."

"How do you do it? The way you eat—"

"Clean living." Reed backed the truck out of its parking space and started down the driveway. "I ate several while she plied me with iced tea. Saved you some to eat on the way."

"No way. My mouth would be flaming and—"

"I picked mild ones to share with you."

"You didn't!" I opened the paper bag and pulled out a foil-wrapped package. "These are bigger."

"Two in a package. You can never—"

"—eat just one!" I chanted with him.

I opened the corn husk wrapper, peeling the corn mash stuck to the strands and popping it into my mouth. Reed tuned in a country western radio station, only interrupting the music long enough to tell me about the bottled water and sodas in the small cooler on the seat between us.

"Good thing I'm not in front of a camera," I told him later. "Those tamales are the best I've ever eaten!"

"I know! And you needn't worry, by the way. You eat more than any female I've ever seen and you're still scrawny."

"Good genes!" The words couldn't be retracted, and they hung in the silence that followed.

Reed changed the subject. "I'm still having trouble with you having worked and lived in Houston. It seems like you've been a part of Saddle Gap for a long time."

"I was a military brat. We lived in a variety of places—some tiny, some big, some foreign."

"Hard to make friends."

"Not really. We were settled by the time I was a teen, which is the most awkward time to start friendships. Besides, I have this insatiable curiosity about everything—and most people like to talk about themselves, so it works."

Reed grinned, his eyes showing he'd decided commenting might be unwise. Instead, we listened to the twangs of the guitar as a woman sang about lost love. I unzipped the small cooler, offered Reed a bottle of water, and took one for myself, gulping almost half of it.

"I figure we'll stop for gas in Lordsburg," he said after a while. "Not much between here and there. But if you need me to stop, there are a few bushes."

I didn't dignify that with an answer. I drained the small water bottle and looked out the window, ignoring his chuckle.

Bushes, cattle, and some gorgeous red dunes and hills lent an air of peace. An occasional car passed us, and we passed a few clusters of mobile homes and signs pointing off to large ranch homes in the distance. This place could get in one's blood, I thought.

The hand on my shoulder made me jump and I squealed. "Time to stop snoring. We're in Lordsburg." I sat up straight and wiped at my mouth. "No, you didn't drool." A snicker.

Reed had pulled up beside a gas pump. "I'll be a minute," I said.

My walk up to the Quick Stop might have been more dignified had my left foot not been a little numb. I wasn't accustomed to napping, and this had been a long one. I washed my hands and patted cool water on my face. That felt better.

Reed was waiting for me beside the front door. "I figure we ought to eat something," he said, holding the door open. "We'll be turning off toward Silver City before we get to Deming. After that, I'm not sure how long it might be before we're close to a restaurant."

I shivered. It was chilly but I wasn't sure whether it was the weather or a foreboding that caused it. "This place is pretty small," I said, not sure what kind of restaurants we might find in town, "but something hot would be good. A burger or chicken or something like that?"

"Me too."

We climbed into the truck and Reed quickly maneuvered out of the parking lot and followed the directions on the Best Burgers in Lordsburg sign just down from the gas station.

We opted to go inside instead of trying to eat on the road. The place was small, but the kitchen was efficient. In a few minutes, I watched Reed bite into his double cheeseburger before I lifted my own junior burger and took a bite. "I thought you weren't on a diet," he said.

"Not. In fact, I'm lucky not to have to diet much. Of course, since the camera adds pounds, I used to watch what I ate more closely and exercised more." I pointed toward my pile of onion rings. "These are my calories."

"Do you miss it?"

"Sometimes. I loved the investigation—chasing the leads, the excitement of solving one, the camaraderie of the crew. But it isn't all as glamorous as it seems—and it's hard on your personal life."

Reed nodded. "What personal life?"

I offered him an onion ring, which he dipped into ketchup and stuffed into his mouth. "Reed, what do you figure the motivation behind all of this is?"

One of the things I liked about Reed most was his ability to follow my shifts in thought. "I've been wondering that as well. Is John wealthy?"

"I have no idea. He lives comfortably, but you can see that he certainly doesn't have a lavish lifestyle."

He reached for another onion ring. "Does he talk about his family?"

"I've been thinking about that too. Aside from maybe mentioning something he did as a kid, I don't remember him saying much about his background. Of course, I was in the middle of a major personal catastrophe. I'm embarrassed to say that I never asked."

"That's a double-edged sword anyway. Some people are very private. If they talk about their family, that's okay, but asking them questions about it can be tricky."

"This Blood Relations place has me mystified. Are you thinking blackmail or something? Wouldn't it be complicated to send in all these samples? And then there's the whole thing about false names—I know who my dad is—and the expense."

I offered him the last onion ring. "And where's John? What's his part in all of this? Has our friendship all this time been a lie? Or is he—"

Reed stood up. "Time to find out." He gathered up wrappers. "Do you want to refill your soda?" I shook my head and headed toward the trash bin.

As Reed pulled out of the parking lot, he continued, "I know that you can be fooled by people, but John doesn't seem like that sort of person. He's a good listener, quiet and genuine. He may not even know anything about this Blood Relations stuff. Maybe he just went shooting in the area before you arrived and got delayed."

"You mean hurt?"

"Or car trouble. Who knows? It's rugged country around here. Sparsely populated."

"So now you think he wasn't shooting in Missouri on his way here?"

"I'm thinking we need to consider all of the possibilities, including that he may not have any connection to the weird mail you received."

I stared out at the relatively flat land we sped past, marred occasionally by billboards. "You don't really believe that, Reed. Why are you doing this with me anyway?"

Silence. Reed turned up the music. I turned toward him and repeated my question. He just stared down the road.

I reached over and turned off the music. "Aren't you going to answer me?"

"Maybe I have this hero complex about rescuing maidens in distress."

I muttered a succinct reply to which he gasped in mock horror. "My mama would have washed your mouth out with soap!" I crossed my arms and stared out at the passing fence posts. "What? Now you're going to pout?" I concentrated on counting fence posts.

When he spoke, the teasing note had vanished. "I'm not really sure either. Any mystery intrigues me, and I'm not good at just waiting around. Since the department gave me some respite time—in spite of my protests—"

"—you figured you'd once again rescue this maiden?"

Reed's laugh filled the cabin of the truck. Unwillingly, I felt my own lips twitch. He was maddening, but his laugh was the most attractive thing about him. Immediately, I conjured up all the reasons why "attractive" wasn't something I needed. Reed reached over and squeezed my hand briefly. "I can't help teasing you sometimes, Sorrel. It's that—"

"—don't you say my red hair!!"

"—sadness that lurks behind your eyes. And maybe I do have this hero urge. Seriously, I'm taking this drive on a hunch—and I have the time. Something doesn't feel quite right. I thought we could just drive through the surrounding areas, just in case we see something. It's a pretty drive. Have you ever gone to Silver City?"

"No."

"There are two national parks in the area, as well as the City of Rocks and other sights that must be a photographer's delight. John might have thought so."

"So you think—"

"—I think we ought to keep our minds open and our eyes sharp."

He had a point there. I relaxed a bit.

"And . . .“

I waited. "And?"

"Willowby called."

"What? Willowby? And you planned to tell me when?"

"He called when you were in the bathroom. He just asked if we could answer some more questions, and I told him we were headed that way anyway."

"Gee, when were you two big strong men going to let the little woman know all about—"

"I wanted you to eat first. It isn't an emergency, he said. Just something he wanted to clear up."

"And he needs us to come all the way there?"

"This may be the first case Willowby has ever had to be lead for."

"You mean murder case? He surely has to know we have nothing to do with that stranger we accidentally spotted lying dead in the ditch."

"He said there's a development he wants to explore."

I balled my fists in my lap.

"It's probably nothing, Sorrel."

"Are you lying to me, Reed?"

The truck swerved suddenly into a graveled parking lot. A huge sign advertised Trading Post. It was quiet in the cab. I heard him draw a deep breath and then sigh. "I should have told you back there, but I really did want you to eat without upset. Look at me, Sorrel."

I looked into those blue eyes.

"It's Willowby. We both know he's a pompous, self-important little guy. Don't let your irritation at me—and my overbearing ways—distract you. We both need to keep our investigative radar out. I won't patronize you with pretending I'm not worried. Something is going on. And we need to use both of our investigative experience and keep our minds sharp."

"Is this the best you can do for an apology?"

"I need to practice on apologies?"

He knew how to use those eyes to his advantage. "You need to practice on remembering that we're partners—in this venture, at least. I'm no shrinking violet."

He held my gaze a few seconds longer. "I apologize. Partners."

"Partners." I reached over to shake.

Reed took my hand and grinned. "No kiss and make up?"

"Would you ask that of Willowby?"

He grimaced and pulled back out on the interstate.

"Reed?" I asked a few miles down the road. "Are you concerned at all about Willowby wanting us back?"

He didn't answer immediately. When he did, I could tell he did so in the new spirit of partnership. "It doesn't seem as trivial as he implied," he said. "Then again—"

"—it's Willowby!" we chorused.

CHAPTER TWENTY-ONE

"A penny for them."

I jumped at the sound of Reed's voice. "What?"

"Your thoughts. I thought you were asleep and maybe you were—with your eyes open."

"Just thinking." I looked out my window. "Where did the sun go?"

"The weather is turning on us. Hadn't you noticed?"

I hadn't. Reed had turned on the heater, and a fine mist coated the windshield. "My blood has thinned—first living in Houston and then Saddle Gap."

"Are you warm enough?"

"Sure."

"I figure we need to alter our plans a little, go on straight to Bosque instead of the roundabout way through the national parks. After we talk with Willowby—and if we still want to—we can go there on our way back. What do you think?"

Was this Reed? Asking instead of telling? "How did Willowby sound?" I asked.

"Besides pompous and full of himself? Maybe a little nervous."

I sighed. "Then I guess it's better to get him out of our hair. Reed, this whole thing has a sort of Alice in Wonderland feel about it—like I've fallen into a rabbit hole and everything gets stranger and stranger."

"I hear you."

"What's your best guess for Willowby's summons?"

"It's a little quick for tests to be ready. Real life and television aren't remotely related. But maybe he's found a witness or someone who knows something. Why he wants us, though, is still anyone's guess."

"Whatever it is, it must have cut his trip short. His wife said they were celebrating Thanksgiving with her family and then he'd be returning home since he had to work the holiday."

"Police work has no respect for holidays."

"Do you miss your family?"

"Sure." He was silent for a bit. "When my grandparents were alive, we gathered at their house for holidays—a conglomeration of mischief, noise, and delicious food."

I nodded. "We were short of family, but Mama loved to cook. My brother thought venison was disgusting, and I think it must have hurt her feelings. But she never let on."

"Your brother sounds like a challenge."

"Stepbrother. Dad had married his high school girlfriend—she was pregnant and told him it was his. He scrapped his plans for college and joined the military. I don't think my grandparents ever forgave him. I could always sense something."

"Then this kid would really be your half-brother."

"No. Apparently, his mother told Dad that she'd been with someone else but he refused to marry her. She only told Dad that story after the courthouse ceremony. Three or four other husbands followed. Dad never had paternity testing, but my brother only came to us for a holiday once, when she was between husbands. I can understand now why he was so angry and obnoxious, but I didn't then."

"Crazy childhood."

"Sad. He was an angry kid."

"Was he mean?"

"Jealous, I think. Dad and I were close, and he must have felt like an outsider. At the same time, he hated animals and was lazy. Dad told him to help me but he refused. I didn't want to argue."

Reed smiled. "You've changed."

"How?"

"Arguments don't bother you now."

I laughed. "Not when I know I'm right."

The mist had grown heavier, surrounding us with gray. I'd grown up in snow and cold, but sunshine and warmth were much more appealing. I thought of long walks on Crystal Beach with Kevin and hot dogs roasted on a fire.

"What do you do for holidays, Reed?"

"Usually spend them on the job. Or with Jose and Teri."

For the first time, I realized that Reed and I had something in common—both only children and sparse family. I wondered if he missed it. I hadn't—until recently. Holidays had meant working, and I'd been busy as most people had wanted the time off.

The phone rang. Reed looked at his screen and answered. "Hello, Willowby." He put the phone on speaker.

"Reed, I know I told you it would be okay to meet at the refuge, but the weather is bad and it will be dark soon. How about you meet us in Socorro at the state police headquarters?

"Okay." We waited.

"Well . . . see you soon?"

"As we can." Reed hung up. He sighed. "Curiouser and curiouser."

"The road to the refuge is good, Reed. I'd say this was Willowby's original set-up, not the alternate plan."

Reed didn't answer right away. "They may want to question us again," he finally said.

"But why?" I turned toward him, as much as my seatbelt would allow. "This is so crazy, Reed. Lots of people find someone dead. And there is absolutely nothing tying us to this guy! This is just a coincidence, so interrogating us over and over is a waste of time."

Reed nodded. "Maybe they have some information on John."

"If they did, why not tell us on the phone?" No answer. I shifted and gazed out at the scenery.

"If so," Reed finally said, "we won't have long to wait." He signaled and turned off the interstate at the Socorro exit.

CHAPTER TWENTY-TWO

"Ms. Janes, would you tell me again how you know this man?"

"I've never seen him before." I stared down at the photo of a corpse. The man may have been handsome, but death and lying out in the elements had taken their toll. "I just saw a figure lying face down in the ditch when I was focusing my camera for a shot." I'd repeated that statement several times, and it felt sing-song by now.

Silence.

Don't say anything more, I cautioned myself. Just answer the questions.

"So it was just a chance encounter."

"It wasn't an encounter. I saw him through my camera lens."

"Why were you out there again?"

"To photograph the birds."

"Alone?"

"Yes."

"Wrong! You were with Deputy Chris Reed."

"Well—"

"Isn't it true that Deputy Reed and you are lovers?"

"No, not true."

"And you called Deputy Reed to give you an alibi?"

"He called me—"

"You and your lover drug the body out into the field so that it wouldn't be discovered right away."

"No—"

"And then the two of you invented the story about someone meeting you here—"

"John had planned to meet me here."

"He had reserved a single room. There was no mention of your joining him."

"Of course not! I reserved my own room, as I know you have checked. We aren't a couple—"

"Why else would an older man be meeting up with a younger woman like you? You have a colorful history, Ms. Janes. Men don't live long around you."

Careful, I reminded myself. It was a hurtful statement, designed to make me react. Don't let the questions draw you into something, I told myself. "Do I need a lawyer?"

"Not if you'll just answer my questions."

"I have answered them. I think we are approaching that time when there is nothing left to tell you." I looked into Sheriff Garcia's unbelieving eyes.

"If you're the good person you claim, you'll want this young man's family to know why you killed him."

"What proof—?" Stop! I knew better than to say anything.

Garcia opened his file and handed a sheet of paper toward me. Even at a glance, I recognized the logo. Blood Relations.

"Not another word."

I hadn't heard the stranger enter the room. She was petite and probably in her early 50s, although her hair held blonde highlights instead of gray. The word that popped in my mind was *classy*. She walked over to me and put her hand on my elbow then turned and smiled beguilingly at the sheriff

"We'll be leaving just now, Joe," she said, giving him a smile that could only be described as friendly yet firm. "Unless you intend to charge Ms. Janes with a crime?" She posed politely and looked quite a distance up at him, even with the three-inch stacked heels she wore.

Sheriff Garcia slid the sheet back into his folder and stood up. He had noticed the appealing picture she made, even though he kept his gruff tone. "No," he said. "Just trying to make sure we have all of the information."

"Then you'll have to look elsewhere," she told him. "My client has never seen this man before. She certainly knows nothing about a complete stranger!"

He picked up his folder and offered his hand to my attorney and then to me. We walked to the door and he held it open. "I'll be in touch," he told me before turning down the hall.

I turned toward the lady. She spoke quickly, "We'll talk in a bit." I followed her through a door into the lobby. Reed met us there and opened the outside door.

I shivered.

"Your coat's in the truck," Reed told me. "It's right over there."

Now that I'd stood up, I felt myself swaying, whether from the headache settling on my forehead or the hunger.

I felt a hand on my elbow. "You must be tired, but I'd like to talk with you some and we have some paperwork to go through. I'm Patience, by the way." She smiled. "A totally inappropriate name given to me by my mother." She turned to Reed, recited an address, and gave him directions. "It's my home," she said. "My office staff is already gone for the day; but Maria, my paralegal, is waiting for us there." She headed toward a vintage Volkswagen Beetle.

"My mama had one of those," I murmured.

"What?" Reed unlocked the truck with a click and opened the passenger door. I pulled out my jacket and slipped into.

"Not important," I said.

We climbed into the truck and Reed waited while I fastened my seatbelt. He reached behind the seat and handed me my purse. "Do you want something to drink? I think the ice is melted, but we still have some bottled water."

I shook my head, leaned my head against the seat, and closed my eyes.. "Did they keep you long?"

Reed pulled out onto the street. "Not at all. They just wanted to talk to you. Willowby—"

My eyes flew open at the name. "I don't want to talk about Willowby! Why wasn't he just open with us—say the sheriff wanted to question me more—instead of acting like he had information for us?"

"I'm not sure Willowby knew Garcia was going to get so intense."

"Intense. Right. I'm not afraid of questions, but his attempted television-style interrogation is not my choice of recreation, especially after several hours of travel. And this lady—"

"A top notch attorney, apparently."

"Says who?"

"Willowby."

"Willowby? God help me! I have fallen down a rabbit hole!" I leaned back and closed my eyes again, only to have them fly open at Reed's chuckle.

"I'm glad you're entertained!" I snapped.

We lapsed into silence as Reed concentrated on the unfamiliar streets. I leaned back against the seat and closed my eyes until Reed parked the truck.

Reed chuckled. "Not what I expected."

I opened my eyes and saw the large two-story house perched on a large corner lot next to an imposing brick mansion. The house, however, could hardly be called a mansion. "Tweety's grandma," I murmured. "I'd have expected the mansion for Patience."

Reed wisely kept his mouth shut.

The door opened before we could ring a doorbell. "Hi, come on in. I'm Maria." Maria was classically beautiful—and Black. She laughed. "I know. You expected Hispanic. Everyone does with my name." She shook hands with each of us and led us through a formal living room and down a hall to the right. "The office is in here. Ms. Montgomery is making tea."

Patience Montgomery's home office was surprisingly cozy. Maria sat behind the smaller of two desks and opened a file. She gestured toward a chair. "I'll start you on some paperwork."

Patience appeared with a tray on which she'd arranged a teapot, lemon, milk, and cups. She was followed by a tall, slim fellow carrying another tray heaped with sandwiches cut in half, chips, cookies, and fruit. "Reed, come on over," she said, arranging things on the coffee table. "I imagine you could use a snack. You join us, too, Sorrel, as soon as you finish."

The tall gentleman stuck out his hand toward Reed. "I'm Earl, the husband," he said. Soon the two were seated in armchairs, eating and chatting.

I signed the retainer and wrote a check. "Join me on the sofa," Patience said. "Maria, you can go on home to your family. Thanks for staying late."

Earl rose as well. "It was good to meet you, Reed," he said and then smiled at me. "Hopefully, we won't become too well acquainted." We all laughed as he headed toward the kitchen with his cup.

"My husband has his own brand of what he calls gallows humor," Patience apologized.

"It likely comes with the territory," I told her. "Is he an attorney also?"

"Goodness, no! He's terrified of courtrooms, he says. Although I'd be terrified of his job. He's the physics chair at the university here." She handed me a plate. "Here, get something to nibble on. You too, Reed. I'll do the talking. I usually do anyway. Usually that's adequate."

I bit into half a chicken salad sandwich and realized how hungry I was. We'd expected to eat an early dinner after visiting with Willowby. That had been almost five hours ago!

Patience—as she insisted we call her—sipped her tea while we ate and then reached for her IPad. "Don't stop," she said. "I'll talk."

As we drove away an hour later, both of us felt calmer. She'd reassured us that Sheriff Garcia had simply been hoping we would solve his murder and his wife wouldn't be angry that he might have to work over Thanksgiving. He was fairly new to the job and, as far as she knew, this was his first suspicious death. "Although," she corrected herself, "it's a murder. And I doubt he has anything much except for this piece of paper from a strange place. Blood Relations." She looked at me. "Have you heard of this group?"

"I wish I hadn't!" I'd said.

After a quick outline of her plan—largely researching the company—and her confident reassurances that she would likely be returning a large portion of my retainer, we'd left.

"I'm glad she has a plan," I told Reed. "No wonder Tweety's grandma handled Sylvester so well."

Reed scoffed. "She doesn't look like Tweety's grandmother, Sorrell, even though the house does."

I had to give him that one.

CHAPTER TWENTY-THREE

The day ran through my mind like a bad movie as I stood in the motel's hot shower. We still had no word from John. This crazy accusation regarding some stranger I'd seen lying dead at the refuge was more an irritant than a problem. I'd been in tight spots many times as a reporter, so this one didn't put me in a panic. But John's disappearance? This was a first. If not for his continued silence, I could think of any number of scenarios to explain it—except for the fact that John didn't do this—at least, he hadn't.

I did admit that Patience Montgomery earned Willowby bonus points. She seemed to be a good attorney; and although my inclination had been not to hire one, I wasn't totally sorry that she had intervened when she had.

In spite of my hot shower and exhaustion, it was well after midnight before I finally slept. What seemed to be only a few minutes later, I awoke to someone hammering on the door.

Reed didn't look much more rested than I felt.

"Go crawl back in a hole!" I pushed the door, but he stuck his foot on the door jamb.

"Meet me for a run. Unless you're too tired."

Then I noticed the sweats and sneakers.

"Five minutes." He headed toward the lobby. In under four minutes, I was running out to the truck, where Reed sat waiting, the motor running.

"Coffee," he said, pointing to the cup in the holder between the seats as I climbed in the cab. I had barely clicked the seat belt before he started backing out. I grabbed the Styrofoam cup. "Careful! It's hot!" he warned. Too late. I'd already singed the tip of my tongue, but he was never going to know that.

We turned onto the highway toward the refuge. The dark orange horizon had begun its transformation to gold. By the time we negotiated the distance to the refuge, we would have visibility for our run.

I sipped my coffee as we sped down the two-lane highway. Reed slowed occasionally for a rabbit or a scurrying kangaroo rat but didn't seem inclined to talk—and I certainly wasn't. Instead, I studied the landscape. Dozens of sandhill cranes were hunkered down in one of the ponds we passed, dark shapes blending together as they each balanced on one foot. Even in the closed cab, I could hear their raspy cooing.

"You'd think their feet would be frozen," I said.

"Better than being breakfast for some coyote."

A few moments later, Reed swung into the entrance and showed the pass. "Do I need a new one?" he asked.

"No, we're honoring the festival passes even though it has been cancelled."

At the first observation platform, several birders had already gathered. "This okay?" Reed asked.

"Sure," I said.

Reed turned the truck into a side park. I drained the coffee cup and climbed out. Reed locked the truck and we began our stretching.

"I forgot to ask if you want your camera," he said.

"I've got a small one in my jacket pocket, but I don't usually shoot when I'm on a run."

We started off slowly. The sky brightened bit by bit, like the lights slowly coming up on a theatre stage. Little interrupted the hush save our footfalls and the occasional rustle or flapping wings. Our breaths made puffs into the cold air as we settled into a comfortable rhythm. The tension from yesterday's nightmarish events and my restless night gave way to the exhilaration I always felt. Even my grumpiness toward my often bossy companion began to evaporate.

Reed reached out and grabbed my elbow. "Look!"

I would have tripped had his grip not been stronger. I righted myself and looked toward the tree where his finger pointed. Almost to the top was a small furry ball. A porcupine! I knew they were reported to be here, but I'd never seen one. Its head moved slightly.

"We need to move on before we spook her," Reed whispered.

I nodded and started on, with Reed following.

"How do you know it's a girl?" I finally asked.

He snorted. "I recognized her!"

"Jerk!" I took off running amid his laughter.

He caught up with me easily and we finished our run without another stop. During the silent trip back to the motel, I checked my phone for messages and then returned to watching the scenery.

"Are you going to pout all day?" Reed asked as he pulled into the parking lot.

"I'm not pouting. I'm thinking about things."

"And?"

"I need another shower."

"We need to do some serious collaborating."

I opened the door and stepped out. "This trip back was a wild goose chase," I said.

"Maybe. But I think we need to go over what we have one more time. Then, if you want, we'll head back to Saddle Gap."

I nodded and walked into the motel lobby. Things just weren't adding up. Although the festival was only for one weekend, John and I had planned to stay until the following Friday. Photographing wildlife—at least to us—was best accomplished without large crowds. It required watching and waiting for those golden opportunities that come when you least expect them. Sometimes we'd only speak a sentence or two in an hour's time. But we communicated—and shared—the experience in the silence. I'd missed his being there. Maybe I was even hurt at the idea that he'd gone off somewhere else with little regard for our plans.

With everything that had happened, I'd missed the main part of the festival running all over. I couldn't afford any more wild goose chases—especially with my shop's first Black Friday sale fast approaching.

Seated at the table in my room, I repeated these arguments to Reed. He listened as he finished a cinnamon roll he'd picked up at the breakfast bar in the lobby. "Sure you don't want one?" he asked. I shook my head. "Okay, I'll make the He's Fine—Just Absent-Minded list. You start the He's in Trouble list."

I took the tablet he handed me and wrote: *Wouldn't stand me up without calling.* I thought a minute: *Wouldn't neglect Van Gogh.*

Reed peered at my list and added to his: *Cat minder didn't do his/her job.* Then he waited expectantly for my next note.

Neighbors worried, I added.

Neighbors just nosy, Reed responded.

I wadded up my paper. "This is a waste of time!"

Reed wadded his paper as well. "Okay, let's go home." He stood. "We have a couple of hours until check-out."

"Reed? Are you sure? You were the one who suggested we come back here! I know you well enough to believe you had something you wanted to clear up."

He tossed our paper wads into the trashcan. "I've had time to sleep on it. Look what this trip has done for us. You were grilled by the sheriff and forced to hire an attorney all over some stranger that you happened to spot while photographing birds at the refuge! John hasn't communicated with you at all. And we still don't have anything concrete to go on. So you're right, this trip has been a waste of time."

"I can't believe you're just giving up!"

"Who said I was giving up? I just said that this place—right now— is a waste of our time."

He was out the door before I could speak. I hated to admit it, but he was right. What else could we possibly find here? Funny how we had almost reversed our original feelings about this trip. Now, as much as it went against my nature, I realized that our best option, logically, was to go home and wait.

I'd never been accused of acting logically.

CHAPTER TWENTY-FOUR

Another quick shower and packing done, I called Vicente and left a short voicemail asking him to let me know what he'd learned about John and Blood Relations. Then I called Teri. She answered just as I reached for the button to hang up.

"Teri! Sorrel here. How are things going?

A pause. "Pretty good."

That was odd. "Are you okay? Kids doing all right?"

"Just a virus. I've been helping Tia make tamales, but this bug hit and I'm taking the rest of the day at home."

"Boys have it too?"

"No. They're spending the day with my mama and my *abuelita*."

"Bet they're not a bit upset about that!" I waited for her giggle. "Are you sure you're okay?"

"I will be. How about you?"

"Long story. It'll keep until we get back."

Her voice took on a bit of animation. "We?"

"Just wanted to check on the cats and any messages," I said. "Expect to be back there this evening or tomorrow."

I could hear her yawn. "I want to hear it all. Any news of John?"

"No—"

"Gotta go!" She hung up.

Something wasn't quite right. Teri was the liveliest person I knew, but she'd had her hands full covering for me lately. I hoped she wasn't sicker than she'd said.

A knock on the door drew me back. "Sorrel?"

Reed looked in when I opened the door and saw my overnight bags. "Good. I've got mine too. Figured we could talk here in privacy and still meet the check-out time."

"Sure." I opened the door for him to enter. He dropped his bag beside mine and followed me to the small table in the corner. "I just talked with Teri."

"How is she? Chasing brats?"

"We didn't talk long, but she said she'd caught some kind of bug."

"They're going around." He pulled out a chair and waited until I'd settled into mine. "Now that we don't have cops and lawyers and nitwit game wardens around, what's your feeling?"

"Something's off," I said, "but I also feel a little foolish. We made that mad dash to Branson—and I'm glad we did as Van was in trouble—but . . ."

"We may have jumped ahead too quickly?"

"Yes. John is so independent, and he has no one to really answer to. The unusual part is that he has never cancelled plans we've made without letting me know. On the other hand, he's often late when he gets caught up in shooting. It's almost addictive. The lighting and the critters are just right, and you focus so heavily on it that you forget about everything else. I can imagine him telling himself that I'd wait for him."

"And his phone may have run down by the time he finished." Reed leaned forward and held my gaze. "What about that letter?"

"That's the part I can't explain away so easily." I sighed. "Someone seems to be playing a hoax on me. But why? What could possibly be the motive? I called Vicente, by the way, to see if he'd found anything; but I had to leave a message."

"I was going to ask about that." We were both silent a moment. "So are you ready to go home?"

I hesitated.

"This other stuff—the sheriff and the victim they found at the refuge—they were just going through the motions of eliminating you as a suspect," he said, reading my mind once again. "Sort of crossing the Ts."

"What a waste of time! I'm sorry I didn't just wait and let somebody else notice him!"

Reed chuckled. "No, you're not. You're too much of a busybody—excuse me—journalist to ignore a body lying in a ditch. And just so you know, they have absolutely nothing to even suspect you."

"They certainly treated me like a suspect last night!"

"Sure. This is probably the only crime scene either of these guys has ever handled. Can't deny them their dramatics. Besides . . ."

He stopped speaking until I finally prompted. "Besides what?"

Reed's eyes danced and he struggled against a smile. "Your lawyer saved the day."

I tried but neither of us could tamp down the laughter. "She reminds me of some television lawyer . . . only she writes her own lines, all the while looking like nobody's idea of a grandmother," I tossed out when I could speak again.

"She's a classy grandmother," Reed agreed. He glanced at his wrist. "We need to finish up if we're leaving—"

"Yes," I interrupted him. "Surely you can't stay away forever and neither can I."

"I'm being put on the schedule for the sheriff's office again, so I do need to get back. And neither of us seems able to keep out of trouble here—"

I glared across the table at his dancing eyes.

"—so I wondered if you'd like to take a different route home. Maybe just drive through some of the interesting areas where John might have gone and gotten too enthralled to leave." That, of course, had been the plan before Willoughby's call needing us to come directly to the police station in Socorro.

"I'd thought I'd do that after we got home and you could—"

"Waste of time and gas since we can check as we go. Besides, it might help to have a second pair of eyes." He grinned.

I nodded.

As I climbed into Reed's truck, I glanced around the parking lot.

"No cops," he said. "I told you they didn't seriously consider you a suspect, but I figured if I called in an attorney they would shut down the show. And if something were to develop, an attorney already on board might not be a bad idea."

Having someone taking care of me raised my hackles. Since I'd lost my parents as a youth and had no close relatives, I'd learned early on to care for myself. Reed must have sensed my displeasure because he continued, "I know that's what you would have done, but when you're in those interrogation rooms and they keep you for hours, you don't have much opportunity. I hope I haven't offended you."

"No," I said. "Thanks."

Reed nodded and backed out. "Do you want to check the GPS? I know Elephant Butte might be a spot for photography, and the guy at the check-out counter reminded me about City of Rocks and the national forest."

Within a few minutes, we turned onto the interstate. Preholiday traffic kept Reed's attention while I checked my phone again for any messages. None. But just as I reached to put it in my pocket, the phone rang. I looked at the ID. "Vicente," I told Reed and answered it.

"Sorrel, sorry I missed your call. I wanted to talk to you anyway about Blood Relations."

"Good. What do we know, Vicente?"

"They seem to be legitimate. I approached them as a potential customer. Figured that would work better than as a television news producer." A chuckle. " It's a straightforward ancestry tracing outfit. For a fee, you receive a cup to spit into and return to them. When the results are compiled, they send you a choice of where and how you want them made available."

"That's what they told me when I called about the results I received recently. But how would they have mine?" I asked. "I certainly haven't spit into any cups."

"I asked about their privacy settings. They have a sophisticated set-up to ensure safety against hackers and other illegal distribution."

"It didn't work."

Vicente agreed. "Hackers are just working harder. The motivation—if strong enough—proves that almost nothing is foolproof. Are you being blackmailed or something?

I thought of the letter but glossed over it. "No. Must be mistaken identity then."

"I thought you left us for the wide open spaces to simplify your life!"

"So did I."

"You could always come back," he said.

"Right!" I laughed. "And pull knives out of my back from my replacement!"

We chatted a few more minutes before another call came for him. "Let me know if—or when—this story comes out," he said.

I mulled over the information Vicente had passed on and had to agree with him. What possibly could motivate someone to set up a scam like this one? I'm a thrifty person by nature and had earned good money during my years in television journalism. Still, the lifestyle wasn't cheap and I'd only recently sold the house Kevin and I had bought in Houston Heights. After paying the realtor and the existing mortgage, I hadn't banked much profit. I'd invested Kevin's life insurance in the stock market. It might bring some long term security but not now. So money wouldn't likely be a motivation.

"Can you reach the cooler? I'd appreciate a bottle of water." Reed's voice broke through my thoughts.

"Sure." I got one for each of us. Only then did I notice the music filling the cab of the truck. "Mariachi?"

"Yep. Helped me stay in character for my undercover."

I couldn't be sure, but his lip seemed to twitch. I turned it off. "Do you have anything like the *Addams Family* or one of those science fiction shows?" I asked. "That seems more appropriate as mood music for this trip."

He ignored me. I took a long gulp of cold water and glanced at the desert landscape we'd entered. "Isn't it amazing how you can be in forests and then in the desert in such a short time?" We were headed toward Elephant Butte Lake State Park, just north of Truth or Consequences.

"Truth or Consequences was originally named Hot Springs," Reed said, answering my unasked question. "People—especially retirees who had arthritic problems—came here for the baths."

"Why did they change the name? It's a weird name."

"Some early television game show had that name. I don't know how the producer convinced the town to change the name—or why."

"You're joking!"

"I'll bet the old timers said the same thing. We'll be there in a half hour or so. Why don't you take a short nap? I'll need your sharp eyes then."

I glanced at Reed but he kept his eyes focused on the highway. I leaned back in my seat. Bossy men irritate me, I thought, as I obediently drifted off.

CHAPTER TWENTY-FIVE

The truck jerked me awake with a sudden turn. I sat up straight and rubbed my neck. "I thought cops drove better," I grumbled.

Reed chuckled.

"Where are we?"

"Truth or Consequences. Thought we'd nose around a little."

I looked at the museum-like building in front of us. "Chamber of Commerce?"

"Uh-huh. They likely have all sorts of brochures for the attractions around here where a guy might photograph wild critters. You coming?"

I combed through my hair with my fingers and hopped out. Reed held the door and followed me inside. A cute young lady smiled at us from the reception desk. "Hello. Can I help you?" she asked Reed. Her desk nameplate identified her as Tami.

"I hope so, Tami," he said, and turned up the wattage of his smile. "A friend of mine told me to meet him here, but I'm a little late and I'm afraid I may have missed him."

"You're the first people I've seen this morning."

I glanced toward the back and noticed an elderly man watching through the glass of a small office on the left. "Do you have any brochures for local attractions?" I asked.

She pulled her eyes away from Reed. "Sure," she said, and gestured toward a small table near the door.

I walked on over and glanced through them while Reed made small talk. "You interested in fishing or camping?" I jumped and turned toward the voice. It belonged to the elderly man.

"Photography, actually."

"Well, now, we have a lot of desert critters around here, as well as interesting formations. You'll find everything from Elephant Butte Lake—folks say the island in the center resembles an elephant—to the City of Rocks and the open pit copper mines at Silver City."

He'd gathered up a few brochures and held them out to me. "Thanks! I've heard about them from my friend John. He's a photographer—much more experienced than I. We planned to meet up with him but I was delayed and now I'm afraid he gave up on me."

"Tall guy? Older?'

I tried to keep the excitement from my voice. "Yes."

"He was here a few days ago. Said they were planning to take photographs and he asked about campsites."

"Oh, that wouldn't have been John then," I said.

"Who was with him?" Reed stuck out his hand to shake the other man's hand. "Chris Reed. And this is Sorrel. We didn't realize he'd decided to invite some others along, but we haven't spoken to him in a few days."

"Sam." He shook Reed's hand. "The other two weren't very friendly. They stood near the door, kinda antsy." He was silent a moment. "Truth is . . . I was a little uncomfortable. Wondered if they were planning something. Your friend—if he's the one you're looking for—was chatty. Nervous like. The other guy and the gal interrupted him and said they had to get going. She didn't look much like the camping type."

"You said this was a few days ago?" Reed asked.

"Yessir . . . about a week, in fact."

We thanked Sam and asked him, if John stopped back in, to let him know he'd missed us. Then, as we started out the door, Reed turned back as if he'd just thought of something. "That could have been Steve and Kim," he said casually. "Was she a blonde? About 20?"

"Hardly," Tami answered. "She was blonde with dark roots and 40s. So was he."

"Oh," Reed smiled and flashed another smile. "Guess Steve and Kim couldn't make it."

They watched as we got in the truck and pulled out. About half a block down the street, Reed spoke. "I'm sure that was John."

"I'm sure it was. But he wouldn't usually have been with a couple like that. John usually goes on his own—or, at least, with serious artists."

Reed thought a moment. "So he may not have chosen to be with them. They stood by the door. He was chatty—something I don't remember about John—making sure they'd remember him."

He was right. John would have expected me to look for him if he didn't cancel or show up. He would have dropped clues where he could. I turned to Reed.

"Campsites! There must be dozens of them!"

"Unfortunately," Reed agreed. "Elephant Butte is right here. Let's just sort of drive by the campsites in that area while we're here."

"Great idea! I have a brochure here listing the more popular ones. But there's one major problem. How will we recognize John and his companions? If he's been taken, he'd hardly be in his own truck."

"Maybe he would or maybe he wouldn't. If he were kidnapped after he reached the area, he'd have his truck. But Sam said he was pulling a little camper trailer. Does that sound familiar?"

"Yes and no. John has a camper, but he'd booked a room at the bed and breakfast. Why do that if he's going to camp? I don't think the camper was John's." Then I said, "But John may have given a ride to someone with a broken down vehicle—particularly if he thought they were honest—"

Reed interrupted me. "Some people are just natural cons, Sorrel. You've met as many as I have."

"Yes, I have. The part about the people who so easily play the victim is that they are especially ruthless when victimizing someone else. Did you get a date when they were here?"

"Not really. The girl—Tami—thought it was about four or five days ago.

"Do you think the campsites would even be open at this time of year, Reed? I didn't think to ask Sam."

"About the only way to know is to drive around the area and see for ourselves."

We wasted the next hour and a half cruising around campsites and talking to people. No one had seen the trio Sam had described. Reed finally turned back toward town.

"Where do we head next?" he asked. I opened one of the brochures just as Reed's phone rang. He pulled over and answered it. I could hear a loud voice.

"Jose?" I asked but he held up his hand and continued to listen.

"When?" he asked. "Is she all right?" Finally, he said, "We'll head right out. Should be there tonight. Thanks, buddy, and tell Teri to hang in there." He hung up and stared ahead.

"Reed?"

"It's Teri," he said. "She'd gone out to feed the cats and someone jumped her. Hit her from behind as she was unlocking the door."

"Is she all right?"

"Well, there are other complications. She's pregnant."

"Pregnant! She never said—"

"She wanted to surprise us. Do this fancy reveal thing. You know Teri. Miss Drama Queen."

I took a breath and forced myself to ask. "And the baby?"

"All right just now. But she's in the hospital overnight for observation."

"Do they know who hurt her?"

"Not yet. And it gets worse, Sorrel. Someone faxed a photo to Randall Byrd of you coming out of the police station in Socorro with the headline "Local Celebrity Questioned in Bosque Murder." And your Jeep's been vandalized. Someone painted the words *Blood Relations* on it in what seems to be real blood."

CHAPTER TWENTY-SIX

Neither of us felt inclined to talk much on the long drive home. Aside from bathroom or gas stops, we drove straight through. Even though Jose had reassured him that Teri was only in the hospital as a safety precaution and would be home tomorrow, Reed was a quiet worrier and had this massive protective streak. I could understand Reed's distress over Teri. He also took his role as the twins' godfather seriously.

Of course, I'm a worrier too. Our visit to the Chamber of Commerce had confirmed the answer to one worrisome question: John had not cancelled his trip to New Mexico. In fact, he'd been in the area during the same time we had planned to meet. But who were these people who'd accompanied him? Were they friends from Branson? Or had he met them at some campsite? Was he in danger? And why hadn't he just given me a call?

And if all that wasn't enough to worry about, we had someone who had attacked Teri outside the shop. It didn't sound like teenaged mischief either. Teri and I had first become friends when I began taking photos for the local newspaper where she worked, but our friendship had really blossomed when she became a consignee for my store. We were an unlikely pair: she a wife, mother of twins, and related to half the town and I single, no family, and career oriented.

As Reed steered the truck onto the two-lane highway, he slowed a bit. In spite of the moon, it was a dark night. Critters, depending on their size, could cause quite a bit of damage even to a vehicle this size.

I couldn't help comparing the sparse traffic to Houston. "Don't you miss the city?" Teri had asked recently. "Shopping? Restaurants? Always something to do?"

"I miss the beach at Galveston," I'd told her. "But never the traffic . . . and I never made any real friends there. My job meant irregular hours and was so competitive that I thought of little else."

"That would be hard on a marriage," she'd observed.

"It was." Kevin had hated my job after our marriage, although he'd first been attracted to me through seeing me on television. And he'd enjoyed the attention we received when we went out.

I smiled. As a teen, I'd complained endlessly about small towns and dreamed of the kind of life I'd recently left behind. Yet it wasn't strange that even though I'd lived in Houston for almost a decade and here for less than a year, I felt no urge to return. Saddle Gap, nestled near the Mexican border, had become home. Life here was more . . . sedate.

"Penny for them."

I laughed. "Not worth it. Just thinking about how good it will be to be home."

"I want to talk to you about that." Reed swerved to miss a rabbit. "I think you ought to stay at the bed and breakfast in Saddle Gap for a night or two."

"Why would I want to do that? The cats will be ready for company by now—and I'm ready for my own bed."

Reed laughed. "Now that's a grandma statement if I ever heard one!"

I ignored that. "And you're taking a grandpa attitude. You should know by now that I don't hide out. I installed a security system—"

"—which has been breached before—"

"—and Saddle Gap is one of the safer small cities in the Southwest."

Reed sighed. "Okay. I'll give in, even though it's against my better judgment. But I'd like to take a quick look around at least. I'd bunk on your couch, but I need to check in—"

"—on your own life, without playing nursemaid to me!"

Both cats gave us a warm welcome when we finally stumbled into my house. I cuddled them briefly and then opened a can of cat food before hauling my bags into the bedroom. By the time Reed had checked things out to his satisfaction, I'd scrambled eggs and baked a can of biscuits. He sniffed, reached down to rub a furry back, and headed to the bathroom.

We ate quickly and cleaned up together.

"Tasted great!" Reed unplugged the sink to let the dishwater drain out and dried his hands. "Your security system doesn't appear to have been tampered with at all. But your motion sensor lighting isn't working on the far side. It doesn't look like anyone disturbed the wiring, so a bulb may have gone out. But I still wish you'd—"

"—stay right here in my own home!"

"Stubborn woman!" Reed's cell chirped. "Jose," he said, punching a button. I went into the bedroom, unpacked my bag, changed into pajamas, and cleaned my face and teeth.

Reed tapped at the door. When I opened it, he looked at me for a long moment. "I think I prefer you this way . . ." he started to say and then stopped. "Teri's doing well. They're giving her some fluids and bed rest, but she'll be home tomorrow. She has a bump on her head."

I followed him through the kitchen and living room combination to my front door. Reed glanced at the door leading to the enclosed porch area which I'd turned into a work area. Then he rechecked to see that it was locked. "I won't patronize you by going over security measures with you, Sorrel," he said. "You've lived and worked in a dangerous city—or two—at all hours of the night. But you're just far enough out of town here—no close neighbors and a highway out there—not to mention the traffic from illegal border crossings. So be careful. Calling 911 doesn't apply out here, so call me if you need me."

"Are you going by Jose's?"

"No, he's wrestling the boys. I need to check in at the office, have some messages. Then I'll go on over to my place."

I wrinkled my nose. "Musty!"

He laughed. "I'm waiting outside until I hear all the locks clicking." As he stepped through the door, Reed looked at me a moment as if to add something. But then he just nodded and pulled the door closed.

I locked it immediately, set the security code, and made a face at the door. Still, it felt good to know he was waiting. In fact, his truck didn't pull out until I'd turned out the lights everywhere but the bedroom.

Flash and Van padded behind me and leaped up on the end of the bed. I soon followed them, but my mind wasn't shutting down so easily. In the dark of the night, I found it more difficult to rationalize John's recent behavior. First, he was conscientious. Not having someone reliable to care for Van while he was gone was unthinkable. Then not calling to let me know his change of plans raised a major red flag. Finally, that couple who had accompanied him to the Chamber of Commerce sounded out of character for John. Where had he met them? John certainly wasn't a snob, but this couple hadn't sounded like people he would choose as camping buddies.

I snuggled down and Van padded up to curl against me. "Wish you could talk, old buddy," I said. He purred and I buried my fingers in his thick coat. As I finally began to doze off, somewhere in the somnolent haze I thought I heard music.

CHAPTER TWENTY-SEVEN

I'd slept better than the night before—likely due to my own mattress and the two cats pressed against my spine. I glanced at my alarm clock. Six o'clock. Way too early, I thought, and snuggled back under the quilt.

Before I could doze off again, though, my eye registered a flashing light. A missed call. That must have been the music from last night. I raised up, picked up my cell while I mentally rehearsed what I'd say to Reed. Hadn't the crazy guy had enough time to tell me everything he knew already? I entered my message code. No message. A hang-up.

Both cats had perched on my hip and were glaring at me. "Okay, okay. Coffee, food, and then I'll get back to this."

I threw the quilt back and slid my feet into the cat slippers John had given me for Christmas last year. Within a few minutes, amid the cats lapping up their breakfast and the brewing coffee spreading its appetizing aroma throughout the house, I'd settled into my comfy chair and reached for my phone. No message on the last call, but I did have a text message—from John!

I clicked on the message: "Sorrel, foxes in the hen—." I checked my received calls history. The missed call and John's text both had come from his cell phone.

Foxes in the henhouse! It was our code for caution about people around us. But the only people around me were Teri and Reed. Of Teri, I was absolutely certain. Of Reed? Reed had rescued me more than once. John surely couldn't have been warning me about them.

Maybe the foxes were his, not mine. Either way, he'd been interrupted and was in trouble. I wanted to think—no, I had to believe—he was still alive. I had no time to consider anything else. I needed all of my strength to find him—and I would!

Two cups of coffee and a granola bar later, I hurried through the shower, dressed in jeans and a sweater, and opened the door that led from my kitchen into the shop. I locked the door behind me to keep the cats out. Teri had collected mail while I was gone and dumped it into our mail basket on the desk.

Calling it an office was optimistic. When I'd redecorated this small shop that my aunt had created from two thirds of her home, I'd kept her vision of the big open area and this tiny corner office that consisted of a counter, a desk top computer, and a filing cabinet. Someday I hoped to glass in the office area.

This morning I caught my breath as I looked out again at the Winter Wonderland Teri had created while I'd taken off for the Bosque Festival. How lucky I was to have Teri—and John! The thought of losing either felt like a fist wrapped around my heart.

When I'd walked into my home and found Kevin's murdered body, John had been there. After years of investigating and reporting other peoples' tragedies, I'd been completely unprepared to handle my own. That seemed like a major inconsistency, actually, as I wasn't new to loss and handling it on my own. I'd been a young teen when my dad died, and my mother had followed only three years later. But even though their deaths had left me grieving, I'd pushed on toward school and career. Occasionally I caught myself tearful at the injustice of the accident and the disease that took them far too soon. But Kevin's murder had felt personal, and I couldn't be sure whether or not I'd indirectly caused it. I'd made a fresh start largely due to the help given me by Teri and John, these two people who now needed mine.

I glanced through the mail, tossing junk and filing a utility bill in the To Be Paid folder. At the bottom of the stack was a black envelope with dramatic red lines running down it. The return address read Blood Relations but the envelope certainly didn't look like the ones I'd received earlier. Was this authentic? I opened it quickly and scanned the letter, which was from Quality Control. The form letter was their response to my telephone inquiry about the results I'd received earlier:

> *Dear Ms. Janes:*
>
> *We have reviewed your files and find that our company has provided you with your test results following your initial inquiry for a test, and your submission of your saliva for testing. Results were mailed to you via certified mail. I am enclosing a copy of your signed receipt. Please contact us if we can be of further help.*

Like most form letters, this was of no help. Whoever had sent a sample of saliva had listed it under my name. Why? Except for the dramatic envelope, which seemed odd. Why would Quality Control play up the drama when the other communications I'd seen from the company hadn't? No signature, not even a facsimile. Just a name typed in with a title beneath it. The company probably had thousands of these printed to send out in reply to people's complaints.

I folded the letter and stuck it in my pocket. On my list of priorities, I decided to keep this puzzle in the top half but not at the top of the list. I wasn't totally convinced that someone hadn't sent in my information—either mine or someone else's—to freak me out. At the moment, though, John had to be my top priority. If he'd been truly kidnapped, I knew time was crucial.

To shake off nervous tension I strolled around the shop, looking at the artful displays my consignees had created for the Black Friday sale. Teri had placed door prize forms on each table, along with colorful garland around the table skirt. What a picture!

Picture! Photos! That was one of the chores Teri had assigned to me! I hurried back for my camera, plugged in the twinkle lights, and flipped on the overhead lighting. After a few shots, I flipped off the overhead and focused again. Some displays needed less light.

I could feel the tension easing as I worked. I needed some time to think about how to continue my search for John. Finishing the preparations for the Black Friday sale gave my brain the respite it needed to start sorting out where I needed to go from here.

I also knew that, of all people, John would understand. With a new business, you needed to capitalize on peak sales opportunities—and Black Friday certainly qualified as one of those. And I owed my consignees the best opportunity to sell their crafts. A great many of them were seniors whose sales provided the extras they could no longer afford otherwise.

On the other hand, my inner conscience reminded time was crucial. And wouldn't I—were I a captive—want John or the authorities to make me a priority? I needed to set up a back-up plan for Black Friday on the off-chance that something intervened.

My cellphone sang "Grandma Got Run Over by a Reindeer." Reed. A quick glance showed that it was already twelve thirty! Could that be right? I answered on the second verse.

"Sorrel? Have you spoken to Teri yet?"

"No. I wanted to check mail, pay bills, and do the photos she needs for the ads so I could tell her I was taking care of my assignments. She's next on my list."

"Good. I've been told to pick you up. We've been invited over there for lunch."

"No way! She doesn't need to be cooking—"

"Of course, she doesn't! Neither do she and Jose need to eat the mountains of food her family have hauled in. Jose sent out an SOS."

Teri's family cooked delicious dishes in huge quantities. They were in high demand at community events. In fact, they would be selling food in stands just outside the store on Friday—a huge draw for our sale. And when suffering or illness befell anyone, especially family, they swarmed in with food to help in the way they knew best. To refuse their gifts would hurt them deeply. Teri and Jose likely had so much food it wouldn't fit in their refrigerator.

"I'll just meet you there," I told Reed. "No need for you to drive all the way out here."

"I'm sitting out front."

Of course, he was! I peeked anyway. Reed waved.

"It will take me a few minutes—"

"It always does. I'll wait."

I purposely took longer than I needed. Chris raised his eyebrows a bit when he saw my camera bag and casual—okay, ratty—jeans. I didn't want him to get the idea that I considered this lunch anything more than a way to check on friends, not a date. He'd gotten out to open the door for me but wisely kept his hands and comments to himself.

CHAPTER TWENTY-EIGHT

The ride over to Teri's was nearly silent. Aside from saying hello after I'd settled into the truck, we hadn't said a word to each other. Reed seemed preoccupied. I suspected it was about work. I hoped it wasn't, because Teri wasn't feeling as well as he'd told me and I wasn't much in the mood for talking either.

As Reed turned onto Teri's street, I noticed a sheriff's car.

"What's up?" I asked.

"Nothing. Just invited a new deputy along. Teri was begging me to bring anyone I knew to help eat some of that feast her family brought."

I laughed. "So you obliged with a big, hungry, single—"

He nodded.

"—guy to help us out!" He coughed, preventing an answer. Clearly, Reed didn't seem to be in the mood for light conversation.

He parked and I hopped out. Before I could even close the door, a giggle floated our way from the cruiser. "Beat ya!" a distinctly feminine voice called.

"See you found your way!" Chris said. He turned toward me. "Sorrel, this is Deputy Lucia Montez. We call her Luz."

I stuck out a hand toward Luz, but she just stood there with her hands on her hips and studied me. "You don't look like a horse."

Reed snorted and tried to turn it into a cough.

"You don't look like a deputy," I replied, withdrawing my hand. "How long have you been one?"

Reed interrupted. "Luz just started today. She's new to Saddle Gap. In from training in Albuquerque. So you and Teri will have the opportunity to fill her in on things around here."

"Teri is better at that than I," I said and turned toward the house.

Luz put a hand on Reed's arm. "Reed, I need to talk to you for a minute—in private."

"Can it wait until after lunch?"

"Not really." She smiled prettily up at him.

"Don't mind me," I said. I walked up to the door and knocked.

Teri opened the door and pulled me into a big hug. After we'd stepped inside, she nodded toward the other two. "Who's the—"

"—deputy? Lucia—Luz—Montez. New from Albuquerque."

"A lady deputy?" Jose rose from the table and walked over to the window to take a peek. "Wow!"

"She said I don't look like a horse."

Jose swallowed a chuckle. "I'll check on the boys," he said and walked quickly down the hall but not before the roar of his laughter burst out.

"Don't worry," Teri told me. "Chris Reed has always attracted women. He doesn't even seem to notice it. For sure he won't start anything up with a co-worker—"

"He can marry her for all I care," I said casually. "In fact, it might be just what he deserves. A sharp-tongued wife to keep him in line!"

Teri led me to the recliner. Then she sank into the sofa. "I'd hoped when I discovered you two had gone to Branson together—"

"—that he'd make wild, passionate love to me?" We both giggled. "Hardly. In fact, he probably thinks I've chopped John into bits with an axe."

Teri's eyes widened. She smiled behind me. "Hi, Chris. Forgive me if I'm too pooped to get up."

My cheeks grew hot. Reed drew Luz forward. "Our new deputy, Luz Montez," he told Teri. Luz smiled at Teri and shook her hand.

"I'm Jose," boomed the traitor's voice from the hallway, "and these are our brats."

I shooed Teri back into her seat when she started to get up and motioned to Reed to help me set out food and paper plates. Luz's giggle sounded often amid Jose's charm and Teri's chatter.

"Axe murderer?" Reed murmured as he passed by me with a platter of tamales that had been warming in the oven.

I ignored him, pulling guacamole from the refrigerator and grabbing a bag of corn chips. When he stepped back in the kitchen, I thrust them at him and turned to pour beans from the pot on the stove. He leaned in close and whispered, "She's just a kid, Sorrel. Be nice."

"Why wouldn't I be?"

Lunch—or any meal—at Teri's table was always a lively affair. I'd watched Teri during the meal, and she didn't look like she had sustained any lasting damage. In fact, the glow of her impending motherhood gave her an even bubblier attitude, if that was possible. And Jose hovered protectively, not allowing her to lift a hand.

"Jose is smothering me!" she whispered as we moved into the living room while Jose and Reed—with marginal help from the twins—cleared the table and cleaned up. Luz had prettily excused herself earlier to return to work.

"You need to be pampered," I told her. "I can't believe I didn't even know you were pregnant!"

"I planned one of those dramatic reveals you see on TV," Teri giggled. "You know me and drama!"

I did. But I could also see a new fragility in my friend. "I feel so guilty that you were attacked at my place—right in the parking lot."

"I wasn't paying attention around me, Sorrel. This is Saddle Gap. Jose is always reminding me that with people sneaking across the border, we need to be more careful."

"And, of course, she paid close attention to my warning!" Jose dropped a kiss on Teri's head and carried a coffee cup over to his recliner. "Ice water? Milk?" he asked her. "No caffeine for you."

Teri made a face and gave me the "what can we do" shrug.

"Sorrel? Coffee?"

I hadn't heard Reed enter. "Thanks but no. I'm stuffed."

A loud clatter sounded down the hall. Teri started to rise but Jose was already up. "Better see if the bunk beds have been disassembled," he said.

"I'll check in with you later," Reed told him. "Gotta get back to work."

I rose also. Even though Teri sounded like her bubbly self, she looked tired. "You need to get some rest," I told her. "Little girls take more rest."

She giggled. "My luck, there are a couple more boys in there." She raised a fist at Reed. "Get ready, because if there are, I'm sending them to Uncle Reed!" He grinned.

"Oh, I almost forgot! Here are the photos you wanted for the ads!" I pulled them out of my camera bag. "Do you want me to drop them off at the paper?"

"No, I want to look at them first! Jose can drop them off." She rose to hug me. "What do you think of the store?"

"Gorgeous! I can't wait to see everyone's reactions when we reopen for the sale! You've done too much!"

"I have some ideas—"

"—which can wait until after you take a nap!" Jose had slipped back, swung her up in his arms, and winked at us. "I have to do my Tarzan tricks with this one."

"We completely agree that you need to rest!" I said. "Don't go near the store!" Reed and I smiled on the way out, Teri's protests—though weaker than even she knew—following us.

I swung the camera bag into the floorboard and climbed into Reed's truck. "Hope I'm not interrupting your work too much. In fact, how about we put our minds together later today? You must have things to catch up on at work. Any out-of-town investigations among them?"

"Nope. I'm assigned to the sheriff's office just now as a liaison, their term for extra help and paper pusher."

"I doubt they're thrilled with our road trips. Anyway, we can meet after you spend some time there with that wonderful paperwork."

He didn't argue, just started the engine and pulled out.

Before I could continue probing, my cell sang out. "Hello," I said. A pause. Then a click. I checked the number. WITHHELD.

"'Grandma Got Run Over by a Reindeer'?"

When I didn't answer, Reed turned onto my highway and we rode in silence until he turned into the store lot and pulled over in front of my house.

"Sorrel?"

"I think John—or someone with his phone—is trying to reach me."

CHAPTER TWENTY-NINE

"When?"

"I've gotten two calls, one last night and one today."

"What did he say? Is he okay?" Reed ground out the questions. The flat, deliberate tone of his voice masked the anger he was keeping leashed at my not telling him sooner.

"I never spoke to him. The calls were hang-ups from his cellphone."

Finally, he asked, "And you were going to tell me this when?"

"When I saw you, but with Luz there—"

"What does she have to do with it?"

"Well, she had something to discuss with you and—"

"—and you were jealous."

I felt my temper rising. "Give me a break! I didn't want to talk about it in front of her because I doubted you'd filled her in!"

Reed sighed. "She doesn't know anything about it. But you could have talked to me after she left."

"If you'll recall, she left while we were still at the table. And I certainly didn't want to share it with Teri and Jose!" I hugged the door and stared out the window.

Neither of us spoke. A few seconds later, I began gathering up my camera bag and the bag of food that Teri had sent. Reed sat hunched over the steering wheel. I yanked the handle open, but by the time I'd stepped out and turned to close it, his big hand closed over mine.

"I'm sorry, Sorrel. It's just—"

"I wasn't asking for help!" I snapped. "We'd just agreed to share information as it came in." I pulled away and started toward the house, but Reed got there first and stepped between me and the door. I stepped back a little.

"Sorrel, the case I was working on has some new developments. I lied about the office paperwork. I've actually been called away for a couple of days."

"And?"

He sighed. "And you're the most stubborn, hardheaded redhead I've ever had the misfortune to be tangled—"

"You're not tangled up with me! I merely let you know about the calls as a courtesy and you blew it up into some sort of—of—!" I turned around and tried to insert the key into the lock. "I've been in charge of my life for a long time now, and I haven't been considered a misfortune to anyone—except maybe my murdered husband . . . or my missing friend!" I jiggled the key but the darn thing wouldn't fit! "So consider yourself lucky and just point that truck in the opposite direction and—"

"Would you just unlock the door?"

"No! I'm enjoying playing with it!"

We glared at each other. Then the corner of Reed's lip twitched and we both spoke together.

"I'm sorry," he began.

"I'm being pigheaded!"

He shrugged and grinned. "You can say that, but I wouldn't dare. Would it offend your feminine pride for me to open the door?"

I stepped back and waved him over. "God made man to do these intricate procedures," I smirked, "and gave us females the brains to get him to do them."

The door swung open easily and I hurried in to punch the security buttons. "Would you like something?"

"Sorry. No time. I need to get back to the office. "

I'd forgotten amid our spat that he was leaving. "When are you leaving?"

"Late this afternoon. I have a meeting first. I may be back late, but I know I'll have some meetings and paperwork to complete for the rest of the week. Thanksgiving next week is putting a squeeze on some of it." But he remained standing at the door, his hand on the knob.

"Godspeed," I said and busied myself storing the leftovers in the fridge. Still, he didn't move. I closed the fridge and looked at him questioningly.

"Sorrel . . ."

I waited for a couple of beats before I finally prompted. "Reed, what's up?"

"I just feel so uncomfortable taking off right now." I started to speak, but he held up his hand and continued. "I know you're smart and savvy and experienced in looking after yourself as well as investigating. But this thing, this surprise at every corner and no real confirmation of anything . . . I just would feel better if you at least had a partner."

"Right. Like the one I had before? I almost didn't survive that partnership!"

"You mean Jason, your partner who turned out to be working for the cartel?"

"Among others. The hardest part is when you don't know who the bad guys and the good guys are!"

Reluctantly, he grinned. "But don't forget who came along in the white hat—"

"Never." I patted his shoulder, letting my hand rest there a moment. "So you need to get along to work and finish what you need to do before you change into your superhero role. I'll try to concentrate on my work as well, in spite of the image of you in tights floating through my brain."

He had a sexy laugh, which I listened to as he turned to leave. I then closed—and locked—the door behind him. Too bad I didn't have time to think about those tights.

Instinct directed me to make a list of how I needed to proceed. So I curled up in the big old chair Teri's cousin had found for me last spring, pulled my electronic pad from my purse, and began:

1. *Check Facebook.* John and I had used it as a
   communication tool to alert each other if one of

us needed help when I left him in Branson and started my life over here in New Mexico.

2. *Call John's neighbor in Branson who was keeping an eye on his little house.*

3. *Return calls*—the answering machine was flashing—*and glance through the mail.* I knew one of the calls could be from John, but it was more likely some of my consignees checking in about Black Friday. Besides, if it was another hang up, I'd rather not make myself any more upset about what was or was not happening.

4. *???* Who knew what might come next.

My list complete for now, I snuggled into the chair's lumpy cushions and began addressing each item in turn. I started by logging onto Facebook. An hour later, I stood up and stretched. No progress really, but I'd reminded myself that a methodical approach works best for me. Facebook had yielded nothing—no activity at all—so John either didn't have Internet access or chose not to send a message.

His neighbor had collected his mail and to avoid future problems had decided to pay his utilities. She knew he would repay her and the damage broken pipes would cause! But to her surprise, John had set up an automatic payment plan with the bank. Not such an unheard of thing, she rattled on to me, except that John had always been so guarded about giving access to his bank account. She was happy he'd planned ahead, she explained, but she couldn't understand why he hadn't made better plans for Van. John loved that cat—and on and on. She was a sweet lady, but I gently disengaged myself as I'd done before when I'd stayed with John, who had once said she spoke in volumes.

As I suspected, most of the calls I needed to return were to consignees for the store. Many of them lived at the senior living center. Even though they'd retained most of the information about the persons they'd been, they had difficulty retaining who they currently were. Teri had less patience in dealing with the seniors than I did, but then she had both sets of her grandparents living close. I'd not known any of mine and I enjoyed these substitutes. It was time to deal with them now before life became any more hectic. So I started on the list of calls, dealing with each of them quickly, mostly reminding the seniors of the schedule for Black Friday and listening to their excitement. I also reminded each one—and would probably do so again—that the ads would be printed next week in Wednesday's Thanksgiving edition.

The last phone message was from Ranger Willowby. I sighed. Maybe I ought to make a glass of iced tea before calling, I thought as I dialed the number.

Willowby answered almost as if he'd been waiting by the phone.

"Ranger Willowby? Sorrel Janes returning your call."

"Uh, hello, Ms. Janes." A pause. "Sorry I called. I think I just blew it up out of proportion."

"Blew what up?"

Another pause. "Sorry I wasted your time."

"Time I have. What did you blow up?"

"Well . . . the wife reminded me that you sell your photos in your store."

"Yes," I answered encouragingly, tamping my own impatience. "I also sell them to newspapers and have submitted some to wildlife magazines. No luck so far." I hoped my rambling a bit would calm him down enough to say why he'd called.

"So that might explain it."

I held my tongue.

"Had you mentioned that you'd be coming here for our fall festival? Maybe promise them some photos?"

"I might have," I lied.

"Well . . . maybe I should turn this in anyway."

Another pause. I mentally counted to ten. Luckily, Willowby wasn't close enough to strangle.

"Turn what in? Did I leave something there? Maybe drop it while taking photos?"

"No, you didn't."

"Someone else?" I probed. Mrs. Willowby must have the patience of a saint. "Is it a note?"

He cleared his throat. Maybe he'd sensed I'd like to wrap my fingers around it. "More like a notebook."

"A notebook?" I felt a giggle somewhere trying to bubble to the surface. Was the note that long? Why did it take Willowby so long to pass the message?

"Well, one of those little notepads . . . the kind that fits in a pocket."

"Why would you think it was mine?"

"Like I said, I think it's yours. But . . . I hope I'm not out of line here. Mrs. Willowby insists—"

"—what does Mrs. Willowby say?"

"She says since your name is there—Sorrel is just a little too uncommon for it to be someone else—maybe I should call." I heard a relieved sigh. Maybe Willowby's or maybe mine.

"My name?"

But Willowby clearly was finished. "I can mail it to you," he said.

I made a lightning decision. "No, I'll come and get it," I said.

"All this way? It's no—"

"I was planning to come out there anyway. Of course, if it's just an empty notebook, I don't see any reason to rush."

"I see some names and dates but nothing much. There's no rush—"

"I'm sure there isn't," I soothed him. "But I have some photography projects I need to discuss with a studio in Socorro, and it's easier if I do it in person. With Thanksgiving next week, I'm anxious to get things tied up before the holidays."

"Oh, sure. The refuge offices are closed most of next week—"

"I'll run by tomorrow. Will you be there?"

"No, but I can leave it behind the desk in the gift shop."

He sounded relieved to have it off his hands. Willowby must certainly be better with wildlife than people, I thought after we'd hung up.

I spent the rest of the day writing checks for bills that had come in the mail, doing laundry, and generally tidying my small house. That finished, I called Teri. We'd not had much chance to talk at lunch with everyone there.

"Sorrel, I'm so excited about next week!" She bubbled.

"Teri, have you been resting at all?"

She giggled. "Sorrel, please don't join the watchdogs! Jose and my family are smothering me!"

I laughed. "We're just so excited about the baby. It is 'baby'?"

"Oh, God, I hope so! No one should have another set of twins!"

"I feel so bad about what happened, Teri. I never would have forgiven myself if—"

"We won't even think about it! And I don't need to be watched over constantly! The doctor said I could resume my normal activities."

"Good! By the way, how far—"

"Thirteen weeks."

"I hadn't a clue!"

Another giggle. "I'm blessed with no morning sickness and lots of loose sweaters! Now, what do you know about this new deputy?"

"No more than you. Reed says she's fresh out of the academy."

"She's fresh, all right!" Teri's infectious giggle quickly enveloped both of us. When we caught our breath, I could hear a bit of fatigue.

"Time for us to get off here," I told her. "But I have a favor to ask. I'm taking a quick drive to Socorro tomorrow—may have to stay overnight. I know I have good security out here, but with all of the advertising and extra merchandise, I wondered if we needed someone to stay overnight. And there are the cats as well."

"I know just the guy! I have a cousin in from Afghanistan—"

"Aw, Teri, we can't take his leave—"

"He'll love it, Sorrel. My aunt drives him crazy! And he wouldn't need to be out there all the time."

"True. If you think he'll—"

"—love it? I'll hang up and give him a quick call."

"And Teri? Reed doesn't need to know!"

Half an hour later the plans were set. Teri's cousin Pete had called and said he would meet me at eight in the morning. He sounded nice and assured me he liked cats.

Just before I turned out the lights, I patted Van and Flash, curled up at the foot of my bed. "You'll have company this time, fur babies," I crooned. "But you're still in charge! Go easy on him, just in case he isn't as understanding as Reed."

CHAPTER THIRTY

I really hadn't needed an alarm, I thought as I looked out my kitchen window at the pink, orange, and yellow of a glorious sunrise. Silence surrounded me, broken only by the coffee dripping into the pot. A rabbit stopped and looked around before continuing his grazing. Trucks sped along the highway, their colorful lights resembling the Christmas lights that would soon be twinkling everywhere. Christmas had always been my favorite holiday.

I love this life, I thought. Then—almost immediately—I felt guilty. Guilty for how things had worked out for me but not for everyone. How could so many changes have filled the past few months?

I had no regrets about the move. Saddle Creek was smaller by far than Houston; but it had a college, adequate shopping, a host of good people—as well as a few bad apples as John liked to say— and much less traffic! I shuddered at the thought of the hours I'd spent in Houston's traffic.

Christmas would be different this year. I'd spent most of my Christmases in Houston working. In fact, I'd volunteered to work so that my colleagues could spend time with their families. And after Kevin and I married, I'd volunteered to work to avoid Kevin's parents.

I'd flown to Florida with Kevin after we became engaged. His parents had called several times and we had spoken briefly, but I'd still been surprised by the reception I'd received. Kevin's parents had seemed excited and welcoming. Later, I'd tried to recall when things between us had chilled. It always circled back to when they'd asked about my family. Kevin hadn't told them anything about me except that I'd graduated from the University of Missouri and now worked as a news anchor/crime journalist. I told them I'd spent my childhood on military bases and then on the ranch where Dad had grown up, that he'd died when I was a young teen—a farm accident—and that Mama had been a teacher until her death my senior year. When I finished, Kevin's mother had taken a deep breath and said, "Well, at least you attended a good school. And your sorority?" I'd shaken my head. Silence followed.

Looking back now, I couldn't remember another conversation with her. Instead, she talked over me or at me, never waiting for my answer. "Just ignore it," Kevin advised. "Mom will grow to love you. I love you and you're hot. My friends can't believe you're mine."

I'd told myself it was enough. Only now, on this November morning way out in the mountains of New Mexico, I acknowledged that it hadn't been enough—and would never have been.

Weird! I don't think I'd ever truly acknowledged that. In the months after Kevin's death, John had told me I'd realize someday— John. Where are you, John?

A coyote howled. Such a lonely sound. Or was it? Like most things, loneliness is a state of mind, I told myself.

I inhaled. Coffee. First things first. I poured a cup and headed toward my favorite comfy chair. But only a sip later, the phone rang. I looked at the phone. Reed.

"Hi!"

"Sorrel, I don't have but a minute. Have you heard anything new?"

"Not yet." I heard a feminine laugh in the background. "Are you at the office?"

"On the road. I'll be out of touch for a couple of days. Leave a text and I'll answer when I can."

I opened my mouth, but he'd already hung up. When had he decided I needed his advice for every move I made? I was well able to do my own investigation. In fact, I'd seldom shared an investigation! When Reed had arrived at Bosque, it had seemed natural to team up. But now Reed had another teammate—that giggle in the background—and I needed to get moving on my own.

I didn't linger over my coffee. I needed to shower and dress before Pete arrived.

Flash and Van climbed on Pete's lap the moment he sat down. Like Reed, Pete addressed them easily. "Aren't you a gorgeous pair," he told them. Van immediately preened and purred. Flash blinked flirtatiously.

I snorted. "Look at these kiss-ups!"

Pete laughed. "I'm going to enjoy this job." He followed me into the kitchen so I could show him where the kitty supplies were stored.

"Feel free to eat whatever you find," I told him. "I haven't been home much lately."

He groaned and rubbed his stomach. "Food! My mom acts like I haven't eaten in weeks! I'm so stuffed I can hardly waddle." I laughed. He didn't have a spare pound on him as far as I could see.

"I made a cheat sheet for you," I continued, pointing to the paper tacked on my note board. "My cell number and the vet's number are there. Flash is easy with change. Van isn't mine and he has his own peculiar routine."

"Just another guy thing."

That phrase followed me onto the road as I turned out of the driveway a mere thirty minutes since Reed's call. I needed to apply this statement to John. He'd been single all the years I'd known him, and he had a routine that he followed in most areas of his life. He shopped at the start of a week, he liked shooting on weekdays to avoid the weekend crowds, he loved hosting casual evenings for friends and students at his home, he was loyal to a fault, and he never—ever—stood people up. Unless, that is, he became absorbed in a project or shoot. Then he could lose track of all time. I smiled when I thought of the time our whole class had shown up at his shop after he'd forgotten class all week. He apologized profusely.

Had that happened now? Logical Sorrel, a childhood nickname my dad had given me, spoke up. John had seemed excited about our shoot at Bosque. But maybe something else had wiped the whole event from his mind. Or maybe he'd planned to let me know but just hadn't done so. He was probably tramping through some wilderness area, enjoying the solitude, his mind filled with the shots!

Not solitude! Worry Wart Sorrel chimed in. *Remember the couple with him at Truth or Consequences? Had he started the trip with them or just collected them along the way?*

Doesn't matter, Logical Sorrel replied. *He hadn't seemed stressed or reluctant to be with them, according to the people we'd spoken with.*

They didn't think the people had looked like photographers, Worry Wart shot back.

How do photographers look? Logical Sorrel replied.

As the miles flew, I worried the Blood Relations thing in my mind. An elaborate hoax? What would motivate someone to go to such trouble? Surely the joker knew I could disprove it easily enough—should I even take it seriously. And having John for my father? My mother had died before I entered the university.

Another possibility could be money! Money motivated so much. How would it fit in with this company? What if the results were false? What if someone was just pulling names from a phone book and scamming innocent people? Nah. That was just too cheesy.

It was a waste of my time, I decided, to worry about some foolish prank.

By the time I reached Bosque Del Apache Wildlife Refuge, the sun was high overhead and the sandhill cranes and snow geese had landed in cornfields to eat. I hoped the offices hadn't closed for lunch. I whipped my Jeep into the small parking area and parked beneath a large tree. The sidewalk curved left; a Gift Shop sign pointed ahead. Willowby had said he'd leave the notebook behind the counter there should he be gone. I crossed my fingers.

Silly of me. Willowby wasn't a bad sort, really. I'd probably smile at his obsessive tendencies in different circumstances.

A bell jangled when I opened the shop door, startling the cheery older lady who hovered over a table of books. She straightened up and smiled. "May I help you?"

"I hope so. Ranger Willowby called about some notepad I'd left here during the Fall Festival. I'm Sorrel Janes."

"Oh, yes." She walked behind the counter and pulled a brown envelope from a drawer. "I have a paper for you to sign acknowledging receipt of it, and I must check your ID before that."

I pulled out my driver's license and handed it over. She glanced at the photo and at me then passed the receipt and a pen. I signed it and casually put the envelope in my purse while I scanned the shop. "You have a nice selection here," I said. "Attractive arrangements."

She gestured toward the book table. "I'm trying to rearrange these books, but it doesn't take long to create chaos." I walked over to it and saw that the books were children's books.

"That would be a constant job," I agreed.

She laughed. "Keeps these idle hands busy."

I thanked her and left, careful to keep a casual air even while I was dying to look inside the envelope.

A couple of other cars had pulled into the lot, but I didn't want to wait a moment longer. I climbed in the Jeep and pulled out the envelope. Willowby had printed my name on the front. I tore it open and pulled out a small, black spiral notepad. I turned it over and over in my hand but could find no distinguishing marks. Belatedly I wondered if I should be wearing gloves. Immediately I tossed that idea in the mental dust bin. Who knew how many fingers had touched it by now? A tag on the back in the lower right corner held a price sticker but no indication of which store had sold it. Then I opened the front cover and gasped.

I forced myself to breathe as I flipped through the notepad, counting as my eyes skimmed page after neatly printed page, each filled with the details of my life.

Why hadn't Willowby told me this? That was the question that registered first, followed by the next logical question. Did he now consider me a serious suspect in John's disappearance?

CHAPTER THIRTY-ONE

Growing up as I did, moving often from one military base to another and then out on the ranch with no close neighbors, I'd learned self-reliance at an early age. Looking at the details of my life, printed neatly by a stranger, I felt a sense of calm envelope me like a warm blanket on a cold winter's night. Someone had decided to bully me. I'd dealt with bullies before. True, they were easier when one could face them down; but one thing I'd learned for sure: Bullies are basically cowards. They can be dangerous and hurtful and ugly; but somewhere deep inside, they are cowards—and I'm not!

I started my Jeep, backed up, and drove down the highway. I needed to think a bit and I knew just the place.

No cars were parked by the pond. It was too late for the dawn take off and too early for the evening returns. I pulled out my camera, locked up, and buttoned my jacket against the November chill. It was a shallow pond where the cranes stopped for the night, standing on one leg and tucking their heads under a wing. Now, while they ate in the nearby cornfields, only a few ducks glided across, turning bottoms-up to catch a snack just below the surface. Straight ahead and above this tableau—like an oil painting—stood the majestic mountains.

I snapped a few photos—just couldn't resist. Then returned my camera to its case and leaned against the fence. The ducks ignored me as they foraged for food, happy for the huge herd of transients to be out of the way. One duck sneaked up on another and stole his food. The victim quacked a bit then moved on to a new spot.

Pity that human bullies aren't more like duck bullies. I remembered that my mama had told me to "just ignore them." I'd tried, willing myself to close my ears as they chanted "carrot top." Loneliness had made me laugh with them until some other poor person diverted their attention.

Finally, my dad had intervened. Mama had yanked the stocking cap off my head as I tried to scoot out the door to the bus stop. I'd screamed, "I hate you!" Then I waited for the world to fall in.

"Sorrel," he'd said quietly. "Don't lie. You don't hate your mama. That's a hurtful lie."

I'd run into Mama's open arms, both of us in tears. "It's okay," she'd whispered.

"No, it's not okay," Dad had continued. "Sorrel, you have to understand something about bullies. They're cowards. And they don't like themselves very much. So they find someone else and try to make them miserable."

"You don't understand, Dad. I hate school. I hate going every day and having those kids run into me and pass ugly notes and say—"

"Cowards, Sorrel. Something is making them hate themselves. You have a tough job. First, you have to pity them. Not openly, of course, because they will really hate that. Then you have to see what it is that makes them hassle you. What's their motivation? Then you find a way to let them know their ugliness not only isn't working but has to stop."

"So am I going to clobber—"

"Violence doesn't do it, Sorrel. How about complimenting something they do well? Or ignoring them—and truly not letting it get under your skin?"

"And if it doesn't work?"

"If it doesn't work, then we go higher up. But the biggest trick is to like who you are. Bullies are intimidated when they see someone who isn't afraid to be herself."

We'd not gone higher up. Some of the bullies had just joined the crowd and turned out to be all right kids after all—and ashamed of themselves, I hoped. Others had grown tired when the reactions weren't what they wanted.

But this didn't feel like that sort of bully. First, this notepad documenting my life movements had been left purposefully. It wasn't an accident that it had been dropped inside a building where someone would find it. Secondly, what was the motivation? To intimidate me? To let me know I was being watched and followed? To make me afraid? To have me look over my shoulder wherever I went?

Could the dead body that had shown up here be part of all this? Even as I started to dismiss it, I had to entertain the idea. The body had been in the most popular shooting field. Anybody who knew me would expect me there—especially when attending the Fall Festival. Reed—he'd been the wild card. No one had expected him there unless—wait! What had he said about John having sent him a text? So Reed wasn't a wild card after all. But why had he been included? Reed was a good detective—intuitive, calculating, and smart. Surely including him stacked the odds against this bully. Unless . . . unless the bully had researched Reed as well and knew he wouldn't be readily available. But why? Why?

John's disappearance must surely be connected to all of this. I hoped this was just one of those times when he'd taken off and gotten too preoccupied—but I knew it wasn't.

I shivered. The wind had picked up, blowing my hair across my face. I reached up and pulled it back. A prickle ran up my spine and I whirled around. Out here, with not a soul close by, I felt eyes watching me. I tensed then purposely shot several more ducks diving and taking off. For good measure, I shot scenery, all the while fighting the urge to look over my shoulder at each new sound. Finally, I put the camera away again and walked toward the Jeep, careful to maintain a casual attitude while keeping my guard.

"Wildlife refuges can be dangerous for a lone photographer," John had warned many times. It was the first time I'd fully appreciated his warning.

My stomach rumbled. It was time to eat and make other plans.

At the end of the two-lane highway, I turned left and then slowed at the Owl Creek Bar and Grill. As always, I had to search for a parking place.

Inside I was assaulted by loud music, laughter, and the heavy scent of roasted green chilies. The waitress led me through a maze of small rooms crammed with booths, tables, and diners. Finally, she settled me at the back of the last room in a corner booth. When she went to hand me a menu, I said, "Iced tea, unsweetened, and a green chili cheeseburger."

My iced tea arrived right away, and I drank thirstily while I glanced around the room. Of the eight booths, only one remained empty. Most contained two or three people, and everyone was eating or talking, straining across their tables to hear or be heard over the music.

My phone lit up. I'd received a message. The good thing about the music was that—if I could hear the caller—my conversation would be more private.

"Hi, Sorrel. Vicente. Just to let you know, I heard from this Blood Relations place. I don't know if my questions alerted them or they were just doing routine checking, but they called to let me know they had had a security leak. Call me."

I redialed. He picked up right away. "That was quick! Where in the world are you?"

I laughed. "I'm in a place in New Mexico called The Owl Creek Bar." I had to repeat myself twice before he heard me.

"Sounds like you just need to listen, since you seem able to hear me. The guy I'd talked to earlier called to let me know about the security breach. I think he was fishing to find out why I'd called in the first place."

"Thinking maybe you knew something?"

"Or was connected. It took some fast talking to convince him I was only considering it at a friend's request. By the way, my friend is planning a surprise for her grandmother at a family reunion."

"And he believed that one?"

"I doubt it. Anyway, apparently the area that was breached was the—"

"—samples?"

Vicente sighed. "I really wish you'd clue me in, Sorrel! You owe me big time!"

"Did he give you any more?"

"Not really. He spent quite a while convincing me that a television station wouldn't find much interest in something this minor. I played nice and agreed with him. I think I frustrated him." He laughed. "Anyway, he promised to get back to me with more details. I miss you girl!"

"Ditto. I can tell I'm frustrating you. But I promise if there's a story here, you'll get it."

Vicente sighed. "Okay. Truth is . . . I may have promised to mention him should a story develop. I have to trust you . . . sort of."

My food arrived so I hung up with a promise to call. It was the biggest hamburger I'd seen in a while, and the green chili was hotter than I'd had anywhere else. The waitress had to fill my glass twice and brought me a to-go box.

Once back in the Jeep, I had a sudden impulse and turned toward Truth or Consequences. I didn't know whether or not she would say any more than she had before, but I felt the girl at the Chamber of Commerce had had something more to say that she hadn't felt comfortable saying to Reed. Maybe our manner had intimidated her. Maybe she didn't feel free speaking with her boss there. But I'd seen a look on her face that told me something hadn't been said.

I glanced at my watch. I could get there before five o'clock. With luck, I could catch her leaving work.

CHAPTER THIRTY-TWO

For once I was in luck. Not only was it close to closing time when I parked in front of the Chamber of Commerce, but Tami also seemed to be closing on her own. I had a couple of choices: I could approach her now and risk someone coming in and interrupting, or I could wait and catch her just as she was locking up. I mentally flipped a coin. Lock up won. So I rummaged through my purse as if looking for something and kept an eye on Tami.

She lifted the phone, spoke into it briefly, punched a couple of buttons, and hung up. Okay, I thought, the phone is set to a message. She systematically began shutting down the computer on her desk and then walked over to do the same to the copy machine. Finally, she disappeared a moment and returned with her purse and a jacket in her hands, locked the front door, and flipped off the lights. I'd already started opening the door when it hit me. She would be parked in back!

I started the Jeep and pulled into a parking spot on the side closest to employee parking. I opened my door and called across just as she was closing the side door. "I guess I'm too late!" I told her. "I was afraid I wouldn't get here in time!"

Tami glanced a bit nervously and then smiled as she recognized me. "Well, we close a little early during November and December, with all the holidays. It's posted out front, but the sign is small. Can I help you?"

"I don't want to hold you up." I turned as if leaving.

Tami hesitated then walked toward me. "I wondered if you'd be back—with everything in the papers and stuff."

I didn't try to hide my surprise. "Papers? I've been away."

"Oh." She was clearly uncomfortable. "Well . . ."

"Do you have time to share a cup of coffee?" I asked. "I felt when we were here before that you weren't comfortable talking too much. Reed is with the sheriff's department and sometimes he can put people off." I smiled encouragingly.

"Well . . . ," she said again, glancing around at the street, deserted save a lone, empty pickup near the corner.

"I've been driving most of the day and I'd like a cup," I continued. "If you don't have a child to go home to, maybe we could get out of this chill. You name the place."

She fought an inward battle a moment longer before she said, "There's a little place down Main Street here."

"Why don't you lead and I'll follow," I said.

She nodded and headed toward her car, looking back once as I stepped inside the Jeep and closed the door. She pulled out and I waited until she had pulled to the light before I followed. A sweeping glance in both directions reassured me that our short conversation had gone unnoticed. So we hadn't raised suspicions. But then why would we?

Tami had flipped on her left blinker and had started to pull through the light by the time I reached it. A couple of blocks later she again signaled to the left, and we pulled into a crowded lot behind a shabby building. I parked a few spots down and she waited for me.

"You go on in and get us a booth or table," I called. "I need to answer a quick phone call."

She nodded, looking relieved. She obviously was nervous about even being seen with me, which surprised me a bit. Whatever she'd meant about the papers didn't sound good. I lifted the phone and called Teri.

"Hi!" she said.

"You sound breathless. Are you doing too much?"

"Ah, it's my hourly phone call from Nurse Ratchett!"

"Really! I heard that giggle you tried to swallow!"

"I'm okay, Sorrel. In fact, I'm on the sofa with my feet propped up while Jose and the boys do who knows what to my kitchen."

"Good for them! What's cooking?"

"Brownies," she said a bit guiltily. "I just can't get the thought of them out of my mind."

I laughed. "Okay. Just checking."

"Are you still at the refuge?"

"Leaving," I lied. "Not sure whether or not I'll drive back tonight though. I'm not looking forward to driving in the rain." I kept my eyes averted from the very dry ground around me.

"You just left this morning and you know the cats are okay. Maybe you should get a room and come in tomorrow."

"What I was thinking." I'm not sure she heard me as she immediately chattered about the tamales the whole family had been making in anticipation of selling them right after Thanksgiving.

"Gotta go," I interrupted. "They're here with my dinner."

After we exchanged a couple of quick goodbyes, I jumped out and locked the Jeep. I felt a twinge of guilt for lying to Teri, but she surely didn't need to stress. Besides, she might just feel the urge to call Reed. I wasn't sure what his commitments were just at this moment, but I knew he couldn't break loose and chase across the state to me—again! And I was enjoying working on my own. True, he was handy. But I loved chasing the story—or person—on my own as well.

I found Tami tucked into a worn vinyl booth toward the back of the restaurant. Chilies and scorched tortilla chips hung in the air as I squeezed between tables and booths.

"Sorry," I told Tami, sliding across from her. Unfortunately, she sat facing the door—my preferred spot.

"No problem," she said. "I already ordered a Dr. Pepper and chips and salsa. I didn't know whether you wanted a coffee or something cold. But she'll stop by in a minute."

As if on cue, a pleasant looking older lady stopped by. "Coffee, please," I told her. "And a glass of iced water." She nodded and zipped away again.

"Busy place," I told Tami.

"Good food. It's all family here and they cook like they eat. I've never seen it empty."

"Sounds like my friend Teri's family."

"Must be nice. My family was fast-food royalty."

My drinks arrived and I added a spoonful of water to the coffee. "Are you from around here?"

"Not originally. But my grandma is and I moved here to help out with her after I finished high school in Albuquerque."

"Is she . . ."

"Fit as a fiddle she says," Tami finished. "But her memory seems to be a little weird sometimes. So she went to a specialist and they diagnosed early onset Alzheimer's. She is fiercely independent, though, so I pretend to need time away from my ex-boyfriend and she thinks she's doing me a favor."

"How sweet." She looked embarrassed. " No, I mean it. I was raised that way—family taking care of family."

She sipped the Dr. Pepper. "So is this guy you asked about your family?"

I hesitated. "Sort of." Then I explained that he'd been one of my college professors who'd had any of his students who wanted over for chili and cornbread or just to talk. We'd kept in touch ever since. "He was supposed to meet me at Socorro, the refuge there, and we missed each other. So I thought I'd just check to see if he'd changed his mind . . . or got lost or something." I sounded a little lame even to myself, and apparently Tami thought I did too.

"Do you want to eat something?" she asked. "It's Gran's night with her Scrabble buddies and I usually eat leftovers at home. "

I grinned. "I've been having trouble ignoring the wonderful dishes being served around us," I admitted. "But I insist you eat and let me pay."

"I—"

"Please."

Tami signaled our waitress, who convinced us to try the specialty of the day—smothered chimichangas.

"Now," I said as she left. "What do you mean about the papers?"

Tami dipped a chip in her salsa and bit into it. Finally, she looked at me. "I don't really know anything more than my boss told you."

"But you mentioned the paper?"

She took another drink. "They both died."

"Who died?"

"The man and woman with your friend."

"Oh my! How did they die?"

Tami seemed to lose some of her warmth. "You know, I don't know if I should eat here. My grandma—"

"You're okay, Tami," I told her. "I'm just a nature photographer and so is John. He retired and moved to Branson a few years ago, and now he sells his photos in his own shop. John's the gentlest man I know. He would never have hurt someone."

"But—"

"How did they die?"

Our food arrived just then, and we spent a couple of moments settling it on our table. I made myself eat a bite then gasped and took a drink of water.

Tami giggled. "You'd be better off with the coffee." She dug into her own plate then, seemingly immune to the peppers. "You get used to them," she added. "Aren't you from New Mexico?"

"No." I took another bite, adding some of the refried beans on the plate, and managed to swallow, although I had tears in my eyes.

In an unspoken agreement, we waited until she had eaten and I'd struggled through part of my plate before we spoke again. My waitress, in passing, placed a glass of milk by me. I took a soothing sip.

Tami leaned toward me and spoke softly. "They were drowned, according to the paper. They're not disclosing many details except that they'd been seen with an older guy before. It's an ongoing investigation."

"Drowned!"

Tami must have renewed her trust in me because she continued. "They didn't seem like they'd be out on the lake. Elephant Butte is really popular for fishermen, but these people didn't seem interested in fishing. In fact, I'd put them around a pool, not a lake."

"Did the paper say anything about where they lived or any family?"

"No, that's another strange thing. No one seems to know them. Your friend said that day in our office that they were camping, but the police were asking any campers to stop by if they knew them."

"Any other mention of John?"

Tami leaned back and refused to meet my eyes. "Police want to know if anyone has seen him. The television newsman said he may be a witness and they just want to talk to him." Then she looked up at me. "But when they were in our office, he seemed worried. I mean, when he reached for some of the brochures, his hand shook."

"Did he say anything?" I asked.

"Besides looking for good camping sites and wildlife areas?"

"Yes."

"Well, he did ask about riding stables."

"Riding stables?" I asked incredulously. "I don't think John has ever ridden in his life!"

Tami lowered her voice until I could hardly hear her. "He said he'd once had a sorrel horse."

"Did he say anything else?"

"Not really. Not that I remember. We gave him some brochures for things in the area."

I made myself take a drink of my coffee. Carefully, I asked, "What were you wanting to say when my friend and I were here before?"

She had taken her napkin off her lap and her fingers worked with it, folding it and unfolding it. "I need my job."

"I will never say anything to your boss."

Her eyes searched the restaurant anxiously. "This wasn't a good idea, with so many—"

"Please tell me."

Finally, she sighed. "I found the brochures in that pot of cactus out front." She locked eyes with me. "Why would you take them unless you were interested?"

"Tami, he would never have hurt them."

She almost whispered. "As they almost were out of sight, the guy put his arm around your friend's shoulder and punched him in the ribs. Then he looked back and I jumped back out of sight." Tears rolled down her cheeks. I found a tissue in my purse.

"Did he see you?"

She sniffed. "No . . . maybe . . . I don't think so. But now they're dead. At least, two of them are."

CHAPTER THIRTY-THREE

When I thanked Tami for her help, she impulsively gave me a quick hug. "We'll see if I've been help or not. I've been accused of being a drama queen," she said. "Your friend is probably sitting around a campfire sharing stories right now."

"That sounds like him," I agreed.

"I'm afraid I told most of this to the police," she said. "I—"

"—you did exactly what you should have done. You'll need to take care though."

"They told me that too." Tami opened her car door and quickly slid inside.

She hadn't checked the back seat, I noticed. "They probably will file that in some cabinet and forget it," I said, "but until this blows over, you might take care about being out at night. You know, watch where you park, let someone know where you plan to go, check the back seat of your car before you open the door." She glanced over her shoulder quickly.

As we drove away, one after the other, I decided that we were more than likely candidates for liar queens. Neither of us really believed that John was sitting around a campfire.

John could get caught up in a photography project and lose track of time, but I had never known him to be intentionally rude. Not appearing—or calling to let me know he wouldn't be there at Bosque—was rude. Especially when he had invited me to join him!

I couldn't ignore the most troubling developments. He'd been here with those two unlikely companions—and now they were dead. I wondered what Reed would—stop! Since when did I need to consult with the police?

I stopped at the light, watching Tami's taillights disappearing. I hoped she had listened to my warnings and used precautions. The thought of her and her grandmother living alone unsettled me. I also wondered whether or not John was being considered a suspect in the two deaths. Tami had told the police that she'd seen them together. Maybe I should contact Patience Montgomery. I pulled over onto a side street and dialed.

Patience picked up on the second ring. "Sorrel," she said. "Thanks for returning my call!"

"Well, not actually. I'm away from my home phone and haven't checked messages. I was just about to do that."

"Where are you?"

"In the area." Something about her tone made me choose caution.

"Have you had dinner?"

"Yes."

"I'm on my own. Why don't you come by? We need to catch up."

"I'm about forty-five minutes away. Will that be too late?"

"No. I'm a night owl and I have a few things to finish up." Again I sensed that she had been unduly cautious—or my imagination was working overtime. Maybe both. Despite wanting to do this on my own, it would have been nice to run a few things by Reed right now! Even though he irritated me at times, I could trust his analytical skills. He could step back from emotion—something that was hard for me to do with John.

John knew I'd try to find him. He'd left that obvious clue: the sorrel horse. Anyone who really knew John would know he had never ridden a horse. In fact, he confided in me that horses were a phobia of his after he'd seen a cowboy thrown and killed by a wild horse in a rodeo when he was a young boy. His reference to horses, particularly a sorrel horse, was a clear call for help.

Ms. Montgomery opened her door before I could ring the bell and herded me toward the back of her house. "I hope you don't mind, Sorrel," she said, "if I finish my meal while we talk. My husband is attending a faculty dinner; and when he does that, I tend to eat leftovers and combine it with work. He invariably gets into some long-winded discussions and makes a late night of it."

I followed her—and the delicious smells—into a comfortable, roomy kitchen. "How cheery!" I told her. I hadn't expected bright red, black, and stainless steel—or such a modern touch. Yet amid the efficient designs nestled bright multicolored pottery and potted plants and flowers. Somehow it didn't clash.

She gestured toward a breakfast nook littered with folders and her partly eaten meal. "I'm having jasmine tea," she said, "but I can make you coffee if you'd like."

"Jasmine tea sounds perfect."

I sat across from her unfinished meal. "I'm so sorry to interrupt your meal—"

"You didn't. I'm the one who chased you down." She set a glass of iced tea down and gestured toward a bowl of sugar and sweeteners close by.

"No thanks." I took a sip.

She settled across and picked up her fork. "I'll finish this while you catch me up on what you're doing here," she said.

I took a long drink. "I needed another look around." I told her about our visit to the Chamber of Commerce before we'd left. "The office worker seemed to have something to say but didn't want to do so while her boss was there. I wanted to talk to her and, I guess, just wanted to snoop around a bit more. Reed had received a call from work and had needed to return."

"Did you discover anything new?"

"We learned that John had visited the chamber office the day before he and I had planned to meet at Socorro. A man and a woman waited for him by the door."

"Did he introduce them?"

"If he did, the manager didn't choose to tell us. He said John asked for information about camping and fishing."

"I'm not an avid fisherman, but I'd think November wouldn't be prime time for that sort of activity."

I reached for the tea and then drew back. "Ms. Montgomery—"

"Patience."

"Patience. Something just didn't sound right. John is a photographer. Why would he suddenly decide to go camping and fishing with an unlikely pair of companions when he'd made plans to attend the Bosque Festival? And he'd made plans to meet me there. Even if he changed his mind, he would have called me. John just isn't the sort of person who would leave me waiting there while he took off on an adventure like that."

"So I assume you were able to talk to this young lady?"

"Yes. I waited until she left work and we had dinner."

She didn't say anything more, just finished the last few bites on her plate while I sipped on my tea. Then she carried her empty dishes to the sink, rinsed them, and put them in the dishwasher. Finally, she refilled her glass of tea and tilted the pitcher toward my glass.

"I'm fine."

"Let's move this to the study then, if you don't mind," she said.

Her study felt as cozy as the rest of the house, but she seemed to belong here. I sat down in a comfortable chair upholstered in southwestern print while she walked over to the desk. "Would you mind if I recorded our conversation, Sorrel?" she asked. "I want to make sure I don't forget details, and my handwritten notes are becoming more and more difficult to read as arthritis has descended."

"Do you want me to repeat—"

"Please."

When I finished, she asked, "Have you heard anything more from John? Calls? Messages?"

"No. But I do seem to have an unusual number of hang-ups."

That seemed to give her pause. "What did the young lady have to add?"

"She told me that the couple had been murdered."

Patience waited while I took another drink. I noticed that my hand shook a bit and took a deep breath. "She said that John had asked about riding stables in the area. He said that he had once had a sorrel horse." I watched as she made the same connection I'd made, but she remained silent. "Then she said that when she was leaving work the day that John stopped by, she noticed that the brochures John had picked up had been thrown into the potted cactus outside."

We both sat silently for a moment longer. Then I added, "Her boss told her not to mention anything if we returned."

"He made the connection between John's horse questions and your name?"

"She didn't think so. But she said that John and this couple might have been involved in a crime and he didn't want the chamber involved." I caught her eye. "I promised her I'd keep her out of it as much as I could. She's just a young lady, living with her grandmother."

"Do these people sound familiar to you? Any family or friends John might have known?"

"Why don't we discuss why you called me?"

Patience clicked off the recorder and picked up her pen and a tablet. "I need to know the timeline again for your activities during the last forty-eight hours."

I told her, watching as she jotted notes.

"And what is your connection to John again?" She continued to write as I talked.

When I finished, I asked, "Why did you call, Ms. Montgomery?"

She didn't answer but asked, "Who can vouch for your whereabouts?"

"Why?"

She didn't answer, just waited patiently. Finally, I told her. "Good," she said.

"What's happening?"

Patience took a deep breath. "John is considered a person of interest in the murder of these two people. And you might be considered an accessory."

"That's crazy!"

"Not really. And I don't want to hear any talk about guilt or innocence. We may not have a long time, and I need to go over how you need to conduct yourself during the police interview when it comes."

She spoke quickly and I forced myself to listen as best as I could. "The important thing is to answer their questions unless I interrupt."

"I'll go," I told Patience. "But could I wait until the morning? I well remember how long they can keep you and it's already late."

CHAPTER THIRTY-FOUR

Patience Montgomery had urged me one last time to go to the police station. "They'll only question you again and let you go because they won't have anything on you," she said, "and then you can go on home for Thanksgiving. There's nothing more you can do, Sorrel. Let the police handle this."

Her argument was logical, but her logic and mine weren't the same. I could see in her eyes that she thought John was dead. Maybe she even thought he had killed the couple. But I couldn't agree with either. In her eyes, I was being illogical; but somewhere out there I felt that John needed me. Unless he was fighting for his own life, John would never take the life of another—and with the clues he'd left behind, John was fighting for his life. If only I wasn't too late.

I felt my phone buzz and pulled it out. Reed. I hesitated. I really wanted to answer and share the latest information with him; but, instead, I watched as it went to message. Reed would only argue that I shouldn't do what I'm doing—following my instincts . . . and my heart.

I pulled up beside the Quick Stop gas pump and hopped out to fill my Jeep. While I stood there holding the hose, I once again reviewed what I knew: John had changed his plans either willingly or unwillingly. Someone had been in his house in Missouri; and because Van had been left there alone, John may have been abducted. He had visited the Chamber of Commerce in Truth or Consequences and left clues behind that he needed help. Amid all of this, someone was playing mind games with this DNA stuff. And how did this all connect with the dead body I'd found in Bosque?

The pump clicked off. I walked into the store and grabbed a pack of nuts, peanut butter crackers, and water. I needed to get back to Truth or Consequences. Another visit to the police station here in Socorro right now would just waste valuable time—and I had nothing to say that they wanted to hear.

I had just turned onto the street when Reed called again. I pulled over and waited until he'd finished another message. Then I punched play. "Sorrel, I need you to call me. Some new developments." He gave the time and his number. In the second message, his voice had changed to more of a growl. "Sorrel, where are you? If you're hearing this message, call. We need to RSVP to a party invite."

His cryptic messages would have been difficult to ignore had I not heard a high-pitched giggle somewhere in the background as he spoke. The new partner? A party?

I'd imposed on Reed long enough. Time to use my own investigative skills. I checked my mirror and pulled back out onto the road toward the interstate off ramp.

As I sped along, John's words echoed through my mind: sorrel horse. He was blatantly hoping to get a message to me. But what about the riding stables? Had he just thrown them in to make the sorrel horse reference? Or were the stables the message and the *sorrel horse* to get my attention?

I clicked a button on my phone. "Find me horse stables near Elephant Butte, New Mexico," I said.

"There are two public riding stables within thirty miles of Elephant Butte," the mechanical voice intoned.

I glanced at the dashboard clock. It would be too late to visit them by the time I arrived tonight. I'd check them out first thing in the morning.

What next?

Camping sites. He'd asked about camping sites. The pair was with him at the time, so surely he wasn't intimidated. Or was he? If they'd abducted him, surely the woman would have gone into the chamber alone while the man kept John in the car. I could make a case for either argument—except for the discarded pamphlets.

I spent the next hour mentally reviewing the facts as I drove along the dark highway. It was hard to organize details—and, frankly, I was beginning to suspect they didn't all link together. What if I had three separate mysteries here? The dead body at the refuge, Blood Relations, and John? Maybe that's why nothing seemed to be linking up.

One thing was certain: I needed to prioritize, and John had to be my first priority. After all, the dead guy might not even be identified for months or years. And, except for the fact that the police had tried to connect me with him, he really was a dead end. "No pun intended," I murmured. And this Blood Relations stuff? It was just bizarre.

John. I had to concentrate on John.

As if on cue, my phone buzzed. This time I picked up, expecting Reed again. No use trying to keep avoiding him.

"Sorrel? Where are you?"

"John?"

CHAPTER THIRTY-FIVE

I counted three beeps. A quick glance at the screen showed CALL ENDED. That call could have originated anywhere. Frustration rose and I fought the panic that had surfaced with it.

"Sorrel, keep your focus!" I muttered. "Someone—for whatever purpose—is depending on you to react emotionally here. You're not even sure that was John."

It sounded like him! my heart argued.

"Someone handy with electronics can manipulate situations any way they wish. You're tired, worried, and scared."

Call Reed.

"Think, Sorrel. Reed is a cop—and he's on some case in some undisclosed location. What would he tell you if you called him? He'd tell you to go home and let the police handle things. And, by the way, when did you need someone to help you investigate?"

My heart rose to my throat. *The police know what to do. What if something I did caused John's death? What if—*

"Sorrel, you have worked with crime and criminals for several years now. How many times do the police complicate matters—or jump to the wrong conclusions? You know John; they don't. Would he ask for your help?"

For the first time, my heart listened to reason. *No, he wouldn't. He wouldn't want me exposed to danger.*

"Exactly! So either that wasn't John—"

—or it was taken out of context!

While my rational and emotional sides argued, my Jeep Liberty whizzed along the interstate. Signs advertising businesses in Truth or Consequences popped up, and I turned onto the exit for the second time in a few hours—only this time I headed toward Elephant Butte instead of town.

The streets were just as narrow as those near downtown had been. At almost every cross street I encountered a stop sign or a yield sign. As I neared the lake, the houses were smaller and the garages often housed boats. I slowed down even more as street lights became scarce. Many of the houses looked like they'd been closed up for the winter months.

I had the street to myself, so I pulled to the curb and spoke into my phone: "Campsites for Elephant Butte."

Almost immediately, the mechanical voice began reciting names. At the pause, I gave the first name, Desert Delights, and waited for directions.

"This should have been called Desert Mirage," I said, as I pulled up to the site. The camp had half a dozen trailer hook-ups and two larger ones that had boat lean-tos. Anything delightful had to be in the viewer's imagination. Even as dark as it was, I doubted John would have rented here.

Out hopped my reasonable self: *He may not have been the one to choose it.*

"Look at the campers," I argued. "Only three—and all hardly big enough for one person."

I squinted at the license plates; but short of shining a flashlight at them, I couldn't determine the states.

Then another argument came to mind: Would they have moved John into their camper, or would they have taken his camper as well? "If they're dead now," I murmured, "what happened to John?"

It was well past ten o'clock and I couldn't see any lights. Didn't fishermen get up really early? In spite of my urgency, I knew that I'd have to wait until morning. "Motels in Truth or Consequences," I told my phone as I turned a tight circle and started back the way I'd just come.

The first two motels had No Vacancy signs already lit. Chances were I'd be spending the night in the Jeep in a Wal-Mart parking lot.

Half an hour later, as I adjusted the sunscreen in front and duct-taped the towels I'd just purchased to the side and back windows, I felt like a psychic. Too bad I couldn't be a psychic regarding John. I'd bought a pillow and a cheap sleeping bag as well. I'd parked between two RVs on the outer edge of the parking lot. After double checking to make sure that the windows were all covered, I climbed into the sleeping bag in the back seat, shoes and all, and gripped my cellphone in my hand.

As if on cue, it buzzed. I looked. It was a text from Teri. Teri? It was midnight! "Sorrel! R we still having the B F sale? R U coming to Mom's for Thanksgiving? R U safe? Reed is driving me nuts!"

I texted back: "Yes, yes, yes, and Reed's a control freak! Why aren't you asleep?"

"Was. Woke up hungry. Sugar attack. Milk and cookies."

"Healthy snack. Everything OK there?"

"Yes. Cats luv my cousin. Reed's a pain."

"He there?"

"Jose awake! Hurry home!" She abruptly clicked off.

I giggled. So typically Teri! And a pregnant Teri had pushed the obsessive/compulsive side up a notch or two.

I yawned and pulled the sleeping bag up to my nose. I doubted I'd be able to sleep at all, but I needed to try. My legs would have appreciated being able to stretch out; and even though I'd tried my best to pad the seatbelt latches with my bag, they poked insistently against my back. I probably shouldn't have given up on finding a hotel room so quickly. Even though Thanksgiving loomed near, surely this small town wasn't overrun by tourists. Fishing wasn't usually a winter sport in these parts.

I closed my eyes and reviewed all the things I knew—which didn't take long—and then started on those I didn't know1. After number five, I must have dozed.

The motorhomes started up just after dawn. I peeked out of the towel-covered window and watched one pull out. Three or four cars crept along the street beyond, but a light rain obscured my sight. I should get started. On second thought, I'd just snuggle back into the S position and wait until my neighbors had moved.

A loud tapping yanked me out of an exhausted sleep. This time, I peeked around into the face of a young policeman. I pulled off the towel curtain and attempted an engaging smile. He motioned for me to step out, and his expression didn't bode well for my attempt at charm.

"I need to get out of this sleeping—"

"Ma'am, just open—"

"I'm sorry, but the zipper isn't—"

"Just roll the window down then, ma'am. Then keep your hands where I can see them."

He couldn't be out of high school, could he? I didn't want to scare him, so I carefully rolled down the window and placed my hands on either side of the headrest of the driver's seat in front of me.

"Could I ask what you think I have done wrong?" I asked, careful to keep my voice as neutral and respectful as possible. The air blowing in was so cold that my teeth wanted to chatter. I willed myself to stop them.

He looked down at a small pad. "What are you doing here?"

"The motels were full, so I thought I'd try to sleep a little until morning."

"This is a store parking lot, ma'am."

The "ma'am" was grating on my nerves, but I curled my icy toes in their thick socks and replied, "But there were two motorhomes parked here, so I thought it would be okay for me to park between them."

He had begun to shift from one foot to the other. Maybe the cold was catching up to him—or, more than likely, he wasn't sure what to do next.

"Could I see your ID?" he finally asked.

"I'll need to get in my purse," I said and indicated it in the floorboard next to me. He watched as I carefully reached over, removed my wallet, and pulled out my driver's license. He took it, glanced over it, and excused himself for a moment. While he walked over to his police car and radioed to someone, I extricated myself from the sleeping bag. I located a bottle of water that had rolled under the passenger seat, stretching a leg over to kick it back to me. It took three or four tries, so I was grateful that he seemed to be engrossed in his conversation. Poor kid, I thought. He should have been more careful.

By the time he returned, I had pulled my hair back into a ponytail, and tucked a breath mint into my mouth. I hoped he'd leave soon. I needed to find a ladies' room somewhere soon!

"Here's your license, Ms. Janes," he said, reaching inside the window.

"Am I free to go?"

"Yes, ma'am. Just so you know, you can't stay in the parking lot here in town."

"But, the motels—"

"We have numerous camping grounds."

"And the motorhomes?"

A flush started up his throat. "The store asked us to sort of overlook—"

"—a motorhome but not a Jeep!"

The flush had suffused his whole face by now, and he clearly wasn't sure how to exit quickly enough. "Hope you have a good visit to our town, ma'am." He turned toward his car.

I'd have stayed to argue only I needed to find the ladies room! I looked at the Wal-Mart, but they'd closed. I'd become accustomed to all night ones back in Houston. So I started up and headed down the street.

The clerk in a Quick Stop Market a couple of blocks from the Walmart glanced up from his cell phone long enough to gesture toward the restroom sign to his left. When I approached the counter a few minutes later in fresh clothes, brushed teeth, and combed hair, he glanced up once more and then out into the store lot. I paid for my coffee and packaged sweet roll—no time to sip coffee in the small connecting café—smiled and thanked him, and reached down to pick up my bag. Again he glanced toward the lot. This time I followed his glance—just in time to see a familiar car backing out and turning onto the main street.

CHAPTER THIRTY-SIX

He watched her usually guarded face. Most other people—especially females—would have shown fear. But not this one. Maybe it was her fierce loyalty for her mentor. Maybe it was her curiosity. Maybe it was just the thrill of the hunt, the need to solve the mystery. He saw no trace of fear.

She sipped the coffee and stood there in the parking lot beside her Jeep. She'd be replaying her early morning visit from the cop in her mind. What had she missed? She chewed on her lip a bit. She would be mapping out her plan, figuring whether or not she needed to shift her strategy.

The cop has been risky, he knew. He had taken precautions to disguise himself as a Wal-Mart manager, and it must have worked. She was a gutsy gal, but a little needling might help keep her on edge. He couldn't see it in her just now, but he bet she was churning a bit inside.

A truck pulled up and four noisy teenaged guys spilled out, cutting off his view. He swore and waited until they entered the store. Then he rose from his window seat, dropped a buck for the waitress, and stepped outside. She'd turned, glancing over her shoulder and climbed into her Jeep. He smiled as he slid into his van. "How does it feel to be pursued, Miss Hot Shot Reporter?" he whispered.

He lifted his birding binoculars as a couple passed by, gazing at the sky above the Quick Stop until he heard their car leaving. Then he refocused them.

She tensed and glanced over her shoulder, but she remained in her Jeep. Instinctively, she'd felt danger nearby. But he didn't see fear. Instead, he watched her pick up her phone and speak into it. Was she calling in help? Maybe contacting the sheriff? It hadn't been her style to call for help so far. Maybe she was more afraid than he thought. No, she wasn't talking into the phone, just listening.

The raucous bunch exited the Quick Stop, their hands full of junk food, and roared off.

Her head was down now. She was tapping on one of those electronic tablets. He might have misjudged her. Maybe she was calling for help after all. Disappointing. But help wouldn't save her. His boss had planned too well, dreamed of this too long, set it up too well.

"Not too much longer, Miss Fancy Pants," he whispered. "The party is about to begin. Just waiting for the Guest of Honor to appear."

She backed up and pulled out. He didn't even need to watch. He knew where she would go.

It was almost time. He chuckled again.

"Time to get this party started," he muttered, tucking his binoculars into their case and starting his engine.

He waited another minute before he pulled out and turned onto the street leading to Elephant Butte.

CHAPTER THIRTY-SEVEN

I listened again to the list of campgrounds from my phone genie
before leaving the parking lot of the Quick Stop. Most of them,
both private and state campgrounds, were close to the lake,
scattered either along the lake road or in the area. But the state
campgrounds were closed until the first of March, so it just made
sense to start with the first private campground I came upon and
wander from there.

Logically, I knew I wasn't going to find John; but I knew I had to
do this—what my mama would have called "leaving no stone
unturned." With Thanksgiving only a week away, surely the
campgrounds wouldn't be full and I'd not disturb too many people
with my door-to-door search. My plan was to check on whichever
campers were inhabited, telling people that I was supposed to meet
John Daniels but had forgotten the address of the campground and
couldn't reach him by phone.

As I headed toward the first campground, I thought about the
call from Branson yesterday, updating me on the missing person status
the police had given John. While I welcomed the fact that they were
finally in agreement, my heart hurt.

My heart hurt worse a couple of hours later—as did my pride. I'd
knocked on door after door, either meeting irritated, sleepy faces or
not finding anyone at home. One grandmotherly looking woman
reassured me that I should just go home and wait until he returned.
Another listened to my quick explanation with obvious skepticism

and slammed the door in my face. A bleary-eyed man glanced behind and around me the whole time, interrupting every few words to ask "Are you wearing a camera?" and "Is this a new reality show?"

Finally, I pulled in to the first state campground, parking just off the graveled driveway in view of the CLOSED sign. I took a long drink from my bottled water then slowly swept my eyes across the area looking for any sign of—whatever!

"The Mystery of the Deserted Campground, eh, Nancy Drew?" I whispered. Then I laughed. The worst thing I could do was to spook myself . . . unless it was to take myself too seriously. I got out, buttoned up my jacket, and stuck my cell in my pocket. Then I started walking through the deserted campground, pulling out my phone occasionally to snap a photo to check later for any disturbances or something unusual that I wasn't catching just now.

I peeked in cabins, wandered around picnic tables, and tromped through sand. The only thing I didn't do was hide behind trees—there weren't any.

Finally, I turned the Jeep back toward town.

I drove through Elephant Butte and pulled into the parking lot of a small restaurant. The clock on the wall above the kitchen read five o'clock; but, except for a guy sitting at the counter, I was the only customer. I slid into a booth facing the door and reached for the menu. A tall, thin woman with extraordinarily red hair came out of the kitchen and set a hamburger in front of the guy at the counter. He said something and she turned to grab the coffee pot behind her. I looked back at the menu.

"What can I get for you, honey?" I must have jumped as she said, "Want something to drink? You can take your time on the food if you want."

"Iced water, please."

"I can get that for you, honey, but what do you want to drink?" She pronounced it *drank*.

"I just want iced water to drink," I told her. "And I think I'll have the grilled cheese sandwich."

"It comes with fries or onion rings or tomato slices." She glanced toward the kitchen and lowered her voice as she leaned toward me. "The fries and rings are frozen and covered in cornmeal." Long earrings danced as she spoke and a fine line of gray hair appeared below the amazing red.

"Tomato slices sound delicious."

She nodded. "Wise choice," she said and walked into the kitchen, returning almost immediately with a glass of iced water.

"I'm looking for a friend of mine," I told her casually. "We'd planned to meet, but he forgot to let me know which campsite he'd chosen. His name is John—John Daniels. He's a wildlife photographer. This would be the kind of place he'd likely come to eat."

She stood there for a moment, her shrewd eyes taking inventory of my age, my casual but not grungy outfit, my red hair bunched into a careless ponytail, the light smudges beneath my make-up free face. "My advice?" she said. "Go home. If he stands you up now, he'll do it again . . . or leave you with a half dozen little ones to feed."

A bell dinged from the kitchen and she hurried over to gather my order. "Miss?" The counter guy raised his cup. She raised her finger with a smile, grabbed a handful of menus, and headed to my table. She left my order and my bill and turned to greet a noisy group as they entered. The casual friendliness had vanished and I wondered if I'd offended her. Oh, well, I thought and shrugged mentally.

I didn't attempt to engage her in conversation a few minutes later when she came for my credit card, her eyes focused on the card and the bill as she picked them up. If the conversation across the room hadn't lulled a bit, I might have missed it. "Don't look at me. When I bring your card, casually walk toward the bathroom over to the right. Don't draw attention to yourself. There's an outside door just past the bathroom. That man you're looking for? They're looking for him and a female."

She returned in a moment, her hands filled with drinks for the table across the room, but first she dropped my card casually and quickly. I added a generous tip, signed my name, put the receipt in my purse, and made my way toward the bathroom sign. Maybe I was just feeling paranoid, but the guy at the counter seemed to follow me with his eyes.

Once out of sight, I darted past the bathroom door and through the outside door, closing it silently. A couple of cars and a dumpster were squeezed close. I quickly walked to the left, picked my way cautiously past a cactus plant, paused at the front edge of the building, and peeked around it. A police cruiser was pulling up. I ducked back.

I listened to its doors slamming and the low rumble of the officers' casual voices. What was I thinking? I hadn't done anything, yet here I was hiding around the side of this rundown café, waiting for the officers to go inside before I sneaked into the Jeep and took off— from what I still wasn't sure. But somehow I trusted this stranger with the amazing red hair and unsolicited advice.

Once inside my Jeep, I pulled out as casually as I could manage and drove toward the lake again. Several vehicles were parked along the edge near the boat ramps. I zipped in between a pick-up truck and a van. Then I picked up my phone and selected Patience's number from the contacts. She picked up as if she were waiting for my call.

"Sorrel. Since this is your cell, I assume you're not calling from jail."

"Should I be there?"

"They want to ask you some questions. You need to come to my office and we'll go over. How long will it take you? I don't want to know where you are."

"I can be with you—"

"I'll wait here at the office. I don't need to know how long it will take. If they should pull you over on your way here, just have someone call me."

"Ms. Montgomery, it might be easier for me to meet you at the station instead. Could you do that?"

She paused. "I think that would work."

I backed out as quickly as I'd arrived and headed back toward Truth or Consequences, meandering through the neighborhoods as long as I could before turning onto I-25.

I'd been questioned by the police a few times while working in Houston, especially after Kevin's murder; and I knew I hadn't broken any laws. The police must want to question me about John. I'd certainly drawn their attention with my search for him. Still, Patience's cautious voice had comforted me.

I felt my heart gradually return to normal so that I could pay attention to the road. It was a pretty drive, even with the heavy traffic. I had turned on the radio and was humming along with a raspy country singer when I glanced down and saw my phone glowing.

Teri's name appeared. I clicked off the radio again and activated the hands-free option.

"Hi, Teri!"

"Sorrel, what the h—"

"Reed?"

"Don't you dare hang up!"

"Why would I hang up?" Had he been there, he'd have seen me batting my eyelashes.

"Why don't you return phone calls?"

"Obscene phone calls?"

I heard a snort. "Sorrel, just listen. I already know where you are. And I know where you're headed."

"The cop brotherhood, eh?"

"Just quit smarting off and listen. When you get there, be sure to keep your temper under—"

"Reed! I know what to do! Why did you call?"

"Sorrel, we don't have time to do this. Just listen—"

Hanging up a cell phone doesn't quite give one the same satisfaction that slamming a receiver does. But arguing with Reed had distracted me enough. I almost missed the exit. "Time to focus, Sorrel," I murmured. "You don't need that irritating deputy . . . or whatever he is this week. Everything is under control."

Sometimes lying to yourself works well. As I pulled into the familiar police station, I decided that lying to oneself was highly overrated. My phone buzzed again. I clicked it off and stepped out of the Jeep. A hand touched my elbow.

"Sorrel?" Patience, as always, looked cool and calm.

"Time to get this party started," I quipped. I'd have felt better had she smiled.

CHAPTER THIRTY-EIGHT

"Do I qualify as your biggest drama queen client?"

Patience laughed and sipped her coffee. "Not yet."

We'd spent an hour at the police station answering questions about John. Patience had sat quietly through the interview, her presence lending a sense of reality and objectivity. Here in her comfortable kitchen, I once again felt like I was traveling through an endless maze with no real destination in sight.

"I'm sorry to have wasted your time." I looked down at my own coffee, started to take a sip, and then set the mug on a coaster. "This has rattled me. I've gone soft, I guess, but with the dramatic exit from that café in Truth or Consequences, I wasn't sure what I'd encounter at the station. And you're calmer than I lately."

According to the detectives with the Portable Crime Unit from Albuquerque, they'd simply wanted to "touch base" with me since I was so closely "connected" to John. I'd answered their questions carefully, answering only what they asked. When the questions became repetitive, Patience had stood and thanked them for their diligence in helping us find out what had happened to my friend.

"You did very well," she said now. "You were truthful and answered their questions carefully and calmly."

"I'm so frustrated! The police, who should be looking for John, are chasing around asking me questions about him instead. Then they bounce to the poor guy who ended up murdered at the refuge. The two men are totally unrelated—except that I found one and can't find the other!" I reached for my cup again. The rich liquid warmed my throat.

Patience picked up a cookie tin and held it toward me. "Have one of these. My hubby makes them from his mother's recipe. In fact, he does most of the cooking here. He cooks; I eat. That's why I'm round and he's not." She wasn't round either, but I smiled anyway.

I accepted one and bit into it, cinnamon, oatmeal, and raisins filling my mouth. She sat quietly as I chewed. I could hear a clock ticking, a neighborhood dog barking, and a car honking. Some of the tension began easing in my neck. The companionable silence soothed me and pushed the stressful events of the day into a memory.

When I drained my coffee cup, Patience broke the silence. "Actually, you were on my list to contact today. I'm going to be out of town for the holidays, and I wanted to give you the contact information for Felicia Calderon who will be covering for me. Let me get her card. But I have a couple of other things going, so if she's not available, she'll have someone else there. Either way, you'll be fine."

The mention of the holidays reminded me that I should check on things back in Saddle Gap while Patience was getting me the information. Teri had sounded more and more panicked every time I'd called.

When she didn't answer, I left a quick message to let her know I planned to start home tomorrow. Then, as I hung up, I noticed I'd crossed my fingers like I'd done when I was a kid telling a fib.

"Here it is." Patience handed me a business card. "I feel a little guilty—"

"Don't!" I said. "I'm actually planning to go home tomorrow, where I hope to stay out of trouble and won't need legal help. My shop is having a huge sale on the Friday after Thanksgiving and my second in command is pregnant." I chatted on about the plans, and Patience asked questions or commented in the appropriate places. But I doubted she bought the whole story.

"Why don't you stay here tonight?" she asked when I finished. "I have a small room just off the office. I use it sometimes when I'm working late, which isn't often. Of course, I have other bedrooms; but I doubt you'd accept those, thinking you'd be putting me out. This one is actually just for this sort of thing."

"Oh, no! I couldn't impose!"

"You need to sleep. I have one of those coffee one-cup things in there. You can leave as early—or as late—as you please. We're going to Albuquerque early in the morning—a last minute idea to spend a leisurely day before catching our flight tomorrow night to Hawaii." She smiled. "Our grown children go to their in-laws for Thanksgiving and to us for Christmas. So my husband convinced me to take a few days in the sun."

"Sounds like fun! I've never been to Hawaii. My husband and I planned to go, but his parents lived in Florida and he felt we could get the same thing there." I felt my phone vibrating but resisted looking at it. It could go to message. I rose. "I'll just go to the Jeep and bring in a bag, if you're sure it won't be—"

"It won't. I'll actually sleep better with you sleeping instead of driving around trying to find a hotel room—or, worse—driving all the way home."

"I'm a trouble magnet."

"My specialty." She led me to the front door. " I'll just check to see if everything is okay." She started toward her office and then turned. "Let me open the garage door. It might be a good idea for your Jeep to be off the street. The door off to the right opens into my office, and I'll unlock it from this side."

My Jeep slid easily into the space to the left of Patience's Volkswagen. The empty space to the right of her car would house her husband's SUV when he returned from teaching his evening class at the college. I grabbed my bag, locked the Jeep, and lowered the garage door before going through the door to her office.

Patience locked it and ushered me into the small room. "It's small," she apologized, "but the bed is comfortable. And there's an adjoining bathroom here." She opened a door straight ahead. "It's a shower and toilet only—"

"Perfect!" I interrupted. "How do you manage to make everything so cozy?" The walls of the bedroom were pale yellow; but the quilt on the single bed featured a floral pattern filled with reds, blues, purple, turquoise, and oranges. The wooden floor shone beneath a bright red area rug. A small wooden wardrobe, a narrow table holding the coffee machine and mugs, a comfortable upholstered blue rocker, and a floor lamp with a stained-glass shade filled the small space. The bathroom, also pale yellow and white, had a corner shelving unit packed with bright orange towels. "The only thing I could possibly add is a framed photo of my cranes—"

"Sold! I'm holding you to that! The walls are bare because I just needed the right thing!" She glanced fondly around. "Thanks for calling it cozy. That's how I feel when I'm here, and I hope you'll be able to relax and enjoy your night. We may be gone when you get up, so make yourself at home. My assistant will be in for a short while in the morning. She can answer any questions or direct you to anything else you need."

After Patience left, I made short work of gathering my toiletries and sleep shirt. A hot shower can't cure all ills, I thought, but it helps us survive them. About halfway through, I heard my phone ring and then go to message; but I couldn't hear the message while rinsing my hair. Soon I forgot about it.

Much later, after I'd dried my hair and snuggled in bed, I glanced at my phone sticking out of the top of my purse beside the bed. The light flashing signaled two messages from earlier. "Probably Teri," I muttered. "Hopefully not that pesky Reed."

The first message was from Teri. "Just checking in, Sorrel," she said. "I got your message, but I'm getting antsy about the shop and the holidays. It's just me, you know. And if I see another tamale, I'll . . . turn into one! In fact, I'll probably start looking like one any time soon!'

She could always make me smile. I'd call her in the morning and reassure her, I decided. Between being pregnant and having twins to fill up her day, she was likely already in bed.

Then I selected the second message. The caller ID read UNKNOWN. I pushed the message button only to hear the gray space you hear when someone is on but isn't speaking. Then John's voice, "Help me."

"John? Where are you?" I answered, forgetting momentarily that it was a recording. Then I heard the click as it stopped. But was the click from my phone or from another machine?

I punched the message button again and listened carefully. "Help me!" Was that John's voice? It sounded like him. I listened again. Yes, it was John.

But something bothered me. I listened again. What was missing? Once more I listened. This time I heard it: the slight clip at the beginning of the message as if he'd been saying something else first. What had he been saying?

I took a deep breath. Was he afraid? My first reaction had been that he was. Now I wasn't so sure.

Should I call the police and have them listen to this recording? It would show that John was truly missing and that he wasn't the evil man they were beginning to think he was.

Sorrel, my inner self scolded, *they might actually think you set this whole thing up to cover him and yourself. Then you'd be in even more trouble than you are right now.*

Of course, I knew I wasn't really in trouble. Each time the police questioned me had been more routine than aggressive. My own impatience about their lack of progress in finding John fueled my anxiety more than anything.

I climbed into bed and turned out the lamp, but I couldn't turn off my brain. Over and over, I reviewed the events since I'd driven to Bosque so happily, anticipating the festival and the photography experience with John. I'd been so busy with the shop that I really needed the break. Besides, John and I hadn't seen each other since May; and neither of us was diligent about calling. To discover not only his failure to show up but also a stranger's murder at the start of the festival had clouded my sunny plans.

My eyelids drooped eventually; but just before I succumbed to exhaustion, an idle thought floated by—a thought that manifested itself into the events of the morning: John wouldn't have called me for help. He would have wanted to protect me, not put me in danger.

Should I notify the police? Would they believe me? I'd sleep on it.

CHAPTER THIRTY-NINE

I'm not sure when I fell asleep, but I knew when I opened my eyes that I'd slept late. The rich aroma of coffee—and a whiff of cinnamon and pumpkin—seeped in under the door. Faint computer noises and the low murmur of voices gave me a surreal feeling. Where was I?

I snuggled beneath the cozy quilt, tempted to pull it over my head and luxuriate in its safe, warm embrace. A phone rang. The distinctive hum of a computer and keys clicking invaded. Time to get up!

After changing into clean jeans and a sweater, repacking my satchel, and wrangling my hair into a passable ponytail, I opened the door into Patience's office. The woman I'd seen on my first visit stood at Patience's desk as she listened on the phone. A young man, who looked about twenty, glanced up from the computer at the small side desk and smiled. "Coffee and breakfast goodies in the kitchen," he said. "There's also bread for toast if you wish."

"Thanks," I said but I doubt he heard me as he resumed typing.

I felt a bit strange threading my way through Patience's house without her leading the way, but the kitchen enveloped me with its familiar cozy warmth. I filled a mug with dark rich coffee and took a quick sip so as not to burn my tongue. Then I chose a cinnamon bun and settled at the breakfast bar. The bun was huge, dripping with glazed sugar, just like my mama used to make. After devouring it in just a few bites and nearly draining my coffee cup, I realized I couldn't remember whether I'd eaten anything since that interrupted meal in the restaurant yesterday. So a piece of pumpkin bread, I told myself as I cut a generous slice, wouldn't put me into calorie overload. Taking a bite, I savored its moist richness melting in my mouth.

"I've always appreciated a woman with a healthy appetite!"

I jumped off my bar stool, swallowing the pumpkin bread too quickly and choking. A big hand thumped me on the back. I whirled around and pushed it away. "Chris Reed! Keep—" was all I could manage before my coughing intensified and tears filled my eyes as the crumbs stuck in my throat. I reached toward my coffee, but a glass of water was slid into my hand. I took a long drink, wiped my eyes and nose with a napkin, and set the glass down. Then I turned to face my intruder.

"You don't have to thank me," he said. I closed my mouth. "Just practicing my Lancelot role."

I continued staring at him. "When . . . how . . ."

"I didn't realize those endless hours in senior English would come in handy," he continued as if I'd never spoken. "I'm gaining great appreciation for Sir Lancelot lately. I thought rescuing maidens in distress would be an easy thing. Ride in on your trusty steed, knock some guy wearing a tin-can suit off his horse, lift the damsel up onto the saddle horn, and ride off with her into the sunset."

"Of all the ridiculous—"

"But now that I look back on it," he continued, pouring coffee into a mug and sitting as if he'd been invited to join me, "I doubt Guinevere was an ill-tempered, feisty redhead who refused to answer phone calls."

"There weren't any phones back then!" I snapped then mentally whacked myself on my head at the sound of his loud, delighted laughter. He'd won another round! Reed loved luring me into losing my temper. I gathered as much of my dignity as I could, sat back down on my stool without looking at him, and picked up my coffee. For the next few moments, we ate and drank facing straight ahead.

"Are you going to pout all morning? My mama told me it was a waste of time—and we have a full morning ahead."

"I'm not pouting!" I said. Drat! He'd done it again.

"Truce?"

I glanced sideways, ignoring his outstretched hand and looking up into those deep blue eyes. They'd turned serious but the unbidden thought that they should be classified as lethal weapons sprang into my brain, only to be pushed quickly away.

"How did you know where to find me?"

"I am a detective after all, Sorrel."

I chose to ignore that. "Where have you been?"

He chose to ignore my question in favor of one of his own. "Why haven't you answered my calls?" He picked up his cup, stood up, and then gestured toward mine with his eyebrow raised. I nodded.

"I've been busy."

"So have I." He set my mug in front of me and leaned in close enough I could smell the fresh scent of aftershave. I sniffed. His lips twitched. "I drove through the night. Hope I don't smell too offensive."

I was tempted to shock him by answering, "You smell scrumptious!" Instead, I smiled sweetly. Reed's incredulous look, followed by his calculating stare, was comical. He was so easy to bait—but now wasn't the time.

"Are you here on official business?" I asked.

"Right. A little problem with jurisdiction, but . . ."

I waited and finally had to ask. "Why are you here?"

"You'd know already if you'd ever answer your phone!"

"Reed!"

He just stared at me, all hint of teasing gone. I reached for the edge of the counter to steady myself. Did he have news I didn't want to hear? Was there news about John and someone had sent him to tell me?

"Hey," he said, stepping close and cupping my chin so that my eyes had to focus on his. "I'm sorry, Sorrel. I didn't stop to think how you could misinterpret my teasing. Nothing—that I know about—has happened to John."

I felt lightheaded with relief, but maybe I paled because he drew me into an embrace—just a loose, friendly one. "Breathe," he reminded me, his hands moving to my shoulders and gently kneading them. I concentrated on breathing—in and out—until the dizzy feeling eased away. He stepped back, his hands still on my shoulders, and looked me over carefully. When satisfied, he dropped his hands, picked up his cup, and nodded toward mine. "You finished or do you want another cup?"

I shook my head, picked up my cup, and started toward the kitchen sink.

"You guys can just leave those in the sink. Ms. Montgomery has a cleaning lady—me. I'm Sofie."

I jumped and swung around. Sofie was small and plump and in that fuzzy age range, somewhere between forty and sixty. Her long, graying hair was braided and hanging down her back. Her uniform consisted of an oversized tee shirt, worn jeans, and an oversized bag she was carrying in her hand. "Sorry," she said, brushing by and depositing the bag on the counter. She then began pulling out cleaning supplies and setting them on the bar. "If you two aren't finished here, I can—"

"We're finished!" we chorused. All of us smiled.

"I'm Sorrel and this is Reed. We're—"

"I don't take no notice to the comings and goings," Sofie said. She reached under the sink and took out some sponges and a plastic pail. "It's a lawyer's place, you know."

"Well, I stayed the night—"

"Don't make the bed or anything. I'll change it." She put the pail in the sink, squirted cleaner in it, and turned on the faucet.

"Thank you." She might have nodded.

Both of us walked out toward Patience's office.

"I assume your car is in the garage?" Reed asked.

"How—"

"I'll wait outside in my truck. Pack your stuff and bring it on out."

"But what about—"

"It will be safe there. I'll leave a note while you get your stuff together."

"But what about—"

"Sorrel, anyone ever tell you that less is more, especially when it comes to words? We've got things to do and I think the two of us should join forces. It will be easier to do that if we're in the same vehicle, don't you think?" He raised his eyebrow and waited until I finally gave a small nod. "Good. We finally agree on something! We can come back and get your vehicle later. I'll fill you in on what I know and you can do the same." He quirked his eyebrow again and I gave another small nod. "Now hurry!"

I did, not because he'd ordered it but because he'd just read my mind.

CHAPTER FORTY

He'd almost decided she'd left her attorney's house during the night. He'd been afraid the van would be conspicuous in that neighborhood, so he'd parked in a secluded area of a nearby park. At daylight, he'd started driving by. After seeing the attorney and her husband leave without Sorrel he'd almost changed his plans. But as he drove through a fast-food place for coffee and breakfast, he'd decided to cruise by again. This time he hit pay dirt: The hero cop had arrived and was hurrying up to the door. Maybe she was hiding in the attorney's house after all. He pulled over and parked a few doors down. True, a van was a bit unusual in this neighborhood, but his coveralls and the sign on the side gave it the appearance of a repair vehicle.

He chuckled, his mind returning to his clever planning. Those phone calls must be working. She'd called in the cavalry. Funny, though. His boss hadn't expected her to do that until things heated up more than this. Guess his boss didn't know everything. "Thank you anyway, missy," he muttered. "Two for the price of one... or three..."

Sleeping in the van had created a cramp in his shoulders. He considered stepping outside and stretching but didn't want to draw attention to his vehicle. Then the cramping spread down into his hip. He couldn't stretch it out in the van; he had to get out to loosen it. He started the engine and drove by without turning his head at all. At the corner, he drove a half block down and pulled into the curb.

When he first stepped out of the truck, he stretched, easing the cramp enough so that he could at least hobble. Must be getting old. Time was when he could sleep anywhere.

Several minutes later, after he'd walked casually around the block and gone over the details once again, the cramp eased. But, as he headed back to his van, he saw the woman who had been putting a letter out to mail when he'd parked the van. She was now standing on her porch, eyeing him again. Maybe he hadn't walked so casually after all.

"Morning," he called. "Have you seen a dog running loose? A little one about this size?" He held his hands apart to approximate the size of a Chihuahua. "Blonde?"

"Sorry," she called and stepped back inside.

He nodded and forced himself to return to his van, pretending to look around for the imaginary dog. He swore and hoped she'd been too far from him to remember how he looked. He'd been careless, and he couldn't afford to ruin things at this stage. He'd waited a long time for this job—one that didn't come around often. Couldn't louse it up now! Besides, he'd already taken steps he couldn't erase, steps that would earn him the money to follow his dreams of making it big in Las Vegas—or a place in the Big House if he failed. He'd assured his client that he could handle this job. Couldn't let a careless slip-up ruin it all.

He climbed into the van, started up, and drove down the street, past the house where the lady had watched him. He saw movement at her front picture window and swore again. She was suspicious. He wished she'd just ignored him. That was the trouble with people today. They couldn't seem to mind their own business! And where did that leave them?

He sighed as he turned at the corner and then into the alley behind her house to survey the area. High cinderblock fences. Impossible to see through and difficult to climb. He parked at the end of the alley and started back up on foot. He didn't have time for this, he thought, his eyes scanning back yards as he walked. How nice! They'd put the house numbers on the back gates.

Deviating from the plan wasn't a good idea, he thought. Neither was leaving a suspicious woman—of course, she could just be a nosey woman—who could talk to the cops. He continued down the alley, pretending to look for the lost dog. No one seemed to be home, but you couldn't be too careful.

Returning to his van, he drove back to the street and parked in front of a house three doors down from hers, with a realtor's for sale sign in the yard. Bet they're asking a lot, he thought. This is a classy neighborhood.

He got out of the van and walked toward her house, pretending to look for his lost pet. Nothing was stirring. Everyone must be at work or already traveling somewhere for the holiday. As he approached her house, he thought he saw the curtain twitch again.

She opened the door as soon as he rang the doorbell. He touched the brim of his hat and smiled worriedly. "Sorry to bother you again, ma'am, but could I ask you to make a phone call for me? Mine has died and my wife is going to be walking the floor worrying about Peanut. He's never been out of the house."

He infused anxiety into his voice as he surveyed the street. She opened the door and stepped out beside him, looking as well. He eased his arm around her shoulders and whispered, "You holler and you're dead. Now come along with me and help me look for Peanut." He smiled as he gave her a peek of the gun holstered inside his jacket. Casually moving his arm down to her waist, he propelled her toward the van, his eyes sweeping both sides of the street.

Up close, she looked older than he'd thought. He could feel her ribs through the blouse and sweater, and her hair had more white than any other color. "Smile," he ordered, his eyes constantly sweeping. She managed a sick smile, her lips trembling.

They reached the van without another car entering the street. He opened the doors in back; but when he began stuffing her inside a large animal crate, she came out of her terror long enough to struggle. He slugged her, finished getting her inside, and grabbed the roll of duct tape lying next to the crate. He plastered a piece across her mouth. Then he locked the crate and quickly closed the van doors.

Again he swore. She'd messed up his plans a little. "It's all your fault," he said over his shoulder as he started up the engine. "Why couldn't you just have minded your own business?"

He heard a muffled sound, a hysterical attempt to speak.

"That's the problem with people today," he continued, pulling out and driving carefully down the street. "They stick their noses in other people's business, interfering in lives that are doing just fine on their own, playing God."

He stopped at a traffic light and flipped on his right blinker. The noise from the crate in back had stopped momentarily. He unwrapped a piece of gum while he waited on the light and popped it into his mouth.

This unplanned interruption in his plan wouldn't completely ruin things, but it offered complications that he didn't welcome. With the holidays almost here, he needed to finish this business and celebrate.

The light changed and he started up, flicking on the radio. Christmas music blared. "What's happening to this world?" he complained to the lady in the crate. "This greedy world is so pushy. We should be celebrating Thanksgiving! Christmas can wait. All that peace and joy to the world! Where's the focus on family?"

He needed to focus on the job at hand, he thought, hoping this excursion hadn't set the timeline back too far. The excitement of his latest success—so far—began to fade when he considered the difficulties he might face in the intricate plan in progress. That wouldn't be good.

By the time he'd turned on to the lawyer's street and parked a couple of houses down from his original surveillance spot, the enormity of his impulsive actions made his heart pound. He squinted through the dark glasses he'd slapped on.

"Shut up!" he growled to the whimpering crate. His eyes searched. Good. The hero's truck was still here. He focused on the house and waited. Just when he figured he had stepped into deeper trouble, the front door opened and out she came, followed by the hero.

"Early Merry Christmas to me!" he whispered.

CHAPTER FORTY-ONE

I'd nixed Reed's plan to leave my Jeep in the garage at Patience's house. After all, I'd argued, she wouldn't be home for at least a week and I needed to return to Saddle Gap. After tossing other plans, Reed and I decided that it would be as safe as anywhere else in her driveway. So I backed it out of the garage, stowed my things inside—except for my electronics—and joined him in his truck.

"You're one stubborn woman," he grumbled, as he started the motor and pulled away from the curb.

"Thank you."

"Are you going to waste our time with bickering?" Reed slowly drove down the street, glancing again in his rearview mirror.

"I'm not—what are you looking for?"

"Nothing. Just that van back there. You notice it before?"

I looked back but we'd already turned. "I didn't notice it now . . . or before."

He snorted. "It was there this morning, parked down the street."

"Work-type van? Do you think it's important?"

"Could be. But more than likely someone is just having some plumbing work done." Reed stopped at a stop sign and then turned again at the corner. "I'm just getting jumpy, most likely."

I wasn't buying that, but I'd play along. "Are you ready to talk about your plan for today? Any chance you're ready to explain why you keep appearing every few days with this working together routine?" I didn't try to hide the sarcasm in my voice, but I hadn't managed to keep the quiver hidden either.

Reed didn't answer right away. Instead, he drove with his own destination in mind, glancing around us as if taking note of something—or looking for someone. When he turned onto the interstate, I couldn't sit there quietly any longer. "The refuge? Are you planning to share with me? Or is this just the Chris Reed Show?"

Still no answer. I could feel anger and frustration bubbling up. My face flushed and for the first time in—I couldn't remember how long—I wanted to square my shoulders, throw my head back, and scream.

"Why don't you wait to scream until we stop at the refuge?" he asked. "You have a healthy set of lungs, and this truck cab isn't very big. Might send me off into a ditch or something—raise the truck insurance."

I hadn't spoken aloud—or had I? "Good idea," I muttered.

Reed snorted; but when I looked, he was staring ahead calmly, his face straight except for a twitch at the corner of his lip.

The birds had already flown from their nightly roost, of course. As we turned onto the road toward the refuge, a gangly group flew up from a field. I smiled at their jagged V before the memory of the man we'd seen lying in a corn field nearby only a few mornings ago sobered me.

"I haven't seen that lately," Reed said.

"They were here just a few days ago. I took some gorgeous shots—"

"Not the birds. Your smile." Then he reached over and briefly covered my hand before returning his hand to the wheel.

We soon reached my favorite pond, which was just a couple of miles before the main gate of the refuge wilderness area. Reed maneuvered the truck into the small parking area at the side of the road, where we sat and watched the ducks swimming past a couple of cranes. Reed pointed toward the cranes. "They must be sick."

"I'm afraid they probably are, poor things, else they'd be out with their buddies eating. I doubt they'll survive the winter." In spite of all that had happened recently, I was still drawn to the tranquility here. We settled into silence for a few moments, watching the critters. I felt the tension that continually kept my shoulders tight ease just a bit.

"I've been working undercover for the Feds," Reed finally said. "They'd asked that I not tell anyone. In fact, they chose me because I don't have any family ties—and I speak passable Spanish."

"Your new partner? Also with the Feds?"

He nodded. A vehicle pulled into the lot briefly then drove on toward the refuge.

"She wasn't very friendly," I said. "I thought she just didn't like—"

"You? I'd warned her ahead of time not to become pals with you, Sorrel. This was too touchy a situation. The least slip-up could have put the whole exercise in danger."

Me? I'd slip up? I kept my face straight, but I could feel my temper rising. Of all people, I would be the one person—after all my work as a crime reporter and—

Reed reached out and squeezed my hand, holding on when I tried to pull it away. "Wait!" He turned my hand loose, unfastened his seatbelt, and turned so that he could look into my face. "I can't resist teasing you, you know. Probably because I don't have a younger sister to pester." When I stayed silent, he continued. " And you are so easy to rile." I gasped. " Best of all, you're nosey."

"I am not nosey! I have a natural curiosity—"

His loud laughter filled the cab. I managed not to join in, except for a giggle or two. "Glad to be back, Red," he said when he'd recovered. "Guess it's time for you to fill me in on whatever progress—or lack thereof—you've made while I've been away."

"Why don't we walk?" I suggested. He nodded. We had the place to ourselves—and the birds—and even though nippy, we had a sunny, cloudless sky.

While we walked along the pond's edge, I told him about my trip to Truth or Consequences. His eyes narrowed when I told him about how John had left the pamphlets and about my experience at the café. The police station and the night in the Walmart parking lot set him off a bit, reminding me that I seemed to be targeted by someone and was behaving erratically. But mostly, he restrained himself and listened.

The cranes had watched us for a bit before deciding we weren't interested in bothering them. Finally, they lifted off and flew to the cornfields. I stopped talking to admire them. "Is there anything more graceful?" I asked.

"Besides a beautiful woman? I doubt it."

I opened my mouth to contradict him but closed it again when I looked into his eyes. They were twinkling again—naughty. "Best way to hush you up," he joked.

Just as quickly, he sobered. "We're dealing with a clever individual here, Sorrel. At least I think it's an individual, although he must have accomplices."

"Do you think the couple at the Chamber—"

"Just handy recruits. Maybe locals—cheap. That's probably why they turned up dead, since he'd worry they'd talk at the wrong time or to the wrong people."

"John—"

"—wouldn't have ever been an accomplice, of course. But we have to consider—not believe, not give up hope—but consider the possibility that he—"

"—is dead?" I could hear the quiver in my voice.

"Is hurt and needs help getting out of whatever he has been pulled into. We're dealing with an intelligent psychopath here, I think. He—and I do believe it's a he—obviously has some sort of twisted grudge against John—and maybe even you. That's why I've taken some of the time coming to me and want to team up with you. The two of us . . . I think we can figure this out. Would you want to do that?"

I felt my eyes mist. His use of the word *team* had touched me deep inside. He was offering a truce and a partnership, and I knew that wasn't easy for someone who had grown up under the philosophy that women should be protected. I turned toward him, put out my hand, and shook his. "I can't think of a better partner," I said.

"I may still tease, you know, but I'll try to curb it." His twinkling eyes challenged that last statement.

"Right. When Hell freezes—"

His bellowing laughter drowned me out. The ducks flew up in a wild flutter of flapping wings and complaints. I laughed at their fussy voices. It felt good to laugh, even when my heart was heavy and I felt an uneasiness settling between my shoulders.

"Reed, are you—"

"—finished with the undercover work? Yes. And I don't plan to do it again."

"Can you at least tell me this? Was it connected to last spring?"

He hesitated and then nodded. "Jason's connection to the cartel reached farther than just you. He'd been a busy boy."

I leaned against the fence. "I won't ask any more," I said. "But it's good to have a partner again."

We watched the ducks for a bit longer, laughing at their mooning us when they dived for bugs in the pond.

"Let's get back inside the truck and map out a plan of attack," Reed finally said. But as we walked away, he glanced around sharply.

"Something wrong?" I asked.

"Just a feeling—like someone is watching."

"I know what you mean," I said. "I've been feeling it lately too."

He reached to open the door for me, but I already had my hand on it. "Have you noticed anything strange—someone—"

"No," I interrupted. "I think I'm just overreacting to the circumstances."

He got in on the driver's side and grunted. "How about we drive around the refuge and just sort of give everything a second look? Everything seems to have begun here at this refuge. Even the guy you found that morning. Doesn't it seem weird to you that on the very morning that John doesn't show up—and hasn't shown up since—a dead man shows up here? No one could recall ever having a dead body here before. It's a huge coincidence, and I personally am not a big believer in coincidences. What have we missed? I'd like to look around. "

For once we totally agreed on something.

CHAPTER FORTY-TWO

"Let's drive around the inside of the refuge before we head for coffee," Reed suggested. "'It's quiet now that most of the birders have gone home for the holiday.'"

"Fine with me," I said. This roadside pool, the spot where we had watched the cranes lift off each morning during the festival, calmed and renewed me. Those magnificent birds went on about their lives, despite a coyote having eaten one of their neighbors the day before or another dying after the long journey south. Their business was living. And ours—even though a bit more complicated—was equally challenging.

"And speaking of holidays," he said, flicking on his blinker and waiting for a truck to pass, "Teri is getting antsy about you. I told her you're just busy taking photos. That you'd follow your tummy—"

"Reed!" He dodged as I pretended to whack him. " I haven't been very good about keeping up with things in Saddle Gap," I admitted. "Think I'll make a quick call and check on the kitties and my house sitter."

"I figure those cats will be packing up soon and thumbing a ride to a better place." He grinned. "You've been running around too much."

I ignored him and punched in the number. "Hi. This is Sorrel's stable!"

I burst out laughing. "Teri! What are you doing there?"

"Bringing in mail, watering your Christmas cactus, trying to console these two cats, getting away from the twins and an over-doting father—"

"Is everything okay? How are you feeling?"

"Now don't you start, Sorrel. I'm feeling great, aside from being over-coddled! What about you? When are you coming home?"

"Actually, I suspect I'll be coming tonight unless something changes. But don't keep a light on for me! I'll let you know." Reed didn't smile at my rendition of an old commercial.

A pause. Then, softer, Teri asked, "Are you okay? Have you heard anything more about John?"

"Not much. I'll catch you up when I get there." I made my voice lighter. "Can't wait to eat those tamales your whole family has been making."

Teri laughed. "You got out of working on this batch, so I'll have to drag you in for the Christmas session!" I heard a scuffle in the background and a meow. She partially covered the phone and scolded, "Boys, the kitties do not want to wear your hats! . . . What? . . . I know because a meow in that tone of voice isn't a yes. It's 'I'm going to draw a new design on your hand!'" She came back to me, "As you can hear, the cats are well and . . . usually happy?"

We both laughed. "I miss them—and you most of all, Teri!" I told her. "See you soon! By the way, your cousin—"

"—is great and usually here, but he met up with this girl . . . "

"Say no more!"

I disconnected just as we passed the refuge office. The dirt-splattered truck that Willowby usually drove was parked in its usual spot. Reed followed my glance. "Willowby must be waiting to join his wife closer to the holidays," he said.

"I think I remember his wife saying when they came to the shop that they took off for Christmas, when the refuge wasn't so busy."

Just past the office, Reed slowed and signaled for the left turn into the entry gate.

I didn't recognize the lady in the booth. Reed pulled out his wallet, but she waved it away. "No charge today," she said.

"You sure?" Reed asked.

She impatiently waved him on without answering.

"Not much on people skills," he commented, pulling past the entry booth.

"The refuge uses volunteers," I said. "Some of them are more charismatic than others, I suspect."

Inside the refuge, we encountered a hive of activity everywhere we looked—ducks diving in the ponds for insects, a porcupine waddling across a dirt path, a buck strolling alongside the road, and thousands of cranes and snow geese feeding in the cornfields.

"Busy place here," Reed observed.

"Makes my fingers itch for my camera."

"You didn't bring it?"

I made a face at him. "You weren't exactly forthcoming about the day's plans!"

He chuckled. "Like to keep you guessing. It's the only way I can—" He stopped suddenly in the narrow road. "Look out there." He pointed across the road to my right.

It was a heavily wooded area, with little disturbed except for a narrow path to the right. Although gold and red leaves covered the ground, plenty still clung to the tall trees. "I'm not sure what I should be seeing."

"I thought I saw a reflection . . . like a mirror or something."

I squinted again, my eyes moving left to right, categorizing details. Just as I opened my mouth to deny it, I saw it. A quick flash, almost imperceptible. "A flashlight? A camera? The sun glinting on a piece of metal?"

"I'm not sure," he said. "It just seems odd."

"Well, you know how people are. No matter how many times they're warned about getting off the trails and about not littering, someone has to ignore it all and leave a mess." I squinted. "Do you want us to investigate, Sherlock?"

"Nope. Let's drive on over to the cornfield where you were shooting when you saw the dead body."

I wasn't sure what Reed expected to find but I nodded.

The field was alive with cranes and snow geese intermingled eating corn, jostling each other, and making lots of noise. A few snow geese flew up when we opened our doors and stepped out, but the cranes hardly glanced our way.

"All right," Reed said. "We were standing over there. A little farther to the right, weren't we?"

I thought a moment. "Some guy kept jostling my elbow, so I moved right to get out of his way. I had to do that a couple of times, and I was getting irritated. There were a lot of people here, but it wasn't so crowded that you had to—"

The thought came to both of us simultaneously. "He must have been—"

"—making sure you were in the right spot!" Reed finished.

"Then the man we found here must be somehow connected to all of this! But what's the connection?"

"I don't know," he answered, "but I suspect we need to find out. Let's drive back around one more time."

"What's the plan?"

"No plan exactly." Reed opened my door and walked around to his own, his eyes sweeping the area. "Don't you think it's odd that no one is out here this morning?"

"Not really," I said. "Most birders and photographers have fulltime jobs and only are able to come on weekends or for festivals."

He climbed in and started the engine. "Doesn't seem too safe for you to be out here on your own," he said.

"Now don't you start!" I turned to look out over the field again. "John has already given me the lecture. I'm not a pansy as my dad used to say! Do you treat your new partner this way?"

Reed had become uncharacteristically silent. A strange foreboding crept up my spine.

I turned toward Reed. He was staring into a revolver held by someone wearing a ski mask! A robbery? The only sounds—flapping wings, bird calls, water—formed a weird setting. I eased my hand toward—

"Be still and do as I say if you don't want your sweetie here splattered all over you and this truck," the ski mask growled. "Turn off the engine and hand me the keys," he instructed Reed. "You toss them or try something cute and she's dead. Trust me, I've done this before."

"So have I!" a second voice hissed in my ear. I jerked instinctively and leaned toward Reed.

"Stop!" the second voice snapped. I jerked again then steeled myself to turn my head toward the passenger window. This second guy was taller and leaner than his partner and looked far too comfortable holding a matching gun. Like his companion, he also wore a ski mask. His eyes caught my attention. They seemed familiar. Did I know him? Had I seen him somewhere recently? It wasn't the color—a sort of faded bluish green that chilled me—but the coldness, the almost total lack of emotion. He would pull that trigger without a hint of remorse and enjoy doing so.

My thoughts must have shown because he suddenly smiled. Even with the ski mask, I could see the evil, almost gleeful, curve of his lips.

I heard Reed turn off the engine and hand the keys over, as I stared into the cold, malicious eyes holding the gun on me.

I heard Reed's door open, feeling rather than seeing the door to my left. "Unclip your seatbelt slowly. My finger wants to squeeze this trigger, and I don't need much encouragement."

My ski mask followed the progress, his eyes shifting for only a few seconds before returning to me. I'd hoped to distract him, but he was obviously far more experienced than the common crook.

Reed grunted, causing me to break my gaze. He had doubled over slightly, his hand to his belly. I could see the pain in his face. The creep had obviously hit him hard. He grabbed Reed's hands and tied them behind his back with what looked like wire.

My mind was racing. What did they want? Then it came to me! The truck. Carjacking had risen in the area due to its closeness to Mexico. Carjackers could sell stolen cars there easier than in the state. I started to feel some relief. Carjackers seldom killed their victims.

Another tiny gleam of hope lit inside me. Surely we weren't the only nature lovers out here! Someone either might already be in the refuge or might wander onto us.

The gleam died just as quickly as I recalled our conversation about how empty the refuge seemed. Reed and I had little chance to slow this hijacking for that reason, but any time we could buy might help.

Just then my door was jerked open, and I felt the gun placed against my throat. "Unfasten the seatbelt," the second man growled. I didn't dare move my head. I needed to do as he asked until an opportunity came along.

If he was planning to kill both of us, doing it here would be inconvenient, which gained us a bit of time. Maybe they'd just tie us up and leave us out in the refuge wilderness, thinking we'd die from exposure or be killed by animals before anyone found us.

The hand that grasped my upper arm was intentionally rough, nails—although short—digging into me. He yanked so hard that I stumbled, knocked my ankle on the frame, and fell down hard on the ground. Before I could react, he grabbed my arms and secured them behind me. When he yanked me to my feet, I gasped as my ankle almost gave away, pain shooting up my leg. I clenched my teeth to smother the cry that rose in my throat.

He grinned. The movement showed well-kept teeth and thin lips. I tried to memorize those teeth and lips before quickly glancing down. I didn't want him to notice, but I feared he had already. This guy was smart. That didn't bode well.

Neither did the voice that I heard coming in our direction. "What's taking so long?" I felt my car thief stiffen.

"Get out of here!" he ordered.

"I—"

"Vanish!" His harsh tone made me inwardly flinch. This guy was no amateur.

She must have driven here, but I couldn't see a vehicle anywhere. At his order, she halted and started walking backwards. Finally, she turned and ran into the trees where we'd noticed the flash earlier. But she wasn't wearing a mask and we'd seen her before—working in the ticket booth at the refuge entrance.

I looked at Reed. His eyes registered the same concern. By being able to identify her, our lives had taken a precarious turn.

Reed and his captor started walking along the road; we followed. My ankle started to swell, the pain increasing as I was shoved, sometimes drug, after them. I bit my lip to avoid crying out. Blood ran down my lip and dripped onto my shirt. Several yards down the road, we crossed into the trees and began a meandering course back again. I could no longer see the road. Beads of sweat popped out on my forehead. I could no longer feel my ankle, just a huge throbbing pain.

When I couldn't keep up with my captor, he slapped me several times until I forced myself to go on. He watched Reed with each slap, goading him, probably hoping he'd react and give them an excuse to shoot. I prayed Reed would ignore it.

Finally, just ahead on another section of the dirt refuge loop, we saw a van. We were hurried toward it. I glimpsed the side of the woman's face as she sat in the passenger seat. Reed's captor opened the double doors in the back and shoved him in. Then he turned back toward the way we had come, probably to move Reed's truck. Something about the man's size and shape reminded me of Willowby. Weird to think of him now.

My ski mask quickly shoved me into the van and set me next to Reed. Then he picked up a huge roll of packing tape, pulled off a long piece, and wrapped it over Reed's mouth. He took another and wrapped it over his eyes. Next he turned toward me. "This is going to pull out some of that hair, Red, if it ever gets taken off." When he finished, he shoved me against the other side of the van.

I listened, hoping to hear what these three had planned for us. Then I heard it, a muffled high-pitched cry very near me. Another person—probably a woman—was in the van with us.

CHAPTER FORTY-THREE

My captor had shoved me into the bed of the van so hard that I'd stumbled and fallen face down on the floor, filling my nose with the smells of motor oil and machinery. As I sat there, eyes and mouth taped, I tried to capture the vague memory of the van floating in my brain, but the throbbing ankle and the wire cutting into my wrists distracted me.

Then the engine started up and with it died the tiny light of hope that we might be discovered by some birder. As the van bumped along the refuge road, we bounced with it. I tried to hold my breath against the throbbing pain, but muffled moans escaped through the packing tape on my mouth. Nausea rose in my throat, but vomiting was not an option. I'd choke. So I swallowed and prayed. Then I felt Reed roll against me. He slung his long leg across my thighs and gripped me, trying to hold me still against the continual swaying of the van.

Another odor—urine and human waste—attacked my nostrils, making my stomach roll. I listened, but could no longer hear her at all. It was eerily quiet. More than likely, the person I'd heard earlier had just died. Poor thing!

But my momentary mourning of our companion's death was interrupted by more horrific thoughts. Had someone else died in this van even before we'd entered? Had John died here? Nausea hit and I swallowed hard again.

Think of something else, my mind commanded; so I concentrated on pleasant thoughts: the upcoming Black Friday sale at my shop; the sound of Flash and Van purring in my ear when I awoke; the cranes taking off in the dawn, warbling greetings to the day ahead. I tried to smile, but the tape made that impossible. I sighed. Despite keeping the nausea from erupting, pleasant thoughts weren't working. I could only imagine John lying dead somewhere and Reed and I soon joining him.

Then something nudged my sore ankle. Once. Twice. I moaned. The third time I realized I was feeling Reed's boot. Reed. It's weird how comforting a nudge can be—even if he had been hitting my sore ankle.

The van stopped suddenly and then quickly made a sharp turn, throwing my head against the side of the van. My last thought as I fainted was of John.

The tape being ripped from my eyes brought me out of the blessed nothingness and back into the nightmare. Strands of my hair were pulled out by their roots, leaving me feeling as if I now had only half of my eyebrows. Tears filled my eyes and ran down my face. Seconds later, my captor ripped the tape from my mouth. My whole face felt on fire; my tongue clung to the roof of my mouth. I coughed. What I wouldn't give for a drink of water.

As if he'd heard my thoughts, my captor threw a cup of ice water in my face. I gasped and choked. "Shut up!" he ordered.

I recognized that voice. But when I looked up, I saw a distorted, strange face. The ski mask had been abandoned for a semitransparent plastic face mask dense enough to disguise his features. He wore a cap with the bill pulled so low that I couldn't see his eyes. I shook my head quickly to get the water out of my eyes and caught a glimpse of Reed to my left. His eyes and mouth were also tape-free, but his ankles were now bound. He seemed to be trying to tell me something but looked down quickly.

They hadn't bothered with mine, but then they didn't need to. My left ankle had swollen to at least twice its size. Looking at the ankle, an ugly purplish mess, I thought I might have permanent damage that would affect my ability to walk. More chilling was the thought that I might not live to know.

"I hear one sound from either of you and you'll join your friend here," the man nearer to me said, pointing to the bag. "Understand?"

When I didn't answer right away, he slapped me. I gasped from the sting and I heard Reed shift. "Should I do that again or will you answer? Better still, how about I work on your boyfriend here," the hateful voice continued.

"I—don' talk," I managed through my dry mouth and puffy lips.

He laughed. "Not so high and mighty now, are you? Bet the camera wouldn't love you now!"

His partner stepped up to the van and peered inside. He also wore one of the strange plastic masks, but with a Stetson instead of a cap. His eyes were focused on the grubby, soiled sleeping bag. "Ready?" he asked.

My captor stepped over, reached down, grabbed the side closest to him, and pulled it toward the door. The horrible odor from last night—only worse, if possible—blasted toward me from the top of the bag that had come open in the process.

I stilled myself, focusing on his reference to the camera. The odor had momentarily diverted by captor's attention. I glanced at Reed. He stared back and then blinked once. He'd caught that reference as well. This man knew who I was. This wasn't a random carjacking at all, but was it connected to John's disappearance? Hundreds of threats had arrived at the station while I worked as a crime reporter. Had this guy been one of them?

"Nasty," the cowboy muttered, as he looked at the sleeping bag.

"You drag the bottom of this thing and I'll push," my captor said.

The cowboy grabbed the bottom of the bag with his gloved hands and yanked. As it slid by me, I squinted, hardly daring to breathe. Please don't let it be John, I mentally prayed.

It wasn't. I didn't know who she was. She was older and had obviously been beaten about her head. I could see blackened eyes and bruises even in the dim lighting. Thank you, God, I silently prayed. Immediately, I felt remorse.

I looked at Reed. He'd been staring at me, waiting for me to look his way. Slowly he winked. *It's okay to be relieved it's not John*, his eyes told me. *And I'm sorry about this lady as well.* I could hear him whispering. Was this mental telepathy?

I thought of our immediate future, a glimmer of hope rekindling. Reed and I had proved to be a tough team to beat before. Still, the realist inside me acknowledged that we had a hard fight ahead of us. I winked at Reed. Win or lose, I was glad he was on my team.

Reed's truck had been pulled up behind us. I didn't know where we were exactly, but I didn't think we were still on the refuge or even in that area. What little I could see of the terrain was rocky and hilly—low hills. I couldn't see more without drawing attention to myself, which I wanted to avoid.

Our captors returned and sprayed a pine-scented liquid on the floor of the van. I wrinkled my nose.

"Can't please you, can we, Red?" the cowboy asked. Then he looked at his partner and, after a few seconds, turned to leave the van. "You come with me," he said to the woman, who had remained in the passenger seat while the men removed the body. Weird that I'd forgotten about her!

She glanced back at us and then smiled flirtatiously at the man as she climbed out of the front seat. He jumped out the back of the van and walked toward Reed's truck. When he reached it, he opened the driver's door and stood there watching her walk to the other side and climb in. Then he raised his hand to signal his partner, who was still in the van.

But the man wasn't watching him. He was watching me. My blood turned cold, and I couldn't breathe. He stood there for what seemed an eternity before reaching for a small box behind him. I couldn't see what he pulled out before he shut the box and scooted it back in place.

He walked over to Reed, drove his fist into Reed's face, and watched as his head dropped. I gritted my teeth, forcing myself not to gasp or react in any way. He slid Reed's shirt sleeve up and jabbed a hypodermic needle in his arm.

Then he stepped over to me. "Do I need to give you the same treatment?" he asked.

I shook my head, turning away and steeling myself not to wince as I felt the needle in my arm.

"Sweet dreams," he mocked as he stepped out of the van, slammed the back doors, and walked around to the driver's seat.

My last thoughts as I heard the engine start and felt the jolt of gears changing were of John, Reed, and that poor nameless woman. But mostly, I thought about the bravest person I'd ever known, the person who considered no obstacle too difficult, no person too frightening, and no task too intimidating.

"Mama," I whispered as my eyes closed.

CHAPTER FORTY-FOUR

"Sorrel, wake up!"

"Mama?"

"No, Sorrel. It's Reed."

"No Reed!"

His weak chuckle seemed close by. "Always going to argue with me, aren't you, honey?"

"No honey!"

I concentrated on opening my eyes. My lips were swollen and my tongue so dry that talking was a challenge. Everything sounded as if I was talking with a mouthful of marbles. I needed to get a drink of water! But first I needed to go to the bathroom.

"So do I." That pesky Reed again. How had that he gotten into my nightmare? "Your eyes open yet?"

"I'm thinking about it!"

Another weak chuckle. "Taking you awhile."

"Happy to be your entertainment."

"Shh! Don't get too noisy."

Reed had edged closer. I started to move away, but my legs felt dead and heavy—so heavy.

"It's not a nightmare after all, is it, Reed?" I whispered.

He sighed. "It's a nightmare all right, Sorrel," he whispered. "We just have to figure out how to get out of it."

If we can, I thought. But that thought was shoved aside in a second by a familiar one from my childhood. *Sorrel Janes,* my mama whispered as clearly as if she were beside me, her voice firm and no-nonsense, *it's easy for anybody to get into a pickle. Getting out of one takes determination and cunning—two things you've always had! Your partner here has it too! Time to put your heads together and figure it out!*

"How's the ankle?" His voice sounded weak but was now so close I could feel his breath tickle my ear.

My eyelids finally came unstuck. I blinked a few times in the darkness. I couldn't see even a beam of light. "I think I'll sit out the next dance. And you?"

"Think they may have cracked a rib but probably just bruised," he whispered. "We must be in some sort of storage unit or something. I don't think we're still in the van." He panted shallowly, then continued in an even softer whisper against my ear. "If they undo our hands to go to the bathroom, we need to leave something . . . some clue . . . of ourselves. If they let us use an actual bathroom, leave as many fingerprints as you can."

I moved my lips to his ear. "I'm wearing earrings, but our captors might notice one if I try to leave it behind." My pronunciation had yet to improve and I felt Reed's shoulder shake a little when I told him about my "eewings."

"I'll get you later," I threatened, but it lost its forcefulness when the words came out sounding as if they all began with a W. The shoulder shook again.

Then he stilled, whispered "shh" into my ear, and carefully—albeit awkwardly—eased back. I turned my back toward him and lay still.

Footsteps and hushed voices approached just outside the walls of whatever we were in. Although I strained to make out the words, I couldn't. One voice grew louder, angry, and was shushed by the other. A key jiggled in the lock, the door swung out, and what appeared to be afternoon sunlight spilled in.

The heavyset kidnapper, Reed's captor, carried in a portable toilet and set it close to me. He still wore the plastic mask and the same clothes. He didn't glance at either of us and said nothing as he turned and walked out.

The second man stepped into the doorway and just stood there for what seemed like hours. I bit my lip to avoid thinking about how badly I needed to go to the bathroom, the horrible taste in my mouth, and my unquenchable thirst.

He finally cleared his throat and asked mockingly, "Anyone need to use the john?"

When neither of us answered, he turned as if to leave. Then he spun around. "Oh, I almost forgot." He walked over to Reed. "Since your hands and feet are wired, do you want me to unwire them?" Then he turned toward me. "Or do you want me to unwire your hands? There's certainly no need to undo both of you." He laughed.

Reed remained silent, but I'd had enough. "Flip a coin," I snapped.

In the eerie silence that followed, I mentally screamed at myself. My temper and my mouth might very well have sealed both of our fates. I steeled myself against a fist—or a gun—either aimed at me or at Reed. Instead, he roared with laughter. When he finally caught his breath, he said, "Okay, Red. I'll undo lover boy's hands. He'll find a way in a few hours—if you're both alive then—to get yours loose as well. But not in time for you to use the facilities."

He walked over behind Reed, yanked him to his feet, laughing when Reed almost fell, and stepped back until he'd regained his balance. Then he pulled wire cutters from his pocket. "Try anything and I'm not going to be happy with you—but I certainly will be with her after you're gone."

Reed nodded his head. A few seconds later, he was free and flexing his fingers. His captor led him against the wall to the other side, stepped back, and smiled. "Enjoy!" Then he walked to the door.

We both watched him as he walked through the door and turned to shut it. I noticed a quart jar filled with water sitting on the floor just to the side of the door opening. Then he slammed the door shut, and blackness once again settled upon us.

"Talk to me so I can get to you," Reed said.

"I can—"

"No, you can't. Don't be a prude, Sorrel."

"I'm no prude!"

"Must you always argue, fuss budget?"

"And I'm not a fuss budget!"

A hand reached out and touched my face. "Thanks, fuss budget!" he said softly. "I knew I could rile you enough to lead me here. Now the fun begins. We have to find the toilet."

"We can work on getting my hands loose—"

"Not that quickly. He didn't leave the wire cutters, remember? Now, let's count steps and step to the side—and pray that we don't end up wandering all around this room or knocking over the water!"

"I'm okay, Reed. I can wait to go!"

"Well, I'm not!"

I found that hilarious. Finally, Reed shook me until I stopped laughing. Then he hugged me close. "We can do this, Sorrel. Just trust me and work with me—but let's try to hurry."

CHAPTER FORTY-FIVE

He chuckled when they dropped their voices to near whispers. Surely they knew he had bugged the room—or maybe they didn't! He'd bugged her Jeep the last time she returned to this area and she still hadn't caught on to that—and they thought they were so smart! Members of law enforcement he'd encountered so far in New Mexico—and in Missouri—hadn't impressed him.

All his life, he'd heard the expression "getting away with murder" but never thought it would be so simple. Murder. That reminded him that he had work to do. In an ideal world, someone of his superior intellect would not be dealing with mundane details. One hired people to take care of those nasty little chores. But one had no choice when those people proved to be incompetent. Those two idiots who'd nabbed the photographer had come with great resumes. But they'd been spotted by that undercover cop. Then they'd come up with the brilliant idea to use the dead body to scare Sorrel into leaving without her friend. He hoped they'd thought about their stupidity as the water closed in on them.

He sighed. He needed the cover of darkness for this evening's activities, but there was much to do before then. "Better take care of the preliminaries," he said aloud, climbing into this cop's truck and starting the engine.

He'd given instructions for the van to be parked in an inconspicuous spot in the rocky hills east of town. Surely his partner and the girlfriend could do that. Of course, he'd also cautioned him to keep a low profile during the surveillance; yet he'd managed to kidnap some nosy old lady and haul her around, tied up and gagged but not blindfolded, in the van. She'd seen too much to live. That was inexcusable! Anyone with law enforcement training should know the simple basic rule: Those who can identify must be permanently silenced. On the other hand, too many bodies attract widespread attention—and that was certainly not his intent at all.

As he drove, his outrage simmered. Deviating from the plan had thrown off the rhythm of the whole scheme.

He drove up beside the take-out window of a fast-food Mexican restaurant and bought a couple of burritos. After he pulled back out on the road, he reached into the bag. They'd provided salsa, but he couldn't manage that one-handed. Any other time, he'd have pulled into the covered parking at the restaurant and eaten them there; but he needed the sunlight to find his way to the meeting spot. After the first bite, he was happy he hadn't added the salsa. He swallowed and coughed. How could anyone eat something this peppery hot? Someone like him who hadn't eaten much all day. And so he took the next bite and the next. Eating faster kept the burn down. When he swallowed the last bite, he reached for a bottle of water and washed some of the burn away. The second burrito could wait.

The sun was setting as he pulled up beside a shabby camper trailer nestled beside a couple of scraggly trees. He turned off the engine and surveyed the scene. At least they'd had the foresight to park the van in a draw several yards away from the camper. All the camp sites surrounding the camper were empty. "A Thanksgiving gift," he muttered, unsnapping his seatbelt.

The door to the camper opened cautiously. "Stupid" stuck his head out, squinting into the darkness. Good thing this guy wouldn't need references for future jobs! He got out and walked quickly up to the camper door. As he approached the step, his partner called a greeting. Up close, he turned his head against his partner's beer breath, which stunk worse than the burrito's garlic and onions

Touching his left hand to the brim of his Stetson, he nodded, grunted, and waited until his partner turned to enter the camper. Then he encircled the man's fat neck with his left arm while his right reached up to slice his throat so deep that his head lolled back. It reminded him of slaughtering pigs on Thanksgiving weekends long ago.

He shoved the writhing soon-to-be corpse into the tiny room, dumping it onto the nearby sofa and into the lap of the sleeping girlfriend. She woke with a start, her mouth opening to scream, something he had to pre-empt. He shoved the corpse over, yanked her off the sofa, and put her in a choke hold.

Listening to her neck cracking, he felt a sense of pride and relief. He hadn't lost his touch. One never could be sure as it wasn't something one could just practice. He dropped her onto her lover's stinking body, stepped back onto the outside step, and shut the door quickly. Then he trotted to the truck.

The bag sitting on the passenger floorboard held sweats, running shoes, a hat, gloves, and a quilted jacket. He hummed while his fingers ripped off his jeans, boots and socks, western shirt, and under shorts and stuffed them into a plastic trash bag. Just as quickly, he pulled on the fresh clothes and shoes. He regretfully stuck the Stetson into the bag and donned the baseball cap that replaced it.

The moon and stars provided enough light to make his way down to the draw and to the van. A quick search through the glove compartment offered the flashlight he'd stored there earlier, as well as the van's title—with John's name on it, of course! He smiled at seeing his plan come together in spite of having to work with morons. He hadn't lost his touch.

He continued his search of the van, dropping the bag with his clothes inside. He found the lightweight bicycle in the back. At least they'd remembered to purchase one! The bike looked adequate, but he tested the tires anyway. A sack next to it held a new jumpsuit. Good! Maybe these two hadn't been totally incompetent. He pulled it out of the bag, careful not to drop any tags or paper, and put it on over his clothes. Then he hopped into the driver's seat and drove the van up to the camper trailer.

When he opened the trailer door, he wrinkled his nose at the stench of death inside. He quickly unhooked the electricity, stepping carefully around his former employees. Once he felt confident everything was ready, he stepped back outside, locked it up, and glanced at his watch. He was right on schedule—but he still had work to do.

Fifteen minutes later, he'd hooked the camper to the back of the van and prepared to take off. "Appreciated the ride, Ole' Paint," he told the cop's truck as he pushed the automatic locks and tossed the keys inside just before slamming the door shut. Then, whistling under his breath, he hopped into the van and eased back onto the road. He hoped everyone had already left the area to celebrate the holiday with family.

His lip lifted at the word *family*, but his lighted watch dial reminded him that he needed to pay attention to time.

A couple of hours later, he again congratulated his careful planning as he watched the van and camper sink into the dark waters of Elephant Butte Lake. He took another quick look around the empty camping spaces around the boat dock. Then he climbed onto the bike, pedaled to the paved road, and headed toward town.

"Better check on my other guests," he mused.

CHAPTER FORTY-SIX

We listened while our captor locked the door. Shortly after, we heard a vehicle start up and drive away.

Reed leaned over and whispered in my ear, "It could be a trick."

"And we're whispering because . . ."

"Because he has likely bugged the place."

"I don't know what he thinks he'd learn."

"Maybe he just wants to snoop. He's gone somewhere to take care of other things. There are only three of them as far as we know."

"Maybe more if they have John." I wiggled my fingers, but several had gone numb, and my shoulders throbbed.

"If he's smart—and I think he is—he'll dump the woman. She let us see her face. But he won't be gone long."

"What do you think this place is? And where?"

"Some kind of barn maybe. They've covered the windows, but tiny streaks of light were peeking in the cracks of the door when we first got here. It's night now, I'm sure. "

"If only my hands were free . . ."

Reed whispered even softer. "Let me see how they have your hands bound. Scoot sideways, quietly."

"You can't do anything, Reed. It's wire!"

But he'd already moved behind me, his hands running over my wrists. Then he raised up and whispered, "Great! Finally a break! He used zip ties—those plastic things. Hold still—and for God's sake, stay quiet."

He moved his head down to my wrists. His hands held them as far up as I could stand, and then he started nipping at the tie with his teeth. Each time he pulled the head of the tie and popped it back, I bit my lip to keep from crying out. I stopped counting on the fifth pull. It wasn't going to work. "Your teeth are going to break or fall out," I whispered.

At that instant, the head of the tie popped off. I wasn't prepared for the pain that followed, but Reed must have been. He covered my mouth with his own. I pulled away and sputtered, "Reed!"

"Don't say anything else!" he whispered. "If he's listening, he'll think we're . . . "

"You've got to be joking!" I said.

"Good!" he whispered. "He'd become suspicious if he didn't hear anything at all. Let me ease your arms now. Take a deep breath; then lean against my shoulder and bury your mouth in my shoulder. This is going to hurt; and if you cry out, he'll be alerted to something."

One thing about Reed, he didn't understate things. My shoulder joints and arms had been pulled tightly for a long time. I gritted my teeth so hard I'm surprised they didn't break. Tears streamed, wetting his shirt as he straightened out first one arm, then the other, rotating each gently. My hands stung with the increased blood flow. Finally, I raised one and pushed away.

"The upper half of me is partly in working order," I whispered. "Thanks."

"It's been a pleasure," he said aloud. "Guess we'd better catch some zees while we can."

I leaned into his ear. "Payback when we get out of here." I could feel rather than hear his snicker.

"That's the spirit!" he whispered. "I was getting a little worried, Red!"

We decided the sensible thing to do would be for Reed to crawl along the walls while I felt my way dragging the hurt foot. Reed tore his shirt and wrapped my ankle first, in hopes it would give me some form of support, then lifted me into a standing position.

We made slow progress, especially me, but finally Reed came back to me. "I think this is one of those metal storage buildings," he whispered. "We're in luck."

"How do you figure that?" I asked, but he'd already moved away.

The next moment I heard a huge crash. The door had swung out, letting in the moonlight. Reed ran over to me, threw me over his shoulder in a fireman's lift, and carried me several yards to a fence. While he caught his breath, I looked around. There were no streetlights or houses in sight.

Reed had been thinking the same thing. "We're not getting help from a friendly neighbor," he said. "But we've got to get out of here now! If we were bugged, he's heard the crash and knows what's up."

"Do you know where we are?"

"Not really." He put his arm around my waist and lifted my injured leg.

"You can't carry me, Reed."

"I know that, Sorrel! I'm tired, hungry, and I suspect whatever was in that shot is still in my system. I'm just helping you over this fence—not carrying you over. I don't need to add a bad back to everything else we have to deal with!"

"Thanks!" I would have stomped my foot, but I didn't want to hurt the uninjured one.

Reed chuckled softly. "I knew I could count on your bad temper! Once we're over the fence, I'll help you along. Let me know when we need to stop."

We had to stop sooner than either of us wanted. The ground slanted and we slid, mercifully yet painfully stopped by a tree. "You're going to have a huge bump on your temple," I told Reed.

"How's the ankle? Can you still hobble on it?"

"Hobble or drag—the alternative option isn't any brighter." I made my voice brave, but I privately wondered how much longer I could continue. "Do you want to go on and get help?"

"Save your breath." He stood up and held out a hand. I took it and struggled upright. "Let's go!"

Progress was an optimistic word to describe our next hour. Every step sent shooting pains through my ankle and up my leg. Several times I stumbled and would have fallen had Reed not been quick enough to catch me. I barely had breath to take one step and then another. My tongue felt puffy, swelling up to fill my mouth. And it was so cold my teeth chattered, yet sweat ran down my face, plastering my hair around my face.

I hoped Reed would agree sometime soon to go on without me. Surely our captors had returned by now. Reed might escape if he left me, but I could see no hope of my getting there with him.

I stumbled again. "Sorrel, grab onto my belt. It's hard to see and if you fall, you could cause even more injury to your foot."

I didn't have the strength or energy to argue, so I complied. Time enough later—maybe—to reassert my aversion to his bossy ways.

"What are you mumbling about?"

"I wasn't—"

"Shh!" Reed stopped so quickly that I bumped into him, almost knocking him down. He squatted, pulling me along with him.

I heard it then—a truck or car engine. We must be close to a road or highway.

"Down!" Reed pushed me flat behind a scraggly piece of brush. " Don't move!"

It was a truck, cruising slowly along a two-lane, paved road. But what had given Reed most concern was a spotlight held out the driver's side, slowly sweeping over the brush.

"Face down!" he whispered again. "Stay very still."

We waited in that position for what seemed like hours but realistically was only a few minutes. Finally, Reed looked up slowly. "Clear," he said.

I rolled over and lay on my back. Reed sat on his haunches for a few minutes, watching and listening. "I think we're okay," he said. "The best case scenario is that it was law enforcement looking for someone else. The worst—"

"—is it's our guy," I interrupted. I was so exhausted I almost wished it were the latter.

Reed rose. "I'm . . . uh . . . going to go . . . uh . . . over there . . . for a minute. You'll be okay? Just stay down and listen for anything. Roll under that bush, facedown, if you hear something."

"I know, I know. Go on."

I listened as he moved off and over a rise and then let the tears run down my face. I closed my eyes in relief only to see the hateful mask rise before me. I jerked, opened my eyes and sat up, and swept the moonlit countryside.

Sorrel Janes! Wipe that face, buck up, and help this young man! He can't carry your weight and his too! I raised you better than that! Use your senses. Listen for sounds foreign to the area, keep your eyes moving side to side and down to spot disturbances in the surroundings, sniff for unusual smells. It's no different from when I took you deer hunting, honey. Yeah, it's night but you have moonlight. You can do this.

A light step behind me made me whirl around.

"Whoa, Sorrel! It's me!"

I relaxed. "Oh."

"Are you all right? Do you need . . ."

"No, Reed. Not now."

"Okay. Let's go then." He started forward and then turned back and touched my shoulder. "I thought I heard you speaking to someone."

"No. It was my dad."

Reed looked at me keenly and then grabbed my hand. "Let's hang onto each other," he said. "We're both exhausted."

I meekly followed. Let him think I was delirious. He'd believe that easier than the truth—that my guardian angel had arrived and peace, as much as it could, had settled on my shoulders.

CHAPTER FORTY-SEVEN

We traveled parallel to the road, which was sometimes straight but more often curved. We moved in crouched positions, stumbling often. I was much more awkward than Reed, of course, with my injured ankle.

Neither of us expressed it, but rattlesnakes were also on our minds. Although they tended to crawl more in September and October, stepping in one of their holes could rile up a whole nest of them. Snakes had always scared me—almost as much as the characters who had kidnapped us.

The moon was high overhead and we had yet to see any other cars. The longer we walked, the more we felt that the men sweeping the roadside with the spotlight were more likely illegal hunters than the kidnappers.

"Let's rest," Reed said finally, trying to give me some respite from my injury.

Sweat, whether from the effort or from the pain in my ankle, beaded on my forehead. "There's nothing you can do for it right now, Reed. We need to push on while we have the cover of darkness."

"You sure?"

I didn't waste breath on an answer, just kept on walking. I was feeling slightly dizzy, and lifting one foot and dragging the other took most of my concentration. I felt an arm slip around my waist and almost screamed. "Listen, Sorrel."

I leaned against him and strained to hear what he was hearing. Could that be water?

"Yes, it is." I didn't know I'd spoken aloud.

"Let's go toward it . . . slowly, Sorrel. It could be deep and I don't think I have the strength to drag you out."

Our awkward progress slowed even more.

As we neared the soft rippling sound of the water, I heard gentle swishes and splashes. "Do you hear that?" I asked.

"Ducks?"

"I think so. Reed, we must still be on the refuge."

"But we drove quite a distance in that van."

"Did we? We were knocked out, remember? I didn't stay awake long."

He groaned. "Some police officer I am."

"We must be in some back area, though," I went on. "I don't remember ever seeing that building, do you?"

"I'll have to think on that."

By now we'd reached the edge of the duck pond. The moonlight reflected off the water, and I could see a few midnight snackers diving for bugs.

"I don't recognize this pond, Reed, or maybe I just don't remember it. But since we're near the road, it should be on one of the bird watching loops."

"What if it's that area we were gawking at when we should have been paying attention to the kidnappers sneaking up on us?" Reed had a point. The refuge extended several miles past the areas for visitors. This pond could be in one of the private areas.

"I hope we haven't been traveling in a circle," I said.

He didn't say anything, but I felt his arm stiffen around me at the same time I heard tires creeping slowly along the road. We scooted close to a small tree and flattened again into the high, stiff brush. As much as the moonlight had helped earlier, I prayed a cloud would pass over and help us hide. A little thought, almost a wish, that we could get this over with even if it meant they found and killed us fluttered by occasionally as we hunkered there. Each time it did, I heard my dad's voice call my name in that warning tone I recognized so well.

"Face down!" Reed whispered urgently.

The vehicle sounded like a truck and was rolling so slowly I could scarcely hear it. I opened an eye and squinted as it rolled by. Only the parking lights glowed, but I could see enough to recognize it as one of the trucks issued to the rangers for their use. I didn't need to see the insignia on the door.

An overwhelming urge to jump up and run toward it must have made me stiffen because Reed's hand tightened. He moved his mouth to my ear and breathed so softly I almost thought I was imagining his words. "We don't know who the enemy is any more."

The build of one of the guys had resembled Willowby's, I remembered. Could he be mixed up in this whole thing?

Everything was just so insane! Even if it were someone here on the refuge, how had they known the connection between John and me? And what was the real connection anyway? Longtime friend, as I'd thought, or relative as the Blood Relations paperwork implied? I was sure Willowby was knowledgeable about wildlife and this refuge, but when did he have time to sneak off to Branson and either kidnap John or rummage through his house? Where would he have found these other people, including the couple who'd been with John at the Chamber of Commerce and had then been found dead? He was either a brilliant actor or, at the very least, wasn't the mastermind.

"Good point."

I jerked. "What?"

"You were rambling aloud again."

I no longer had the energy to do more than whisper back. "Plan?"

But he was no longer listening to me. I could feel him alert even though we weren't touching. Then I felt his hand on my back, lightly at first and then urgently. "When you get underwater," he whispered, "hold your breath and try to swim to the other side. Come up for air only when you must. Then crawl away and be quiet—no matter what you see. I'm hoping he thinks any splashing is just one of the ducks diving."

I had only seconds to process what he'd said before he shoved me with one fluid motion. I rolled down the small bank and slid into the cold water. My instinct to come up for air and get out of this icy pond wanted to override Reed's instructions. But I'd never heard such desperation in his voice before. Somehow I stayed beneath the surface and dogpaddled toward the opposite side, disrupting the ducks. With my last strength, I grasped handfuls of brush and pulled myself out of the water and onto the bank. Then I collapsed.

I don't know how long I lay there—it couldn't have been long—but I was losing the battle to be quiet and inconspicuous as my body shivered. The moon had disappeared beneath clouds, and I couldn't see Reed across the pond. Had he planned to follow me? We hadn't had time to coordinate our movements, so I decided to wait a minute or two longer for him to join me.

As I looked out at the water, hoping to see Reed emerge, two large hands grabbed my head, stuffed something into my mouth, then tied a handkerchief or something around my head. I hit out feebly, turning my head from side to side, but was about as effective as a young calf at branding time.

The hands then grabbed me by the shoulders and drug me on my stomach. Pain from the brush scraping my belly as it shredded my shirt and from my ankle bouncing over the rough ground nauseated me. We stopped for a moment and the man crouched down in front of me. The scarf around my head had slipped, allowing me to see. I stared into a pair of ranger's uniform boots and then let my eyes travel upward until I was staring into Willowby's eyes. The blackness that followed was welcome.

CHAPTER FORTY-EIGHT

In those old movies my mama liked to watch, the heroine faints gracefully and awakens in the handsome hero's arms. A full orchestra plays while the two gaze soulfully into each other's eyes, and the audience knows they will live happily ever after.

I, on the other hand, opened my eyes to muddy clothes plastered onto my shivering, aching body and a gag in my mouth. My hair had flopped over my eyes, but I could hear a struggle somewhere nearby— grunts and a cracking sound mixed with profanities. Despite the gag, I tried calling for Reed, only to be frustrated by my muffled, useless attempts.

"How close is back-up?" someone nearby whispered.

"Not close enough," another voice behind me muttered.

Had the police arrived? What had happened to Willowby? I tossed my head a little and tried to focus my eyes through the strands that wouldn't move, but all I could see were shapes off in the distance. My hands had been cuffed, I discovered, and my fingers weren't working at all, affected by the shivering that continued to wrack my body.

Something warm—a coat?—was dropped on me. I sniffed. Cigars. I didn't remember Willowby smoking anything. He must have a whole army of conspirators here—and Reed was on his own. Some partner I'd turned out to be!

"Is she awake?" The voice sounded familiar, but I couldn't place it.

"Shh!" another voice hissed nearby.

More scuffling in the distance spooked the ducks, and the night air filled with their flapping wings and squawking complaints.

"Come on out, girlie! Your lover—such as he is—awaits." The voice floated across the pond, and I recognized it as my captor. He'd found us after all! But, my befuddled brain realized, he was acting as if I wasn't already trussed up like a Sunday dinner chicken.

"Don't be shy! We're waiting for you. You don't want to miss the party!"

We? Did that mean he had even more people? Weren't there just the two of them and the woman? What had happened to her? If Willowby was Reed's captor, why wasn't he answering this guy? Weren't they still on the same team?

Someone crawling by bumped my foot and I groaned. "Shh!" the person hissed in my ear.

"Come out, come out, wherever you are!" the evil voice coaxed.

Surely this is a nightmare, I wished. Nightmares end with the dawn. But every muscle in my body hurt, telling me otherwise.

An eerie silence descended, freezing us in a tableau of pure evil. Just as the orchestra didn't play, neither did my life pass before my eyes. Instead, anger simmered deep inside. How dare some creepy guy kidnap us and wreak havoc on our bodies, minds, and lives! This malevolence had caused John to disappear. It had left me surrounded by thugs reeking of cigars, my ankle throbbing worse by the hour. And Reed?

I couldn't wait for the nightmare to end of its own accord. If I couldn't walk, talk, or crawl, I decided, I'd do what I could do—roll. It wasn't a rational decision, of course, or I would have thought about my gagged mouth and handcuffed hands. Those trivialities surfaced the minute I pushed off with my elbow. I knew for certain this had been the wrong decision when a bullet whizzed by very close. *Mama*, I thought, *see you soon.*

Then chaos erupted. The gun went off a second time. Someone yelped across the pond ahead of me. Someone grabbed my good leg and yanked me back. Bodies scrambled around me, hands grabbing me by the shoulders, pulling me over the brush and dirt. I squeezed my eyes shut. New sounds emerged—tires rolling fast, brakes squealing, doors slamming, feet racing toward us.

"Police!" a voice yelled.

"About time!" I muttered and, hearing distinct words rather than garbled sound, realized the gag had been removed from my mouth, although I wasn't sure how that had happened.

"About time!" My words echoed but sounded deeper.

"I already said that!" I mumbled. "Uncuff my hands and let's get out of here!"

A snicker grew into a laugh, one I was intimately acquainted with. Reed.

"We need paramedics over here," he called as he knelt down behind me and removed the handcuffs.

I rubbed my wrists, trying to restore the circulation. "Are you shot?" I asked.

"Not yet," he answered. Then he stood up and was replaced by another man.

"Ma'am," the new guy said, "how are you hurt?"

"My ankle," I said. "The left one."

He bent down and gently manipulated until he finally removed my sneaker and then my sock. I gritted my teeth to keep from yelling. He then probed it gently. "Can you put any weight on it at all?"

"No. I've been sort of hopping or dragging it."

"We'll need to take you to the ER and let a doctor look at it," he said. "I think it's a nasty sprain, but we need to check it out. Anything else?"

"No."

"All right. I'll be back in a minute."

I looked behind me but Reed had vanished. Another couple of police cars had arrived, their lights still flashing. Across the pond, I could see pinpoints of light crisscrossing the banks and adjoining fields as people searched the area; but I couldn't make out anyone familiar or understand what they were saying.

Soon the man who'd checked my foot returned with another man. "This may hurt a bit," he said. The men knelt on opposite sides of me, interlacing their arms behind my back and under my legs. "Now, just put your arms around our shoulders," the paramedic said just before they scooped me up off the ground. I bit my lip but still moaned as they lugged me across the uneven ground. Finally, they settled me into the back of an SUV. The first paramedic removed his jacket and rolled it up under my ankle before going around to the driver's door. The second one climbed in beside me, his arm around my shoulders to brace me.

"We're short on ambulances," he said. "I'm sorry this isn't more comfortable, but we needed the other one for the other victims."

"Victims? Is someone hurt? Reed? Where are we going?"

"We're taking you to the hospital, Ms. Janes."

"Willowby?"

No one answered. I could hear a siren somewhere. I was so tired. My eyelids began to droop. But before I could sleep, I felt the SUV slowing and turning. "Ouch! That hurts!"

"We need a gurney," someone said.

Getting me out was even more painful than getting me into the SUV. Inside, someone thanked my carriers and I felt a cool hand on my wrist. "How are we feeling, Ms. Janes?" a sweet voice asked.

"I don't know about you, but I'm feeling ready to end this nightmare and go home."

"Doctor wants her in number 3," someone said.

The next hour or so was a blur, with people coming and going and hands probing, questions coming at me.

"Are we going home yet?" I heard my voice ask. "I have two cats to feed." A chuckle.

"Soon, Ms. Janes. Just rest a bit longer right now. The doctor gave you a sedative, remember? He wants you to rest a bit longer before you leave us. Okay?"

I didn't bother to answer. I was too tired. Maybe later.

Someone walked into the room and asked, "Is she . . .?"

John? Was that John? No, I reminded myself. John was lost. But I knew that voice.

"She's resting, Detective Reed. We've given her something."

"Reed? I thought he shot you!" My voice sounded distant. Why doesn't someone answer me? I think I'll just doze a little while.

Wait! I can't sleep now! Why won't my eyes open? Are they glued shut? "Reed, you better answer me!" I mumbled. "I need to know what's going on!"

"What's she saying? Is she in pain?"

Who said that? I don't recognize that voice!

"Nah. She's just not wanting to miss out on anything. Never saw a bossier woman!"

"Just you wait!" I warned, stifling a yawn. "You're going to . . . well . . . I'll . . ." But all I heard was that familiar snicker as I drifted off.

CHAPTER FORTY-NINE

"You didn't interrupt Patience's vacation!"

"Not to worry, the attorney covering for her answered when I called after I retrieved your Jeep, so I didn't disturb Patience. In fact, Patience had already cleared our using her house, if we needed, with her staff; and you need a place to rest, one that is more private—not to mention more comfortable—than a motel. Besides, Felicia is coming into the office this morning anyway and agreed to let us in."

"But I've slept already," I protested. Then I yawned.

Reed laughed as he finished stuffing me into my Jeep—his car had been impounded by the authorities for processing—and climbed into the driver's side.

"I've slept already," I protested. Then I yawned.

Reed laughed.

"I'm hungry."

"I figured as much. So am I." He spotted a drive-through ahead. "A hamburger okay with you?"

"Cut the onions. And add a chocolate milkshake."

I heard him give my order, adding a hamburger and fries for himself, as I leaned my head against the passenger window to wait.

"I'd better write this moment down in my diary," Reed commented.

"Why?"

"You've been quiet for—let me check!" He made an exaggerated show of consulting his watch.

I merely rolled my eyes. Reed chuckled.

A young man soon appeared at the window with our order. Reed paid him, handed the food bags to me, pulled to the street, and flipped the blinker. The clock on the dashboard read 5:00 am.

"Quiet this time of the morning," I commented. "We humans can certainly cause chaos, can't we? Yet the wild critters wake up to glorious mornings like this one and go on about their lives."

Poised to turn onto the street, Reed looked over at me, seeming to read my mind. "Want to take our breakfast out there?"

"Absolutely!"

"You sure?"

"Why wouldn't I be? Did you forget my dad was a rancher? You climb back on the horse that throws you!"

Reed flipped the other blinker and turned toward the interstate. We didn't speak during the short drive to the refuge turn-off. He looked tired but alert and held himself a bit stiffer than usual, the result of sleeping in the reclining chair near my bed in the emergency room. The only thing he mentioned when I asked about his "war wounds" was that they had taped his ribs and patched up a few places.

"Should you be driving?"

Reed smiled. "Stop making me want to laugh, Sorrel. It hurts."

I loved this time of morning. The skies were streaked with red, dark orange, yellow, and pink with touches of pale lilac. My hands itched to grab a camera. The snow geese had already taken off from the pond, but a large number of the sandhill cranes were still hunkered down in the shallow water, each with one foot up and its face tucked under a wing. Reed turned the Jeep into a spot where we could watch them and turned off the ignition. Neither of us spoke, just dug into the bags and settled back to eat and let the refuge work its magic.

As always, the peaceful setting renewed me. "It's almost like the violence of last night hadn't happened."

He nodded, although I could see the shadows under his eyes and knew he was remembering how closely we had both been to death.

"Are you ready to fill me in on what exactly happened last night?" my hunger for information more intense than my need for food. I rewrapped the remaining half of my hamburger and placed it in the bag. Reed hadn't lost his appetite. He thoughtfully stuffed a French fry into his mouth and chewed.

Finally, he swallowed. "What could you see?" he finally asked.

"Not much. After I rolled into the pond, I was covered in mud and duck . . . well . . . I was a slimy mess. And it was dark, remember? The next thing I knew I was handcuffed and gagged."

A bark of laughter erupted from his mouth, causing him to grimace and clutch his side. Despite the pain it had caused him, his laughter was a welcome sound. I'd not realized how much I'd missed the joking, often obnoxious detective I'd come to . . . well . . . expect.

"I figured you'd get a laugh out of that—the handcuffs, the gag, or both?"

Wisely, he didn't answer. "Your friend showed up," he said.

"Alone?"

"Yeah."

"But . . . wasn't Willowby there?"

"Willowby? Why?"

"I saw him."

"You probably did. He came with law enforcement." Reed stuffed the last fry in his mouth and reached for the keys. "You still buckled in?" He hesitated. "We're really not supposed to be discussing too much, Sorrel. They still need statements from us because we weren't really in good enough shape to give them last night. Especially you." He started the Jeep and made a U-turn in the parking lot.

"I thought you'd been shot, Reed . . . it sounded like someone was hit."

He concentrated on the road far more than he needed. "It was your pal."

"Dead?"

"Nope. Might as well be."

"Injured?"

He gave me an exasperated glance. "We're not supposed to be discussing it."

"We're not . . . but I want to know why he 'might as well' be dead?"

"If I tell you, you have to act like you don't know from me." He thumped his hand on the steering wheel. "I can't believe I'm saying that. You do realize that I am an officer of the law? Just forget anything I've told you so far."

"So I just ask whoever interviews me why our creep might as well be dead?"

"Sorrel, why can't you—for once—just wait and talk to the officers?"

"Because I was there, covered in mud and . . . yuck . . . and with this ankle, and I have a right to know if the guy who is mostly responsible for it all is—"

"All right! But if you so much as breathe that I told you, you'll have worse than one ankle to worry about!"

"Detective Chris Reed! Are you threatening a member of the press?"

I waited for him to shrug, smile, and come back with one of his smart-alecky cracks; but he only continued to stare woodenly down the interstate.

"Please, Reed?" I asked softly.

Still staring at the road ahead, he finally spoke. "He chose to remain silent. Lawyered up—some high-powered lawyer. Big money." Now I understood his frustration. This guy wasn't going to talk. He wouldn't help us answer any of the questions that remained unless he was given full immunity.

I thought I'd muttered the expletive under my breath, but Reed clicked his tongue and looked over at me in mock shock. "Sorrel Janes! What would your mama do if she'd heard you right then?"

"Wash my mouth out with soap," I said. "Sorry. That was not only unprofessional but unnecessary. I'm just so tired and confused! Seems like every way we turn, we run into another road block."

"Let's go back to Patience's house," Reed said. I nodded. Neither of us spoke during the fifteen-minute drive. The events of the past several hours seemed surreal and the quiet felt comforting.

Reed turned into Patience's driveway, nodding toward the dark sedan parked in front of her house. "I may be wrong but I suspect we'll have company when we get inside. They'll separate us and talk to each of us separately."

"I know," I said.

He turned off the ignition, got out, came around the Jeep, opened my door, and told me to wait.

"You're not going to carry me, Reed—"

"Hardly," he snickered, "not after the way you've been chowing down."

He continued to laugh as he opened the back and retrieved a pair of crutches. He brought them around and, just barely keeping a straight face, asked, "Do you know how to use these?"

"I'll manage," I answered, my irritation clearly evident. Still, I took the hand he offered to help me out of the Jeep.

"Are you two going to come inside or wait out here and continue to insult each other?"

Sheriff Garcia had walked up during our exchange and, judging by his demeanor, wasn't amused. While I awkwardly hopped along to Patience's door, I tried to remember if I had ever seen him amused . . . or even affable.

CHAPTER FIFTY

Being questioned by Sheriff Garcia didn't give me the nervous flutters any more, but I could think of other things much more fun. His questions were straightforward, as always, and he still raised his eyebrow in a skeptical way whenever I answered. That look probably put fear in most people. I was just too tired for it to work on me.

He asked about the abduction and whether or not I had ever met the three people involved. Of course, I'd already anticipated that question. He also asked my opinion of why they had abducted me. It seemed an unusual question, but I supposed he was wondering if we'd had an ongoing feud with each other or something. I told him that, at the time, I'd wondered if the two men wanted to rob us, given the isolated spot.

Felicia Calderon, Patience's stand-in, had spotted the sheriff's car when she arrived at the office and had called in another colleague, a middle-aged man named Carl Brown, to sit in during the questioning. I began to wonder if my case was evolving into something more complicated that needed an attorney with more experience. Ms. Calderon seemed quite young when she let us into Patience's home and escorted us to her office. However, she delayed Sheriff Garcia's questioning until Mr. Brown arrived, which was only a few minutes after we entered the house.

Mr. Brown didn't say much at first, but when Garcia continued to ask some of the same questions, he called a halt to the interview. "I believe Ms. Janes has answered your questions. She is willing to speak with you again if you need her to clarify, but you can understand that she is not only exhausted but also in pain."

How had he guessed? Then I noticed that my hands were damp and trembling.

The sheriff rose, handed me his card, and instructed me to let him know if I remembered anything else. Then he left. I wondered how Reed had fared but figured he'd done better than I. After all, he was usually the one asking questions, so he would have known how to handle himself.

I spoke with Mr. Brown a few moments. He reminded me to call him if I were questioned again or had anything I needed to discuss regarding the case. By now, everything and everyone seemed sort of fuzzy. I needed to sleep. Thankfully, the small room I'd used before was only a few steps away.

The crutches made my arms sore. I'd used them once in high school when I'd hurt my leg in sports, but I'd never mastered them. I propped them against the wall, hopped to the bed, and lay down. Patience had draped a crocheted afghan onto the chair nearby, and I draped it over me and closed my eyes.

Then the images began. The gun in my face. The evil lurking behind my captor's eyes. The dead man in the field. My eyes popped open. Why hadn't Garcia asked about him? How did he fit into all of this? And why didn't they seem concerned? And no one had mentioned Willowby!

As I lay there, I replayed the whole interrogation I'd just had with Garcia. Something just wasn't right, but I couldn't settle on what it was. He'd been professional. He'd asked the right questions, although he omitted the dead man and . . . John. Why hadn't anyone mentioned John? When I'd been questioned by Garcia before, he'd always seemed skeptical about my "missing friend," as he sarcastically referred to John.

A light tap on the door interrupted my meandering. "Yes?" I called.

Reed stuck his head around the door. "I figured you'd be passed out by now," he said.

"Can't shut my brain down. Come on in."

He stepped in and walked over to the bed. I gestured toward the chair.

When he didn't act like he was going to say anything, I asked, "Have you heard anything about your truck yet?"

"No. I appreciate your letting me use the Jeep."

Silence stretched a bit. He seemed awkward, which wasn't like Reed. Sarcastic, insulting, teasing, confident. Sure! Awkward? This was new. When the silence again threatened to stretch indefinitely, I asked, "Did they mention the guy we saw at the refuge that day? Or John?"

"They didn't. But I asked Garcia. He seemed surprised. Doesn't seem to think that guy is anything more than a random act of violence. And John? I think he had forgotten about him completely."

That didn't feel right! Surely an unsolved crime would be listed as that on the books. He wouldn't just forget about it. "What's your take?"

"I think he was dishing out a load of . . . lies," Reed said. "I'm not sure but he may suspect you still, and I'm so closely connected with you that he feels he should be close-mouthed."

"Whatever for? When I saw the guy in my camera, we contacted law enforcement."

"Sorrel . . ." Reed wasn't looking at me. "I'm getting a weird feeling here."

"What do you mean?" Suddenly he couldn't seem to get anything out of his mouth. "Spit it out! I'm tired and impatient and we've spent—"

"All right!" Reed got up and walked to the foot of the bed. " My take on this is that Garcia is trying to get the guy they have in custody to talk by negotiating a deal and he'll try the same thing when they find the other man and woman who were involved."

"What do you mean?"

"I mean I think he may be trying to get our captors to blame things on us."

I sat up and glared. "No way! This isn't the 1950s, Reed. The science has to agree with their story."

My voice had risen and Reed put his finger to his lips. He cocked his head and listened for a moment, then walked to me, leaned over, and whispered. "If you're not going to sleep, how about we get out of here?" Then, more loudly than usual, he said, "I could use a cup of coffee and a piece of pie."

I nodded. Then wordlessly, I got up, straightened the bed comforter and pillows, put on my shoe, and ran my fingers through my hair.

We stepped out the door into Patience's office. The woman working on a computer at the desk glanced up casually.

"We're going for coffee and pie at Denny's," Reed told her. "Later." She nodded.

After pulling out of the driveway, Reed turned toward the interstate.

"I thought Denny's was the other direction," I said.

"It is. I'm probably paranoid, but I wanted to fan our trail . . . just in case."

"You're definitely paranoid," I told him. "So where are we actually headed?"

"Owl Bar and Grill. It's noisy enough to cover what we say."

The Owl Bar and Grill was busy as usual, so the waitress had to lead us through the maze of tables into one of the back rooms. When I sat across from Reed, he drawled, "Aw, honey, we're not fighting!" and sat on the bench beside me. Our waitress grinned and handed us a menu. Reed winked at her. "Give us a minute?" She laughed and walked away.

I waited until she was out of sight and turned on him. "Just when I was beginning to trust you, Reed, you—"

He leaned forward as if to nuzzle my neck and whispered, "Just play along with me, Sorrel. As I said, I think we're being set up here. I should have thought of it sooner."

"So the police have found—"

"Shh! I don't think so. Garcia is a young hotshot. I think he wants to make a name for himself with this case," he whispered.

"But they have the guys—"

"Just one. The gal and the other guy—"

"—are still missing."

"And I think Garcia is offering him a deal to get him to talk before his lawyer arrives. He can't question him; but he can talk to him about his options, possible jail time, and ways to mitigate his sentence."

”With a deal that implicates us?”

“That’s the feeling I’m getting. So far, however, our kidnapper has continued to do nothing more than listen. But who knows what might happen when his lawyer gets here from Santa Fe.”

Our waitress returned, and Reed ordered a couple of coffees and a green chili cheeseburger. Then he turned to me. “Do you want one too?” I shook my head. “She’ll have fries,” he told her.

When she left, I turned to him. “What about Willowby?”

Reed looked confused. “Willowby? What about Willowby?”

“Your captor, Reed! Surely you noticed!”

“How? Our captors wore those funky masks—”

“—but his body, Reed! He’s the same size!” I took a breath, held up my hand, and counted out my points. “Plus, he was there when I found the body, he visited me in Saddle Gap, he was there last night—”

“Of course, he was there, Sorrel. He’s in charge of the refuge. Besides, Willowby? He’s the least possible—”

“—which gives him the perfect cover!” I saw our waitress heading over with coffee cups.

“Cream?” she asked.

“No, thank you,” I told her. Reed just shook his head and smiled. I could see he had already made another conquest.

“You food will be right out,” she told him.

After she left, Reed took his time sipping the coffee, looking around the room. Then he leaned toward me and spoke barely above a whisper. “Things are not always as they seem, Sorrel.”

“Do you think I’m an idiot, Chris Reed?” I ground out, careful to keep my voice down but moving enough so that I could meet his eyes.

He stared at me for a long moment. Then he again spoke right in my ear. “No, Sorrel. I think you have been through a huge nightmare—certainly not your first—and you are the most loyal friend I have ever known. John probably knows how lucky he is, but I'm still learning. I’m sorry. I don’t mean to patronize you. What I should have said is that there are things I can’t reveal to you right now. But I’m asking you to trust me, and I’ll fill you in completely when I can.”

He straightened up and sipped his coffee. I followed suit, and we sat quietly until our food arrived. I wasn’t really hungry. It hadn’t been that long since we’d had the hamburgers and fries. But Reed happily plowed into his as if he were making up for the hours we'd not eaten—and maybe he was. I nibbled on a French fry and sipped the coffee.

"Have you heard anything more about this Blood Relations outfit?" Reed asked before he took a big bite.

I jumped. "Not really. Not since I got the message that they'd been hacked. I almost forgot about them, to tell the truth. Some crazy joke, sending me some sort of crazy notification that John is my father! I know my dad—not that John wouldn't make someone a super father."

Reed continued chewing. I waited. Then I leaned in and whispered, "You know something, don't you?"

He swallowed and took a drink of coffee. Letting his eyes scan the room, he finally leaned down toward his cup and spoke so softly I wasn't completely convinced I was hearing him right. "His credit card receipts show a payment to them." He took another bite without the slightest indication he'd dropped a bomb.

"I can't believe it! Maybe someone stole his card—"

"I checked that already."

"Why would he—"

"Remember that note his lawyer had? About his looking into something he'd been thinking on for a long time?"

"This is just crazy!" I pushed my untouched fries away and gulped the coffee, scorching my mouth.

"Is something wrong with your fries?" The waitress had reappeared, the coffee pot in her hand. Reed held out his cup for a refill.

"I'm sorry," I said. "I thought I could eat just now, but my leg is hurting and I guess the painkillers have robbed me of my appetite." I smiled. "Could I just have a take-away box?"

"Of course you can."

I turned to Reed as soon as she was out of sight. "Do you think this Blood Relations thing has something to do with John's disappearance?"

"It seems a logical conclusion, Sorrel. John had plans to be here—ones he instigated himself—and he not only stood you up, but he didn't leave his own place well cared for. You said yourself he'd have told his neighbor, made sure the cat was cared for, and certainly let you know if he'd changed his mind."

"This whole thing just hasn't sounded right," I agreed. "It feels like we're in the middle of something even more elaborate than a kidnapping ."

Reed concentrated on his coffee for a bit. He seemed to be mulling something over. Finally, he glanced around the room and said, "I'm going to the men's room. When the waitress returns, will you have her leave the check?"

The waitress brought the check and my take-out box and insisted on taking my credit card to the register for me. I'd just finished signing the credit card slip when Reed returned.

"Hey!" he said. "I—"

"My treat this time," I said. "But I'd appreciate help getting the box to the car."

We threaded our way through the bar, and Reed stepped ahead of me to open the door. "I've been meaning to tell you," he began as we stepped outside.

But I interrupted when I didn't see my Jeep where we'd left it. "Reed?"

"Relax. I had a friend bring us this guy." He started toward a dark sedan. "Figured it would be easier for you to get in and out of."

I didn't say anything until we were inside the car. "Now tell me the truth or I'm opening this car door and calling the police to report mine stolen."

Reed threw back his head and laughed, a loud, infectious laugh that was hard not to join in with. I waited until he sobered. "Okay. The truth is that I wanted to have your Jeep looked over for tracking devices. I'd do the same with mine, only it's in police custody just now. It has to be more than coincidence that we've been so visible."

"I've thought that too," I finally admitted. "You switched keys in the bathroom? And that's why you ordered food! You were stalling until someone arrived. I couldn't imagine how you could be hungry already! "

He started the engine and smirked. "You're right on!"

"Reed, sometimes I could just—"

His laugh interrupted.

I looked over at him but just as I did, I remembered my mama saying that she'd fallen in love with my dad's laugh, not his good looks.

CHAPTER FIFTY-ONE

I wasn't sure why the thought of falling in love for any reason popped into my head. I certainly wasn't feeling romantic—especially about Reed. My close call and John's continued disappearance just had me feeling a little sentimental, that's all. I didn't have time for such nonsense just now.

Besides, law enforcement wasn't exactly an ideal occupation for a mate. The most attractive thing about Kevin had been that his job as an oil executive was demanding enough to keep him happy and allow me to pursue my own career in journalism. I also had to concede that our jobs had also been a source of conflict when I was out chasing stories all hours and he wanted me on his arm for a social event.

"Want to take another run to the refuge?" Reed interrupted my thoughts.

"I love the refuge but don't we have other things to do just now?"

He didn't answer, just turned down the highway. "It's a good place to talk," he said.

"So now you're finally willing to talk?"

Reed pointed to a flock of cranes grazing in some farmer's field. "I wonder if that poor guy has enough grain left to sell after those birds eat there," he said. "I heard once that birds eat more than their body weight daily. Can you imagine how much those big birds can eat?"

"Your undercover assignment?" I prompted.

Reed didn't say anything, but his body language told me he was on alert.

"How did they select you? First, you're a detective with the police department of Saddle Gap. Then after you solve that case, instead of getting promoted and sitting back on your laurels, you take a lesser job as a sheriff's department flunkee."

That caught him. "Hey, now," he said, "don't you think *flunkee* is a little derogatory?"

I ignored him. "Then they select you for some mysterious undercover assignment, complete with a sexy, territorial chick—"

"Whoa! Sexy? Territorial? Why didn't I notice that?"

I had the distinct impression Reed was enjoying this conversation way too much. "You're not going to change the subject that easily."

"Want to stay outside the refuge or go on the loop?"

"How about stopping by to see Ranger Willowby?" I countered.

He didn't try to hide his wide grin. "He's not there."

"And you would know because . . . ?"

His cell buzzed just as we passed ranger headquarters. He reached for it as we turned into the gate and stopped. "Reed," he said and listened as he pulled his badge from his pocket and flashed it at the lady manning the gate. She waved us on.

Reed pulled through but stopped just inside the gate. "When?" he asked. He listened for a minute.

"How?" I could tell he wasn't liking what he heard.

"Did he say anything?" He muttered something under his breath. "Okay . . . Yeah, I'll tell her. She's with me."

He glanced over at me. "Let's drive up to the pond so we won't be in the road obstructing people." I didn't remind him that there weren't any others around that we could obstruct. Clearly, what he'd heard hadn't been anything he'd wanted to hear. Likely, I wouldn't want to hear it either.

Neither of us spoke as he drove to the pond, parked, and turned off the engine. He leaned his head on the steering wheel for a few moments before finally saying, "Our kidnapper is dead."

"Dead? How—"

"Hung in his holding cell."

"But how's that possible?"

"Apparently, he was either afraid to go into the general population and hanged himself or someone got to him and hanged him."

"Wouldn't that be impossible? Didn't they take his belt and things away? What was he hanging by?"

"His shirt."

I crossed my arms and stared out the window. "I guess we should be relieved not to have to testify about our ordeal," I said. "At least not until they find the other two. Did he tell them anything about why they kidnapped us?"

"He asked for an attorney and clammed up."

"Of course he did!" I unclasped my seatbelt and opened the door. "I don't recall anyone telling us his name."

"His current name didn't raise any eyebrows. He was simply Tom Smith. But when they ran his prints, they came up with a different name. He'd served in the military and had been working as a mercenary over the years. His name at that time was Michael Stevens."

"Isn't that—"

"—one of the names on your family tree? Yes, it is."

"Did they double check—"

"The family tree? Hacked. None of the people mentioned are related to you, Sorrel. Apparently, he wanted you to think so. But an interesting fact did surface. There's some connection to John's ancestors tangled with the Stevens. They're still checking that out."

"I need to walk," I said, flung my foot out, and winced as I hung onto the door. "I forgot."

I expected Reed to laugh but he didn't. Instead, he hopped out, came around the car, and gently lifted my injured foot back. "I think it's time—past time—for a painkiller," he said.

"I don't want painkillers! They'll put me to sleep! What I want is a break once in a while! We have things to do—things to discuss—people to find!" A tear escaped onto my cheek. I wiped it away with an angry jab and glared at him.

"Tell you what," Reed cajoled. "Do you have them with you?" I nodded. "Capsules?" I nodded again. " Only take one. We'll talk fast, and then you can sleep."

I crossed my arms. "Forget the pills! I can handle a little . . . well . . . a lot of pain. What I need right now is information! Talk."

"It's police business, Sorrel. And you're a journalist, at least, you were in the past and you still have connections. Unfortunately, journalists, current or former, have a reputation for being nosey and interfering, and you particularly are one with—"

"—a big mouth?"

"—a personal stake in things." He looked off then stared into my eyes. He sighed. "You can never—I mean on fear of death—repeat what I tell you until this is released to the public. And even then you can't let anyone know I told you! Your word of honor?"

"Aren't you being overly dramatic, Reed?"

He put his hand on the key but I stopped him. "Okay, okay!"

"Word of honor?"

"My word."

He sighed. "I'm sorry. I'm so frustrated and I'm taking it out on you."

"And I'm being . . . the same as you."

We both sat silently and just stared at the scenery in front of us for a bit. The cranes and snow geese ate, flew up, flapped, and landed again. They were gorgeous creatures, funny, sometimes awkward, and engaging. "Soothing," I murmured. "No wonder mankind loves to watch natural critters. We think we're so above them, but they could teach us a thing or two."

I heard Reed take a deep breath. "I was approached to go undercover for two reasons: I've become fairly fluent in what we call broken Spanish—local idioms with some of the pure language worked in—and because of the . . . case I'd just worked involving the Mexican cartel—your case."

I didn't realize I'd been holding my breath. I breathed out, staring ahead. "So much for our being open with each other." Then I added, "So I still have a case?"

"Everything was need-to-know, and with your past association with the media . . . Sorrel, the long and short is . . . they suspect the cartel is involved in the death of several prominent ranchers in the state and in the other states along our southern border. It's a huge project with several agencies involved. Everyone is on a need-to-know basis, so I just know some of it."

"So we may have been kidnapped because of your undercover work? That doesn't make sense, Reed. You weren't even here. Did they follow you here? And who is the dead man I saw across the field? Is he one of them too? Do you think John got taken—"

"Sorrel, take a breath. I can't answer all of these questions."

"You said the girl—"

"—is my undercover partner. Yes. One of them."

"So where have you been, Reed? El Paso?"

"Some of the time."

"Why didn't she come with you here?" When he didn't answer, it began to dawn on me. "You came here because of work! You used me, Reed, as a cover!"

"It's not like you think, Sorrel."

"Of course not, Reed. It's never like I think! Here I am thinking we're friends, that we care enough for our friends to be loyal, not deceitful!" I crossed my arms. "I think I'd like to go back to . . . a hotel or somewhere—and I want my Jeep!"

"It's being swept—"

"—for bugs! Right. And I'm running for governor! I want my Jeep, Reed."

"You have to listen to me, Sorrel."

"I don't have to do anything with you! First, you lie to me about coming here with that letter. By the way, is it a fake too? And then you pretend to be worried about John. Are you behind his disappearance?"

"Shut up, Sorrel. You're angry and you probably have a right to be mad, but you're just rambling now. You can't believe all this garbage you're spouting."

I scooted over as far as possible against the passenger door. "I believe you've been playing me—all of us—for the sake of this undercover operation. Were you laughing all the way to Branson? Was that just a ruse to keep me out of everyone's way? Where's John, Reed? "

Reed yanked the keys from the ignition, unclipped the seatbelt, and opened the door. "I'm going to make a phone call," he said. "I'd appreciate it if you'd try to tame that nasty temper of yours until I get back in the car. When I do, I think I can answer some of your questions!"

I watched him walk a short distance along the front of the field, talking into his cell as he walked. He clicked it off after a few moments, stared out at the field for a while, and then turned around and walked back to the car. I looked out my window, pretending to ignore him.

"All right," he said when he got back in the car and slammed the door. "I'll tell you what I know but only on one condition!"

"What's the condition?" I couldn't resist asking.

"That you try to control that temper of yours. I always thought crime reporters were more professional."

"The other crime reporters haven't been kidnapped, half starved, injured, and dunked in a pond filled with mud and duck poop! I expect they might lose their cool in those circumstances too!"

Was that a chuckle? My fingers itched with the urge to claw his eyes out! Reed knew well enough to turn it into a cough. Then he grew serious. "First, the young man you found was an undercover officer."

"You knew all along who he was? How could you—"

"Sorrel, I didn't know him. I only just found out he was one of ours."

"Who killed him? Why?"

Reed chose his words carefully. "We don't know who killed him, although we have our suspicions."

"Was it our kidnappers?"

"Possibly. The general thought is that he came upon John's abduction and broke his cover."

"You said the Mexican drug cartel, Reed. They wouldn't have any reason to hurt John!"

"Sorrel, the cartel operates through several online companies."

I could feel the foreboding building within me. "Don't tell me!"

"Yes, Blood Relations is one of them. I don't know if it was before they were hacked, but I suspect so. You're right, though. They wouldn't have had a reason to hurt John, unless maybe because of—"

"—his association with me? Do they still have a contract or something out for me?"

Reed answered carefully. "I don't have confirmation about whether or not the contract has been cancelled."

CHAPTER FIFTY-TWO

There are moments when you just know that further talk will only exacerbate a horrible moment. So we drove to town in a silence that weighed heavy enough to make breathing an effort. I looked out at the refuge, a place that had given me such beauty and glorious happiness as well as horror, terror, and despair. I mentally violated Dickens: It was the best of places, it was the worst of places.

"Did you say something?" Reed asked.

"No."

His cell phone rang, and he answered it, his voice distant and formal. My whole world reeked of betrayal and distrust. Reed had recognized that name—Blood Relations—but had never even flickered an eyelash. Yes, I'd known he couldn't share department details with me. But I'd trusted that he'd not let me wander out here in total darkness. We could have died together in that nasty old building . . . or crawling through brush in the dark.

Reed interrupted my thoughts with a comment. "Sheriff Garcia needs to see us at the police station. I told him we were heading in that direction to pick up your Jeep."

I nodded, staring straight ahead.

We turned left and passed the Owl Bar and Grill, then on to I-25 and Socorro. It was a ten-minute drive at most. I pulled the last of my inner strength together.

At the police station, Reed held the door as I awkwardly maneuvered my crutches. "This way," he said, pointing to the second door on the right and stepped past me to tap on it. At a brusque "come," he opened it and waited again for my slow progress.

The first person I saw was Ranger Willowby. No, it wasn't Ranger Willowby. It was someone who looked much like him. This version of Willowby wore a well-fitted suit which made him look slimmer. Gone was the shaggy haircut and bumbling air. He could have been an executive, standing up to shake my hand. Or—and I had no idea from where that thought surfaced—an FBI agent!

I extended my hand. He shook it then indicated that I should sit. His eyes—if I could trust my instincts, and I wasn't sure how trustworthy they were any more—held remorse and kindness.

Once seated, I looked across the table at Sheriff Garcia and a couple of other people I didn't recognize. A dark-haired woman in a slim pants suit looked vaguely familiar. The unknown man, probably FBI or from a similar agency, asked if we wanted coffee. I shook my head. Reed sat beside me, shaking his head also.

The room took a surreal tone as the meeting started. I felt like I was in a bubble, watching the expressions and hearing the hum of voices but not really taking much of it in. I shouldn't have swallowed that pain pill, I decided; but I'd been so angry with Reed and I knew I needed the strength to get through the next few hours and then get home.

The new man appeared to be in charge. He started off with introductions. Mrs. Willowby wasn't a missus at all; and although she held a slight resemblance to the woman she'd portrayed, her new professional attitude made her very different. Both Ranger and Mrs. Willowby had replaced the regular ranger and his wife, who had taken a six-month leave to care for ailing parents. Due to the sparse population in the area, their story had been easier for people to accept. It also fit into the operation concerning the cartel; they were not too close but close enough to help with ongoing investigations.

They confirmed what Reed had already told me: The young man whom I had discovered dead in the ditch was also undercover. No one was yet sure, but the consensus was that while conducting routine surveillance, he'd come upon something he shouldn't have seen. The bullet in the back of his head came from a gun with a silencer. The investigation of his murder continued. I glanced at Reed but didn't react. He and I had come to the same conclusion, but I knew better than to mention that we had been discussing this topic.

"Ms. Janes?" I looked at Willowby. He'd obviously spoken to me more than once. The whole room held that air of waiting.

"Yes, sir."

"I'm sorry for your loss."

The words echoed then plowed into my chest, making it hard for me to breathe. I squeezed my hands together in my lap so tightly that my nails cut into my palm. That, at least, helped me know this was real and not some horrible nightmare.

"I'm afraid my ears aren't working as well as they should," I finally told him. "The doctor put drops in and cotton balls. Would you remind repeating what was just said?"

Willowby looked at me kindly. This new Willowby was much more likeable than the old one had been, although he'd been endearing in his own pompous, bumbling way. "We need you to make a formal identification at the morgue."

"I can do that," Reed said.

Then I knew. John. My friend. My confidant. My anchor.

I took a deep breath and looked into Willowby's eyes—or whoever he was, and he'd probably told me earlier—and answered firmly, "Yes, I'll do it. And thank you. It truly is a great loss." Then I added, "But first, I need to know what happened and why."

"That's still under investigation."

We walked to the small morgue. Only Reed came in with me. John was lying on a gurney, covered by a sheet. His face showed the torment he'd suffered, but he was beautiful to me. I reached out and touched his hair then turned. I heard, rather than saw, Reed covering his face again with the sheet. I felt his hand on the small of my back; and in spite of how angry I was with Reed, I so appreciated his quiet strength.

We stepped out of the room into the hall where the others waited.

"It's John," I told them. "Who did this? Why was he tortured? He certainly had no connection to the cartel! Was he alive when I arrived? "

"We know he had no affiliation to the cartel. Time of death hasn't been determined, but we think it was fairly recent."

I waited. When no one seemed inclined to speak, I asked again, "Who tortured him? Why?"

Finally, Willowby—after locking eyes with someone else in the group—replied. "Ms. Janes, your John"—I could have hugged him for saying it that way, and my cavalier attitude of the person he'd been playing died at that instant—"we suspect he was kidnapped by a couple who gained his trust after he arrived here. They may have met him in Socorro or maybe disguised themselves as refuge volunteers. They handed him off to another couple, confidence game types, who were drowned. Indications are the woman and man involved in your abduction, who have vanished off the radar, may also have been involved with him. All of this was masterminded by the man who tortured him. We do not know for sure yet what John would not tell them. That man has hung himself in jail. So you see that we have a large number of unanswered questions. But we will find the answers. And when we do, I promise that you will know."

I nodded and held out my hand. He shook it. "Thank you. Please be sure that I'll not share that information with anyone in the press. But I did promise someone the hacking story behind Blood Relations?"

Willowby nodded. "Would you allow us to handle that one? If you'll give me the name of the person and the particulars, we can give some information that will be a scoop without harming our investigations."

"Thank you again." I looked at Reed. "I don't know who is in charge of John's—"

"You are, Sorrel."

I swallowed. "He always said cremation." I turned to Reed. "I need to go home."

CHAPTER FIFTY-THREE

"Would it be too big an imposition to give me a ride home?" Reed asked. "Your Jeep is processed, but my truck seems to be taking longer. As I suspected early on, you had a simple tracking device planted on your Jeep."

"I had no idea. I wonder when they did that!"

"Early on," Reed said. "Could even have been when we left it by that pond when I arrived and took you to breakfast in my truck."

"What will you do for a vehicle when you get home?" We were just going through the paces. Both of us knew I wouldn't really be able to drive the distance with my ankle injured.

"My old jalopy truck. I'll have Jose give me a ride from your place to home, so I can leave the Jeep there."

"Okay." I stopped at the front desk and asked for my keys. It took a few moments while I showed ID and filled out paperwork. Reed stood quietly by.

He held the door for me while I hopped past, careful not to bump into anything with the crutches. "I don't know what to say, Sorrel—"

"Then don't say anything," I said quietly. "I hope that didn't sound rude, Reed. I didn't mean it that way. I feel your sympathy and it is a comfort to me. But I have so many unanswered questions that need answers. No one has even yet told me the cause of death. Why?"

We'd reached the Jeep and I'd clicked the key fob to unlock it before handing him the keys. He leaned around me to open the door and took the crutches from me, storing them in the back seat along with a satchel I'd only just noticed. At least he didn't try to help as I lifted my leg with my hands and awkwardly settled in the passenger seat. He walked around to the driver's side, checked to see if I had belted in, and started the engine.

Reed pulled onto the street. He finally spoke again as we sat behind a couple of cars at the stop light. "They'll do the autopsy first, of course. And you saw as well as I that different forms of . . . coercion had been practiced." The light changed. He started up and flipped on his blinker. "Maybe . . ."

"I need to know what you know. I have a right to know, Reed. Even though I know that paperwork from that company was lying and that John wasn't my father, he was my good friend."

"Strangulation," he finally said. "They'll need the autopsy to confirm it; but from the signs, John was strangled."

I gritted my teeth and held my breath. Had he been frightened?

"The investigation is still ongoing, Sorrel. And when I find out, I'll let you know. I promise you. I know you're angry with me and don't trust me, but I won't lie to you or cover up anything about John."

I nodded but remained silent.

"I'm going to hold you to that," I finally said. "No more secrets?"

"No more secrets, Sorrel."

"Reed? I wouldn't say I don't trust you. I have a fast mouth when I get angry."

I heard a muffled chuckle.

"Reed? You do realize they didn't address our kidnapping?"

"Yes."

"Is it related to John? A final method to get him to tell them what they wanted?"

"I hope not."

Reed pulled into a gas station a couple of blocks further down the street. "I'll fill the tank before we start back home," he said as he eased up to a gas pump. I reached in my purse, but he waved my hand away and got out.

As we headed out of Socorro, Reed turned on the radio. The stations were already playing Christmas music. I started to tell him what I thought of that, but then I remembered how mad . . . and sad . . . and tired I felt. I leaned back against the headrest and dozed off.

I felt Reed tuck his jacket around me and thought I heard him whisper, "I loved him too, Sorrel." But then I've always been a big dreamer.

Two pairs of eyes watched the Jeep pull out. "Do you think they noticed us?" the man asked.

"They didn't seem to notice anything." She tossed her long black hair and smoothed her hand down her mini skirt over her now much slimmer thighs. "Why would they recognize us anyway? We've lost at least thirty years, Stan!" She giggled. "I'm glad to be rid of those wrinkles and my granny clothes—not to mention that wig!"

"I'm glad you lost them too!" He grinned suggestively and wiggled his brows at her. "When we get out of this backwater state, let's drink to a job well done!"

"Not so well done. What about her—the 'horsey' one? She and her lawman got away. I didn't know the whole plan, but—"

"—and we don't know the whole plan," he interrupted. "All of us were working on a part of the whole. You and I, at least, didn't end up in the lake like some of the others."

"I guess being watchdogs and eavesdropping was safer. But next time I hope the Big Guy has something more glamorous for us!" she complained. "I really got tired of this one. If I hear another bird in the next fifty years, it will be too soon! Give me Phoenix or Vegas!"

"You didn't get tired of the cash. And I doubt he'd appreciate you calling him by that name."

She rolled her eyes. "Who cares? Are you going to tattle?" She pouted a moment then checked them to see if any of her new perfectly polished nails were chipped. "I'm still not sure why snowbirds think it's so much fun to travel around in those huge motorhomes and do volunteer work—or work for almost nothing."

He inwardly sighed. This chick was hot and he'd enjoyed working with her; but like the others he'd partnered with, she was boring and vain. She was also a never-ending chatterbox. He clicked on the radio as he entered the I-25 ramp and sped toward Albuquerque. Per instructions, they would part at the rental car agency and pick up tickets to their destinations.

"Do you ever wonder why we do what we do?" she asked.

He sighed. "I thought we already covered this ground. The M-O-N-E-Y."

"No, I mean . . . what possible reason did we have for luring that old artist into our motorhome and holding him there?"

"Need to know! And I don't need to know. Neither do you, if you know what's good for you."

That shut her up for a while. He began to relax and enjoy the scenery. Interstates were never this straight or had so little traffic in Jersey.

"Well, if you ask me, he didn't seem like such a hot commodity." She unwrapped a stick of gum and popped it in her mouth.

"Because maybe he was a personal hit, you idiot! I'm not sure who we were working for, but I do know they wanted him first and then the girl! Maybe they planned to ransom her. She was a hotshot crime reporter whose investigations helped make some powerful enemies."

He glanced toward her. She sat back, smacking her gum, with a satisfied smirk on her face.

Oh, God! What had he done! She'd been goading and pushing him just for this, and he'd finally slipped up—and someday, when she needed an ace, she'd use it. Then he would be in the same shape as that poor artist stiff. Stiff. The very word sent chills down his spine. People out there with enough money to set up this elaborate operation usually had long memories.

CHAPTER FIFTY-FOUR

We arrived back in Saddle Gap just two days before Thanksgiving. Flash gave me a haughty glare when I peeked into my bedroom, but Van leaped off the bed and started a frenzy of weaving through my legs. I scooped him up, talking softly and burying my face in his fur, which caused Flash to change her mind and pad daintily over for her share of attention.

During our reunion, Reed quietly unloaded my luggage in the living area, called Jose, and waited. It had been a quiet trip as neither of us was inclined to speak. I offered him something hot to drink, finally breaking the hours of silence, albeit awkwardly.

"No, thanks," he said. His phone binged and he looked, down. "Jose is outside. I should get to my place." He then walked to the door and paused. "Will you be at Teri and Jose's for Thanksgiving?"

"I'm not sure." I avoided looking at him.

I decided not to go to Thanksgiving dinner, even though I knew Teri would be disappointed. I begged off, asking her forgiveness, because I was so far behind on preparing for Black Friday. Jose arrived that evening with two plates filled with all sorts of food and an entire pie. "Please take it," he pleaded. "And please take a bite while I take a picture with my phone."

"You're joking!"

"No, I'm not. I don't dare return home without proof that you ate."

I stared at him a moment before a smile pulled at the edge of my mouth. I lifted the foil cover, pulled a fork out of the drawer, and stabbed a green bean. I lifted it to my mouth and smiled into the phone. But just as he started to snap the shot, the bean dropped onto my chest. Both of us froze and then burst out laughing.

Jose snapped a photo and cheered.

"You go back to your sweet wife and those twins," I told him. "Tell Teri she's not working all day tomorrow!"

"Right!" he groaned, heading toward the door. "I hope you have a miracle in mind to make her follow your orders."

Black Friday proved hugely profitable for the artisans who'd consigned their goods to my shop. Teri's uncle brought his cart to the parking lot and sold tamales, tacos, and burritos. The twins set up a hot chocolate stand just inside the doorway. None of us had a chance to exchange more than a quick word all day.

When the day ended, I hugged Teri and bustled her and the twins off to Jose. "You can't continue hiding out!" she said.

John's will arrived the following Monday by certified mail. I signed the receipt and handed it to the mail carrier, who held out yet another letter. John's name in the return address, care of his attorney, made me pale.

I lay them both on the table beside my comfy chair and walked over to the cupboard. "I need a cup of tea," I told the felines. They raised their heads at the sound of my voice, saw nothing edible in my hands, and resumed dozing.

A couple of consignees from the senior center had things well in hand when I stepped into the shop. "I've got some business to see to," I told them. "Buzz me if you have an emergency."

I settled down in my chair, the cinnamon from my tea mug tickling my nose. Both cats rose and arranged themselves, one behind my head on the chair cushion that remained conformed to a cat's shape and one on my feet.

I lifted the letter and held it against my heart. Then I slit open the top and read:

> *Dear Sorrel,*
>   *If you're reading this, then my plans didn't go as I'd wished. Makes me think of Steinbeck's words*

about the "best laid plans of mice and men." (See, I am sort of literary after all.)

When I received a letter from a company called Blood Relations asking for a saliva sample a few months ago, I thought at first it was a hoax. Apparently, you'd asked me to participate, as you were searching for your father. That was odd, as your father was dead and you knew who he was. Then I wondered if you were researching a story and wanted me to participate. I don't know if you remember my call that night, but I asked a few vague questions and soon realized you knew nothing about this company or the request. After I hung up, I almost tossed it in the wastebasket. Instead, I put it in a drawer.

Every time I passed that drawer, I thought of it— and of your sweet mama.

Yes, your sweet mama. We shared a secret, she and I; and I'm only sharing it now because she is gone . . . and, I suppose, so am I.

Did she tell you much about her childhood? I know she mentioned that the aunt who left you the place there in Saddle Gap had fostered her. In fact, she'd actually grown up in foster homes here in the state of Missouri. So did I. We ended up in a miserable home with two other children. The couple was able to show a presentable front to the authorities, but life was abusive behind the scenes. They were quick to slap, punch, and hit and the language was foul. We cooked, cleaned, and lived in quiet terror. Your mother was feisty (so now you know where you inherited that gene) and was most often the victim of physical abuse. She never cried in their presence. I must have fallen in love with her while washing blood away and holding ice cubes to her black eyes. I think she looked on me as her savior. Either way, we survived there several years.

The county finally stepped in and sent all of us to new homes. She went to a farm family by the name of

Stevens. When the woman's family came to visit, they adopted your mother. I was old enough to be put in a sort of halfway house to graduate high school as I only had a year left.

Thus, we lost track of each other until—several years later—we bumped into each other in the University of Missouri library. She'd transferred there from a junior college, and I was finishing my master's degree and teaching freshman classes. How small is our world!

Before I could ask her out, she regaled me with stories about a young soldier she'd met. It was apparent that she had fallen in love. (He was your father, by the way, not I.) We rekindled our friendship, but she married your dad soon after graduation and moved away. Our contact became Christmas cards, where she'd tuck in a photo of you occasionally. The last letter told me of your father's death and her recent cancer diagnosis. She asked if I could keep an eye out in case you needed help. Thus, that full scholarship you received from the University of Missouri, as well as my accidentally bumping into you at the start of school.

But the biggest secret—the one I only learned then just before her death—is the one that has caused this Blood Relations nightmare. Your mother was pregnant when she left with the Stevens family, another abusive bunch. Apparently, the Stevens family had suspected that she was pregnant. The baby was born at home and had been "adopted" before she knew what had happened. She sneaked away from there and wound up on the street. I don't know how, but she ended up in Saddle Gap with the kind people there. She loved Rose, who became her first true mother figure.

In that last letter, she included a copy of the little boy's birth certificate and the adoption papers. She managed over the years, with the help of your father, to locate these two items. But she also received information that he hadn't survived infancy. So she ceased her search. But after your father died, she once again decided to find what she could about the baby boy. The Stevens family, besides being cold, unkind people, made her question the baby's infant death. They had an older son, a troubled child, and your mother feared he had caused the trouble. She was convinced that he'd killed the baby.

However, she scarcely started her search when she became ill. So she sent me that letter and other documents so I would have the option of continuing her search—for our baby. I didn't know or I would have taken her away somehow when I left. But we were so young—so alone.

I wonder if this older son of the Stevens family is behind this Blood Relations thing, so I am following up on my own. I so regret that I could not protect my child. Hopefully, I can do that for you, for you have been the daughter I didn't have.

I'm sorry to leave you, but I take some comfort in knowing that you have found such a nice little nest there in Saddle Gap. You also have great friends to whom you may turn for comfort and family. I'm especially impressed with the young detective, Chris Reed. He is a loyal friend to you. I won't ask if he's more than that. I guess, if what we're told about heaven is true, I'll be watching from afar.

Take care, my little Sorrel.
John

I carefully folded the letter and stored it in the family Bible I'd found in my aunt's chest. The will could wait for a while.

I poured out the tea I hadn't drunk and, in turn, picked up and hugged each cat. As expected, it wasn't appreciated by either; but Van offered less resistance. I figured he knew John was gone now. Then I corrected myself. No, John wasn't gone. He was even closer to us—in our hearts.

I opened the door leading to my shop and called out to a young mother browsing through the display of knitted goods. "Hello! Have you seen our cute mittens?"

Then I turned to the consignee standing nearby. "I'll be back in my workroom. If you need me, call. I've got some gorgeous sandhill crane photos to mat and frame!"

EPILOGUE

"Sorrel, you can't back out now! You abandoned me at Thanksgiving. If you abandon me on Christmas Eve, I don't know if I will ever forgive you!"

I grinned as I listened to Teri's phone message. I'd just pulled into a spot in front of her mother's house and decided to check messages before going inside. From the looks of the cars up and down the street, the whole town had come as well. I scooped up the box of wrapped packages and scooted out. I'd left Reed's at home, deciding to drop it by Teri's tomorrow instead.

I hadn't seen Reed since he'd left me after the long trip from Socorro. Teri had tried several times to bring him into our conversations, but I'd always changed the subject. Once I'd even called with an excuse when I came to her house for dinner and saw his truck. Saddle Gap wasn't big enough to avoid him forever, but I needed a little longer to let the pain and anger heal. The anger, at least, had started to dissipate soon after I'd read John's letter.

I had to understand that Reed had conflicting loyalties: his job and his friendship. He'd tried to balance the two—and maybe he'd managed to juggle the two as well as he could. Maybe someday he could forgive the ugly things I'd said to him in my pain and anger—or maybe someday I'd have the courage to apologize . . . and mean it.

"Let me take that, Sorrel," Jose said before I could step inside. He took the box from me and held it high, the twins scampering after him, begging to open their presents right away. "Teri's in the kitchen," he said.

Teri's mother had a huge table that filled the dining room. She'd covered it with a bright Christmas cloth that I recognized as one from my shop. In the large, connecting U-shaped kitchen, people were lined up at the counters, stove, and another table in the middle of the room. Teri, smothered in a large apron that didn't totally hide the small baby bump, held her sticky hands high as she gave me an air hug.

"Here's your apron, *hijita*," her mother said, tying the strings around my waist as she spoke.

"Oh," I said, "I'm just—"

"—here to eat?" a cousin—Luisa, I thought—called from the stove. "Sorry, *amiga*. Everyone helps with the tamales. Join the line."

She was right. Teri's *abuelita* found a job for everyone and kept the line going with supplies. I joined Teri in spreading the masa on the corn husks. When I asked why they were green instead of the dried yellow ones, her *abuelita* replied, "They give a better corn taste. When we put the corn-on-the-cob in the freezer during the summer, I cut off the ends, save the green husks, bag them and place them in the freezer. When the kids were all home, I did it to save money. Now, I do it to enhance the flavor of the tamales." She explained it all in Spanish, of course; but Teri whispered the translation.

Spreading the masa wasn't as easy as it looked. I soon had a liberal amount down the front of me, as well as in my hair and on the tip of my nose. Teri's aunts and mother stirred up an endless supply of masa. Her brothers and her dad shredded the pork and beef roasts. Her cousins spread the chili. Uncles and male cousins wrapped them all up and Jose stacked them in the pot.

About three hours later amid jokes, laughter, singing, and other banter, we had finished several dozen. The first pot had cooled; the others were in different stages of cooking. We then cleaned up the mess and settled wherever we could find a spot to sample a few.

"No one on my table," *Abuelita* ordered. So we scattered about the living room, while several of the men congregated in the garage.

"Iced tea? Soda?" I asked Teri while Jose settled her in a recliner with a plate.

"Water," she said. "There's cold bottled water—"

"I know," I interrupted. "That's what I want as well."

When I returned with the bottles and a full plate of my own, Jose and the boys had joined her. I passed the water and grinned. "I'll find a spot—"

"Here's a spot. Saved it for you."

The words hung in a room that seemed to have suddenly hushed.

Reed looked a little thinner, but it didn't detract from his handsome face. In fact, his eyes seemed bluer than before. I tried to think of something—anything—to say to ease the silence. But nothing came to mind. Then Jose, his face kindly as he looked at me, said, "Let me grab a chair for you, Sorrel."

I nodded and conversation started up again. I somehow walked over to the corner where Reed had cleared a side table and Jose had set a folding chair. Then Reed sat down on another and gave his attention to the tamales.

I took a bite, felt my eyes begin to water, and grabbed the water bottle. Reed tried to continue eating but was soon shaking with laughter.

"Why didn't you warn me how hot these were?" I gasped.

"Would you have believed me?" he answered, his laughter fading. His eyes held mine for what seemed like hours.

"Are you okay, Sorrel?" Teri called.

"And you're a traitor too!" I half scolded. But as her giggles rose, I just couldn't keep frowning. What an adorable friend I'd made! I glanced all around the room then, hearing bits of conversation and good-natured banter.

When we'd almost finished eating, I looked at Reed. "I want to—"

"Let's talk later," he said.

"I'd like that." For now, we ate the food, responded to the jokes, and relaxed in the spirit of what Christmas was all about. Sometime during that evening, I discovered that what we see is often distorted by past experiences and relationships.

Reed had taken a leave of absence from law enforcement, I learned. He'd bought a small ranch that had been foreclosed just outside of town. Would he go back? I wondered. I hoped so. Reed had that special combination of determination, intelligence, and heart that lawmen need. It was his gift.

Near midnight, the little ones were taken outside to a small lean-to to watch the cow kneeling. "She is waiting for the Christ child to be born," I heard Teri explain to her boys.

"I have never heard that," I told Reed.

He laughed. "I asked my mom, 'What else would we expect a cow do at night—stand?' She said I needed help with imagination and faith." He shrugged.

"Maybe we both do," I said.

I carried leftover bits and pieces to the trash and thanked everyone as I grabbed my bag of gifts and prepared to go home. When I turned around, Reed stood waiting by the door, his arms around a big box. I raised my brow and he shrugged. "You can never leave Teri's place without a doggie bag . . . well, in this case, a box!"

I laughed. "Better you than me," I said.

"Did I forget to tell you that this is your box, not mine?"

"Mine? I'll never get—"

"I'll follow you home and carry it in," he said.

"I have a gift for you," I said, "but I wasn't brave enough to bring it over and then I wasn't sure if you'd want it."

"After you," he said.

Flash and Van smothered Reed with cat love—and fur—the moment he arrived. "They've missed you," I said as he scooped each up and sat in the comfy chair.

"I've missed everyone too," he said.

"Something to drink? Soda? Coffee?"

"I'm stuffed," he confessed. "What I'd really like is to tear into that package over there." Then he grinned. "I'm still a big kid about Christmas gifts."

I'd propped his gift at the end of the sofa, so I reached for it and handed it to him. "You'll probably have help." I grinned. "In fact, they've already unwrapped it a time or two."

Watching the three of them work on the package was hilarious, but Reed finally pulled the framed photo from the wrapping. He stared at it for what seemed quite a long time, and I'd begun to think he didn't like it. Just as I started to open my mouth, he said, "What a gorgeous photo of our cranes!"

My eyes immediately teared up. "I was a little afraid that it would mean—"

"—special memories of wonderful times," he finished.

"I'm so happy you like them, Reed." I held his eyes. "This photo reminds me of why I love these birds. They fly from way up past our borders every year to winter here. Every day they go on about their lives, content with each other and loving their lives."

I took a breath. "They remind me that happiness is out there in the small things as well as the large ones."

He reached over and took my hand in his. "I'll never look at this photo without remembering those happy times and the person who would want us to laugh and love our lives."

"John named me his executor," I told him. "He asked me to oversee a scholarship fund for his school. I was surprised at the amount of money he'd left, including a large amount to me. I want to include it with the other money, in memory of my mama, for the scholarship fund. I thought his memorial service—maybe in the spring—would be a good time to present that." I squeezed his hand tighter. "Do you think you could go with me to that? I think . . . I know John would like that."

"I'd like that too." Then, "Wait! I almost forgot!" He reached in his pocket, pulled out a small package, and handed it to me.

I held it a moment.

"Hurry up!" he said. "The cats are anxious to have new ribbons and paper to shred."

We laughed as I tore into the package to reveal a small box. Inside, lying on a layer of cotton, was a delicate gold chain with an intricately carved sandhill crane charm.

"Great minds think alike!" we chorused. He fastened it around my neck, and I ran to the mirror to admire it.

When I returned, Reed was standing. "Have you heard that Blood Relations has been closed down?" he asked. "Guess the attention from the Feds contributed to that. I just wish we could figure out how John fell into their web."

I ignored that for a moment. "Have you heard whether or not they've caught the rest of them?"

"In Las Vegas. Stan is a compulsive gambler, so he has been hiring out for unsavory jobs to finance his gambling. She was just a call girl. Oh, and they finally IDed the man who was in charge. Our captor. Stevens. No idea why, though. And no one seems to have figured out who the money behind him and these other people was." He paused. "Sometimes you just don't tie up all the loose ends in a neat bow."

"Reed," I said. "Could you sit down a moment and read something before you leave?" I walked over to the Bible and drew out the letter. "You deserve to know what this letter contains. You're welcome to share it with the authorities if you think they need to know. I only received it when I received John's will. At that time, I tucked it away to handle later. Now is the time."

Reed sat down again and drew out the letter. I couldn't sit still, so I walked over and began finding room for the contents of Teri's box in my refrigerator and cupboards.

I didn't hear him rise, but I felt his arms encircle my waist. "Oh, Sorrel," he whispered. "I should have been here when this arrived."

I stood there as images filled my mind: Reed beside me during that dark night, teasing me to make me mad enough to keep going, sending me on even as he planned to fight to the death to give me the chance to escape.

I turned in his arms and hugged him the way I'd wanted to all night.

"Where's the mistletoe when you need it?" he asked.

"You don't need it, Reed," I answered.

TERI'S TAMALES

Ingredients:
    Beef or pork roast
    MASA Marina (cornmeal tamale mix)
    Red chili powderSalt
    CornhusksGarlic powder
    MEAT MIXTURE:

Place a pork or/and beef roast in enough water to cover it. Cook at slow heat (or use a crockpot and cook overnight) until meat falls apart. Drain and save juice. Break and shred the meat, add enough salt, garlic powder, and red chili powder as desired. Use the hot or mild chili, depending on your taste. Meat mixture should have enough juice to spread easily. Set aside or refrigerate until ready to make the tamales.

CORNHUSKS: Use the dry cornhusks found in the grocery store. Soak in hot water until SOFT.

MASA (dough): Using the juice from the meat, mix with enough Masa Marina to make a thick paste. Spread on a cornhusk that has been drained on a towel. Spread evenly one inch from the bottom and one inch from one side. Leave one inch room at the top. Place meat chili mixture in center, spreading evenly and avoiding the edges. Fold side that has masa to the edge first, then other side, and finally fold the bottom (about one inch). Leave the top open. Too much meat mixture will result in a leaky tamale and not enough meat mixture will results in a masa—not a meat-flavored tamale.

STEAMING THE TAMALES: Using a large stew or tamale pot, place a wire rack on bottom with a vegetable steamer or metal cup (empty vegetable can is good) upside down in center. Stand the tamales around the can with the folded side down and open at top. Fill pot with one inch of water. Avoid standing the tamales in the water as it will make them soggy. Bring to a boil, lower the heat and cook with the steam for about an hour. Remove a tamale. Open and check if the masa is too soft. It should be firm when cooled. Remove from pot and place on a cookie sheet to cool. Eat or bag in zipper plastic bag, refrigerate, or freeze up to three months.

ASSEMBLY LINE PROCESS LIKE IN BLOOD RELATIONS:
Take corn husks out of water, dry on towel.
Spread masa on husks.
Place chili in center of masa husk, spread gently.
Fold sides, bottom, and scrape off excess masa from edges
Place around can in tamale pot

Lonna Enox taught high school and college English before pursuing a career in writing. She lives in New Mexico with her husband, three cats, and a husky/border collie mix dog. *Blood Relations* is a sequel to her first Sorrel Janes mystery, *The Last Dance.*